SHOOTING FOR THE STARS
Gravity #3

by Sarina Bowen

Rennie Road Books

Sarina Bowen

SHOOTING FOR THE STARS

Copyright © 2014 by Sarina Bowen

All rights reserved. No part of this text may be reproduced, transmitted, down-loaded, decompiled, reverse engineered, or stored in or introduced into any information storage and retrieval system, in any form or by any means, whether electronic or mechanical, now known or hereinafter invented, without the express written permission of the author or her publishing company.

This is a work of fiction. Names, characters, places and incidents are either the product of the author's imagination or are used fictitiously, and any resemblance to actual persons, living or dead, business establishments, events or locales is entirely coincidental

www.sarinabowen.com

December

One

STELLA LAZARUS LIFTED HER eyes from her snowboard to the shimmer of Lake Tahoe in the distance. She was standing atop a ridge so steep that the spectators below could not easily be seen. But that was just as well, since one spectator in particular might make her knees feel even shakier.

Chill already, she chided herself. *This isn't your first rodeo.*

This momentary panic always arrived, though. At every competition. The scariest part of the race was not the actual descent. Those seventy-five or so seconds of bombing down the mountain were so adrenaline-filled that there wasn't any time for nerves.

No, the worst bit was right now — these last three minutes before her run. From the moment the previous competitor disappeared over the cornice, Stella had to fight the surge of nervous energy fizzing in her gut.

By now, it was too late to rethink her line of descent. And it was too late to decide which of her many snowboards was the best fit for the icy conditions. All the important stuff had already been decided. Yet it was too *early* to exorcise the demons coiled like springs inside her chest.

So the seconds ticked by in slow motion. Each glug of her heart was audible, as was the wind whistling through her helmet. The weather was fierce today. Stella was too pumped up to worry much about the chill, yet the bystanders could be seen bracing against the wind, curling in on themselves during each harsh blast.

The snow underfoot was crunchy, icy stuff. There'd been quite a bit of complaining among her fellow competitors about the crusty conditions California had dished up for the freeriding competition, especially at this resort so famous for its lofty powder.

Bring it, Stella thought, bouncing her body up and down to keep her muscles warm. She was from Vermont, where hardpack was the norm. She'd grown up hearing that scrape of the board against the ice every time she swung into a turn. Today's "poor" conditions actually favored her.

The loudspeaker, garbled by the wind, mumbled out her predecessor's score. So now all eyes would turn to her.

No fear, baby.

A few yards away, the lead judge raised a hand, indicating she was free to begin. He cracked his gum and smiled at her. "Rip it up, sister," he said. "Whenever you're ready."

"Thanks, man."

Snowboarding was a sport that refused to take itself too seriously, and Stella loved that. A freeriding competition was not a race, per se. There was no gatehouse, and no fancy-ass timing equipment. Freeriding competitions weren't about beating the clock. The judges cared about speed, but only as it related to style and prowess.

Stella bent down to check her bindings one last time. Standing tall again, she rocked her feet, testing the fit. Everything was solid.

Shooting for the Stars

Now it was just girl versus mountain, and Stella liked her chances. This was *it* right here. It could very well be her greatest moment as a snowboarder. The Master of the Mountain Championship was the biggest American event of the Big Mountain Cup. Not only was Stella in good shape and injury free, but she'd trained harder this year than any other in her life.

I can win this, she told herself.

The assorted coaches and competitors standing in the wind began to clap for her.

"Kill it, girl!" somebody shouted.

With a deep breath, Stella bent her knees and tipped the board over the edge. Just like that, her whole existence was reduced to motion and instinct.

Gravity kicked in immediately. The top of the course was a wicked fifty-degree pitch. The first three women had taken it with extreme turns, keeping their speed in check by jamming the board back and forth.

Not Stella.

She straight-lined it, pointing the nose of her board directly downhill to maximize her acceleration. She was ready for the course's sudden turn to the left. But when the lip of a fifteen-foot cliff rushed into view, there was barely enough time to flex her knees and watch the ground fall away. Airborne now, she snapped her hips and grasped for the board's edge with one hand — she'd get points for the grab. And then she was spotting the landing, setting the board down smoothly enough to keep herself upright and moving fast.

The landing was *almost* perfect. She experienced a nanosecond of terror when her board wobbled. Clenching her quads, she rode it out.

You've got this, she reassured herself as more terrain came into view. The next rock wasn't as big as the cliff, so Stella used it to throw a one-eighty. Lake Tahoe's icy blue shimmer swung from one side of her body to the other. Landing the jump, she was now riding switch, her back to the fall line below. It was risky as hell, but Stella needed the points. She needed this win. Hanging on for all that it was worth, she dropped switch into another little chute, propelling herself toward the last section of terrain. It wasn't as steep, but Stella was already carrying some wicked speed.

Time to lay down a few more tricks before the finish line.

And here her brain shut off entirely as she jumped and whirled and landed at a velocity too fast for logic and reason. Years of muscle memory and plain old reflex kicked in. There was a final snarl of trees to navigate, and then a sweet little double jump. By the time she landed the second one, the finish line was rushing towards her, the faces of the spectators blurring together as she swept past.

Less than a minute and a half since dropping in, Stella stood panting in the run-out.

Unclipping her bindings, she walked, chest heaving, over to the scoring area. She stood in front of the sponsor board, the corporate logos shining in the afternoon sunlight, trying not to shake. There would be cameras trained on her here. So the trick was to wait calmly for her score, even though her body was still coursing with adrenaline, her synapses quivering from hyper-stimulation.

There was no other rush like it.

It would take a few minutes until she felt fully human again. That kind of speed and danger brought you to a primal place. In high school biology class, when the teacher had explained the fight-or-flight response, Stella had had no problem grasping the concept. By then, she'd already been the most daring female snowboarder in her corner of Vermont.

She *heard* her score before she actually saw it. "Seventy three point five," the announcer's voice said. It took her heart a half second to process the news. But when she did, her giant

Shooting for the Stars

smile could not be contained. On the leader board, she saw her name pop into first place.

This was the moment when an athlete was supposed to turn into the waiting arms of her... boyfriend? Husband? Parents? Stella unclipped her helmet, shook out her hair, and smiled for the cameras. Then she began looking around for her fan club of two.

"You rock, little girl!" someone shouted. But it was a stranger.

"Thanks!" she called, scanning the crowd. "Crowd" being a relative term, of course. Freeriding didn't bring out the masses, like her brother's superpipe events did. Hers wasn't an Olympic sport, which meant that few people even knew what freeriding was. Also, the competitions weren't very accessible. The hundred or so spectators here today had taken three different chairlifts to reach the finish line. Some of the fans were probably on the mountain for an ordinary ski day, and had stumbled on the event while picking out their next run.

When Stella's gaze landed on the face she sought, her heart tripped over its own feet. Her whole life, Stella had been a fierce and graceful athlete. She'd had to be — how else could a girl keep up with a brother who was four years older and his best friend, Bear?

But while Stella's body had always been sure-footed on the snow, her heart was a total klutz. The large object of her affection was now staring at her, a proud, quirky smile lighting up his handsome, scrufftastic face.

What she wouldn't give to be the frequent target of that smile.

This thought was interrupted by something hard crashing into her chest. It was her brother, Hank. "That was *sick*," he enthused, grabbing her into a hug. "The way you ate up that first chute. The jump in switch! The tail grab off that last boulder. I mean, *dayum*." He pounded her back.

For once, Stella just hung there in his arms, eating up the praise. Because there was a chance that the run she'd just put down was every bit as good as Hank said it was.

Then, when Hank set her back onto her feet, Stella held her breath. Because it was Bear's turn to congratulate her. Usually, when Stella knew she was about to come face to face with Bear, she braced herself. Because there was never any point to letting him read on her face how much she cared.

Just once she'd tried to let him know and had been brushed off so fast it had made her head spin. But that was years ago.

Today was special, though. She had just kicked some serious ass up there, and nobody expected her to play it cool. So Stella didn't dim her smile when she looked up into Bear's eyes. She just let it all hang out — her joy at doing well, her excitement at seeing him for the first time in months. Her love.

Not that he'd notice.

When those silver-gray eyes met hers, there was more unguarded warmth in them than Stella usually saw there. That gave her a zing that no drug could ever touch. Her run must have been spectacular to get that kind of approval from Bear. Given the choice, Stella would have stood there forever, soaking up that look in his eye. Instead, she found herself briefly crushed against his side, one of his big arms pinning her.

"Awesome job, buddy," he said in that rumbling voice which she always felt everywhere.

"Thanks," she whispered. Just as her mind formed the words *Bear is holding me*, he wasn't anymore. There was nothing but cold air where his body had just been.

Meanwhile her brother was still singing her praises. "...so fast and so solid. Nobody is going to *touch* that run," Hank said.

"Don't *jinx* me," Stella yelped. Like any red-blooded athlete, she was deeply superstitious.

"Honey, I couldn't," he said. "When you ride like that *nobody* can step in front of you. The first event of the season belongs to you."

"*Stop*, already," she laughed. "Jesus." There were several more competitors to follow. Any one of them could put down the run of a lifetime, too.

But none did.

Thirty minutes later, she took her phone out of her pocket and snapped a picture of the final standings, showing STELLA LAZARUS on top. She forwarded the photo to her parents back home in Vermont. They would probably reply with "great job, Sweetie." But their absence spoke volumes. They hadn't really been listening when Stella told them how important this single competition was to her. Yet they'd bought their plane tickets to the Olympics three months ago. And Hank wouldn't even be named to the American team for another four weeks.

Whatever. She had won this thing, and she was going to be happy about that. "I'm picking the cocktails tonight," Stella announced.

"Oh, man," Bear teased. "Don't pick anything that will lose me my man card."

She socked him in the arm, which was their usual form of affection. "Just for that, there's going to be an umbrella in your drink."

"Great," Bear muttered.

"Stell-Bell, I'm going to have to take a rain check on the drinking," Hank said.

"God, why?" Hank *never* took a rain check on partying. He'd earned his nickname "Hazardous" both on the snow and off.

"I'm flying back to Vermont tonight for the exhibition event."

"Oh, shit," Stella complained. "That's this weekend?"

"Yep. I'm really sorry."

For a second, she was disappointed. But then Stella realized two things. First, her brother had come to Lake Tahoe for no reason other than to watch her compete. And, secondly, for the first time in years, she was going to have an evening alone with Bear. *Well then.* "I'm sorry to see you go, but I totally understand," she said.

"You do? Aw." Hank ruffled her hair. "Will you still be this nice about it if I ask you to drive Bear back to South Tahoe? Then I can take my rental straight to the Reno airport."

Stella laughed. "Fine."

"I didn't check out," her brother added. He fished a key card out of his pocket. "You can have my room tonight, and it's awesome. I got upgraded."

"You always get upgraded." Stella took the card. "For once, I'm going to be the lucky beneficiary."

"The room is penthouse number one. Just like your standing." He cocked his head toward the leader board. Then he hugged her one more time. "I'm outie. Got a flight to catch."

"Bye, Hank!" Stella called after him. As she watched her brother duck under the roped-off boundary, a swarm of people descended to ask him for an autograph. That always happened, and not just on mountains. In shopping plazas and airports, people recognized her Olympic champion brother.

Stella shook her head. "Think I'll be mobbed like that later?"

"I'll fight 'em off for you," Bear offered. He lifted his snowboard off the ground and mimed bashing heads with it.

She gave him another gentle punch to the bicep. "I knew you were good for something." Weirdly, Bear actually flinched. Then his mouth drew into a tense, straight line. Stella watched him, studying his silver gaze, trying to figure out what she'd said to make him frown.

Bear turned away. "Let's ride down," he said. "I mean, if you're ready. Is there a press conference?"

Stella sighed. "Nope. The back-country events don't draw many journalists. And I already spoke to *Outside Magazine* and *Snowboard* today. Which way do you want to head down? I was thinking the Rock Garden."

He hesitated. "There's always Dead Tree."

"Bear, you know where this is leading right?" Stella stuck out a fist. The two of them had always been competitive. Since they were preschoolers inventing stunts on their tricycles, he'd had a bossy, alpha-dog personality. And Stella could admit she was just a wee bit strong-headed herself. Their entire childhood had been a long series of petty disagreements which needed settling.

Even though they hadn't seen each other in months, Bear knew exactly what to do. Removing his glove, he put his fist across from hers. In unison they chanted: *"Rock, paper, scissors, SHOOT!"*

Stella was about to protest that Bear had hesitated when she realized she'd won. "Scissors cut paper! Rock Garden it is." She hiked her board under one arm and ran toward the cornice.

Two

TOGETHER, BEAR AND STELLA *jetted* down the mountain.

Bear was glad for this little respite from his own churning mind. Edging hard, he chased Stella's dark ponytail as it flapped in the breeze. It was like flying, really. The silver-blue of Lake Tahoe appeared and disappeared as they wove and bounced through the terrain.

Stella liked to go fast, and Bear liked pursuing her. For twenty minutes, it didn't matter that Bear was having a really shitty day. Chasing her downhill, everything was a simple balance between friction and gravity.

His best friend's little sister had never been the sort of girl who stopped to admire the view, so the whole thing was over too soon. At the base, they bent over their boots to unclip. And Bear had to work to keep himself from panting like a winded old dog. "I'm happy to drive," he said when Stella turned to face the parking lot.

Stella removed her helmet and shook out her ponytail. "You do know that people with boobs are capable of operating a motor vehicle, don't you?" She studied him with one hand on her hip, flushed cheeks and bright eyes.

He got trapped for a second by all that loveliness. Stella was one of the most beautiful girls he'd ever met. And she always had a challenging glint in her eye. It was comforting, really. On this day when people he trusted had let him down, he could count on at least one person in his life to remain constant. "Easy, killer. I just thought that since I knew where the hotel was, because I *came from there a few hours ago*, that driving would make your load lighter."

She tipped her chin up, considering his argument. Bear had wisely stopped short of pointing out that Stella got lost more than anyone else he'd ever known. She'd probably give in. But first, she would draw out the moment, deciding whether or not to be offended by the suggestion. And that was fine, because he could look at her all day.

With an eye roll, Stella dug a set of rental car keys out of her pocket and handed them to Bear.

Thank Christ. The real reason he wanted to drive was that he didn't think he was going to be much good for conversation. If he was behind the wheel, his poor mood might be less noticeable.

"Omigod, look!" Stella squealed.

On a digital screen at the bottom of the ski lift, there was a picture of her. It had to be three feet tall. "WINNER of the Women's Mountain Masters: Stella Lazarus."

Bear yanked his phone out of his jacket pocket and took a picture. "Wait, Stella, go stand beside yourself." Giggling, she dropped her board on the snow and ran to stand next to her oversize image. He took another shot. "I don't know if the world can handle *two* of you," he said.

"Right?" she agreed cheerily.

When Bear went to stash his phone again, he found a crisp bill hanging out of his pocket. That was odd. He didn't keep money there.

"Careful," Stella said. "That's a c-note."

Bear pulled it into his palm and saw that she was right. He looked down on the snow and found another hundred dollar bill, quickly trapping it under his boot before it could blow away. *What the fuck?*

Oh. *Hank.*

Bear felt a hot spark of irritation. He didn't want his wealthy friend's money.

Scowling, Bear bent down to collect the bill off the snow. The universe had obviously conspired to humiliate him today. The first blow had come just as Bear and Hank had pulled into the parking lot here at Squaw Valley. Bear's phone had rung, and he'd found that the caller was his biggest sponsor. "It's Rafe from Bungee Brands. I've got to take this, but I'll only be a minute," he'd told Hank. "Hi Rafe," he'd said, picking up the call.

"Bear. How are you man?"

"Good. What's happening?"

There had been a pause on the other end of the line, but Bear hadn't really noticed. He'd been watching Hank pull their gear out of the back of the car. And he'd been feeling lucky that they were standing in this beautiful place, with a crystalline lake on one side, and one of the burliest resort mountains in America rising up before them.

"I've got some bad news," Rafe had said into his ear. "We can't renew your contract at New Year's."

New Year's? That was only three weeks away. "What?" he'd asked, stupidly. The Bungee Brands sponsorship was forty thousand dollars, and by far the largest source of Bear's meager income.

"Things are just really tight this year. I'm so sorry. I wanted to explain in person, but I'm not going to make it to any of the tour events until January."

Reeling, Bear had done the math. Bungee Brands would be spending all its efforts — and its money — on the Olympic qualifying events. New champions would be crowned. And even now — weeks before the first flights left for Europe — the whole world had already decided that he was yesterday's news.

"I see."

"I'm putting a little something in the mail for you, though," Rafe had said. "We've been friends for a long time, man. Hope that doesn't change."

Bear hadn't even had a response to that. "I have to run," he'd said. Hank was standing there, his boarding boots already on, watching Bear with a question on his face.

"Call me later, if you want."

"Thanks," Bear had said before ending the call. *Thanks,* he'd repeated numbly afterward. He'd just thanked the guy for canning him. *Thanks for nothing.*

He'd shoved his phone into his pocket again, still stunned.

"What's the matter?" Hank had asked.

"Bungee dropped me," he'd answered.

"What? They cut you back?"

That was the moment when numbness had turned to anger. "They didn't cut me back, they just fucking cut me." But how could Hank understand, anyway? Bear had felt a surge of resentment for his friend of more than twenty-five years. Hank had never lost a sponsorship. Not once. He was one of the highest paid athletes in winter sports.

They'd ridden the lift in a rare uncomfortable silence.

Eventually, Hank had turned to him with a sheepish expression. "Can I ask a favor? Take Stella out tonight? I feel bad that I can't do it myself."

"Yeah. Sure thing," Bear had said.

"And maybe you can take your mind off of… you know." Hank had cleared his throat.

"Yeah, I know," Bear had grumbled, his mood plummeting immediately.

And now? Finding two hundred of Hank's dollars in his pocket did not boost Bear's spirits. Although he understood why

Shooting for the Stars

Hank had done it. He'd asked Bear to take Stella out for the night. Bear would have happily done it anyway. Bear didn't like talking about money, ever. And he didn't like thinking about it, either. Unfortunately, it was about to become the biggest problem he had.

On that glum thought, he followed Stella toward the parking valets.

"Here goes the winner of the American Masters Cup, putting on her sunglasses," Stella said as he loaded their boards and boots into the back of the Jeep she'd rented. "...And here goes the winner of the American Masters Cup, asking you whether you'd rather have the Snickers, or the peanut butter cups." She opened her backpack as she slid onto the passenger's seat.

"The peanut butter cups. Easy choice." He knew Snickers was her favorite. When they were kids, she'd always traded for them on Halloween, when she and Hank and Bear would dump out their booty on the floor of the Lazarus family room to paw through their new wealth.

That was before Bear understood what wealth really was. That it was bigger than a pillowcase full of fun-sized chocolates. And that some people had it, and others never would.

Bear got into the driver's seat, or rather he tried to. Stella was nearly a foot shorter than he was. Adjusting the seat, he warmed up the engine, then maneuvered the Jeep through Squaw's vast parking lot and out onto the roadway.

He was alone with Stella Lazarus. If that couldn't lift his mood, then nothing could.

"Where shall we have dinner?" she asked while fiddling with the radio.

"It was your big day. So you can pick. Anything you want. I'll even dress up if you want to hit one of the nicer places."

After all, someone should be happy tonight. Unfortunately, it wouldn't be him, but so far he was doing a decent job of hiding it.

"You'll dress up, huh?" Stella asked, and he could hear a smile in her voice. "You'll wear your *good* flannel shirt and jeans without holes?"

Since his eyes were on the road, he didn't look at her. But he really didn't need to. He'd been watching Stella smile his whole life. It started with a quirk of those perfect lips. And then those big brown eyes lit up.

"I could whip out a dress shirt, buddy," he said. "Try me." Though hers was a fair question. They'd known each other literally forever. And Stella could probably count on one hand the number of times she'd seen him dress up for something. The whole state of Vermont was strictly casual. The snowboarding world was, too.

"Okay, as much as I would like to see that, a fancy meal isn't what I want tonight."

"No?" He should have been relived, since he really wasn't in the mood for formality. On the other hand, if they went somewhere casual then he'd miss out on the rare sight of Stella wearing a dress.

"What I want is to sit in the hotel bar, and order all the fattening appetizers that I usually avoid. Tonight nothing is off the menu."

"Nothing, huh?" As soon as he said the words, he wished he could take them back. Because Stella was the one girl on the planet that he wasn't allowed to make sexy jokes with. Usually it wasn't an issue because Hank was nearby. Hank's presence always reminded him to keep it on the straight and narrow.

"Not a *thing*," Stella said, arranging the fingers of one hand into heavy metal horns. "Tonight we're going to party like Vikings. Vikings who like tequila."

Shooting for the Stars

"You got it."

Bear wound Stella's rental car down highway 89, which was one of the most gorgeous roads in America. The startling beauty of Lake Tahoe, its frigid waters framed all around by mountains, flashed in and out of view. On the other side of the road, an endless number of evergreens rose into the air. Their trunks performed a visual trick as the car passed by. If Bear turned his chin a few degrees toward the passenger side, the spaces between the tree trunks seemed to gap open in rows as the car flew past. It would make a cool shot for one of the videos he liked to stitch together in his spare time.

Stella fiddled with the radio, settling on a bluegrass station. And Bear drove on in silence, the scenery calming him.

He loved this. Pro snowboarding wasn't glamorous in the traditional sense. Very few athletes actually got rich in terms of dollars and cents. But there were dividends all the same. Bear never sat his ass in an office cubicle and watched the clock for lunchtime. Instead, he passed his days on the most beautiful mountain roads on earth. He breathed the cleanest air. And when he closed his eyes at night — even if it was on the scratchy pillow of a cheap motel — on the inside of his eyelids, he saw aspen trunks framed against the blue sky, or the black cut of the High Sierras standing dark against the clouds.

"Do you mind if I call my agent for a minute?" Stella asked from the passenger seat. "There's five bars of reception here."

"Knock yourself out, buddy. Where was he today, anyway?" Her agent should have been there to see her rock that event.

Stella let loose with one of her killer smiles, the kind Bear often felt in some very inappropriate places. "When I become one of his more important clients, he'll probably turn up more often."

He sneaked another glance at her as she cocked the phone against her sun-kissed face. Stella was so happy today that it almost hurt to look at her. He'd been like that once — full of optimism and the belief that things would just keep getting better. Tonight he needed to make it through the next few hours without poisoning her joy.

"Chad! I won the whole thing!" he heard her tell her agent. "It was beautiful."

And that was the truth, not bravado. Put a Lazarus sibling onto a snowboard and prepare to be awed. He'd watched her event with his heart in his throat, of course. The speed she'd accumulated by straight-lining that first chute had made him almost physically ill. But he needn't have worried. She had chewed up that terrain as if it were her breakfast appetizer. For seventy seconds, he'd been able to forget his own troubles and just love the sport again. Watching Stella carve an artful line down the slope, it was easy to remember why he'd given so many years of his life to snowboarding.

"Do you think StillWater will come through for me now?" Stella asked her agent.

During the long silence which followed, Bear found himself holding his breath. *Please say yes, motherfuckers*, he coached the universe. He could get past the idea that his own usefulness to the sport was starting to wane. He'd been given every chance in the world to prove himself. And then some. But the fact that Stella was having trouble picking up sponsorships was just plain wrong.

"Okay, Chad," she said. "Then I'll just have to win the next one, too." A minute later she set down the phone.

"Everything all right?" he asked quietly.

"Sure," Stella said, but she swallowed hard. "I was just hoping to pick up a decent sponsorship from this win. But Chad isn't sure that it matters."

"Of *course* the win matters," he practically growled. "It's just that in an Olympic year..."

"They're going to throw all the money at medal winners," Stella finished. "I know that. He's going to make another round of calls for me. But..." She let the sentence die.

Bear didn't get it. He really didn't. Stella wasn't just an awesome snowboarder, she was flat-out gorgeous, with thick, shiny hair and cheekbones that most women would sell their souls for. So what if freeriding wasn't a sport that people followed? They would *start* watching it if Stella Lazarus were on the front of their cereal boxes.

"You know what?" he declared. "We're not thinking about sponsorships tonight. This is a sponsorship-free zone. Tonight we're all about the win."

She sat up a little straighter in her seat. "Okay. I can do that."

"Speaking of your win, I got the whole thing on video."

"Thank you! Can I see it?"

"Not until it's edited."

"What?" Stella yelped. "You are such a tease."

He chuckled. "No, buddy. I have to put you to some killer music, okay? And tag on the podium shot, the billboard with your name. The whole package."

"Don't forget to edit out that bobble from the first jump."

Bear shook his head as the hotel came into view. "Other guys I have to edit. But not you. There weren't any bobbles." He pulled Stella's rental car up in front of the main doors to the nicest hotel at the southern end of Tahoe. This was where Hank Lazarus stayed when he came to town, whereas Bear had made a reservation at a cheaper lodge a few miles away.

A valet leaped forward to ask for the keys, but Bear shook his head.

"Aren't you coming in?" Stella asked, one foot on the curb.

"I was going to check in at the lodge so they don't give my room away," he said.

Stella lifted her chin toward the hotel. "Bear, it's cocktail hour. If they give your room away, you can crash in the suite Hank left us. Just come inside. I want a margarita, like, yesterday."

An argument formed on the tip of Bear's tongue. It was a reflex, really. He and Stella had locked horns over everything from pizza toppings to politics for more than two decades. But tonight he just didn't have it in him. Sitting beside her over cocktails was the best fucking idea he'd ever heard.

Bear got out of the car, handing the keys to the valet—another damn thing that Hank was paying for—and followed Stella into the hotel lobby. She rolled a small suitcase along behind her, and Bear knew better than to try to take it from her. In the past, he'd received several lectures on feminism by giving into the impulse to carry things for her.

"Wow, it's jamming in here," Stella remarked inside.

She wasn't wrong. It was après ski hour. Every table in the bar had a group of wealthy Californians around it. Returning from a day of skiing, they'd have a beer or three before deciding where to eat dinner. In their brand new parkas, and the occasional fur hat, they dressed as if they owned the place. (Some of them probably did.)

Mixed in with the A-list crowd was a smattering of ski and snowboard bums, some of whom were familiar to Bear. He raised a hand in greeting to a couple of Canadian kids who'd joined the freestyle circuit just last year. They stood by the door, hands jammed in their pockets, probably waiting for friends. Now that Bear thought about it, they weren't even of legal drinking age.

He'd never felt as old as he did right then. Twenty nine years old, and his days as a pro snowboarder were probably numbered. There was even one kid on the circuit — a Japanese competitor — who was *fifteen*. His mother actually flew around to all the tour stops with him.

Stella hooked her arm through his, steering Bear toward the elevators. "I want to change out of my ski pants," she said. "And check out this hotel room Hank raved about."

"Bryan Barry, hold up." Bear swiveled around to find Dan Lacy, the president of the Fresh Mountain Extreme Freestyle Tour, waving him down.

Damn. It. All. Tonight was supposed to be about drinking with Stella. Not running into this weasel. But when the head of the tour asked for your attention, you had to say yes.

"Can I come and find you in ten minutes?" Bear asked Stella.

"Sure." She gave his arm a squeeze. "Penthouse number one."

"Got it. I'll be right up."

"I NEED A WORD," Lacy said as Bear approached. "Follow me, please?"

His curt manner made Bear's stomach roll. He'd thought that his day couldn't get any worse. But apparently that wasn't true.

Lacy ducked behind the concierge desk and into a suite of offices that Bear hadn't known was back there. Everywhere the tour stopped, Lacy always commandeered an office. The guys (and gals) on the tour referred to it as Airfarce One. And nobody wanted an invitation, because that's where the tongue lashings and the wrist slaps happened. Hank was a frequent flier. Lacy was always chewing him a new one for something or other:

drunken singing in front of reporters or making so much noise at the hotel that it made the local news.

Bear mostly stayed out of Lacy's way, and that was intentional. He hadn't won a tour event in two years. He wasn't a superstar like Hank or a household name. He was basically clinging to his spot on the tour with his fingernails. That's why he hadn't gone to the freestyle exhibition back in Vermont with Hank this weekend. The hometown event had sounded like a great time. But Bear knew he couldn't afford to skip tour competitions. He had to show up for everything. On time. Every time.

Lacy led him into a windowless office with just three chairs, a table and a laptop. "Close the door," Lacy said.

Ouch. Bear closed it, and turned to face the president.

"Sit."

Bear sat.

The president made a tent of his fingers. "Bryan, I'm sad to say that with your scores where they are this year, this will be your last season on the tour."

For a moment, Bear merely replayed Lacy's statement in his mind, trying to find a loophole in those words. But there just wasn't any way out of that simple statement. Even so, he didn't flinch. He would never give Lacy that satisfaction. And he didn't say anything, either. Because what was the point?

"I know this is difficult for you," Lacy went on. "But there isn't *anyone* on the tour right now who isn't eventually going to hear the same thing from me."

Now Bear did flinch. Because even though Lacy was right — nobody was immune to the ravages of time — Bear hadn't expected this conversation to happen just yet. Hank, for one, was older than he was. But Hank was Hank. He was in a class all his own. He'd accomplished everything that Bear had ever wanted in the sport, and then some.

And now it was all going to end.

"We want you to ride every event through the third week of February," Lacy was saying.

"The third week of February," Bear echoed. He caught up to the president's words, and realized what they meant. They wanted to keep him around through the Olympics. Because the superstars would be going for the gold then. And Lacy needed the also-rans to hold down the fort while they were off chasing glory.

"That's right. That's more than half the season, anyway. You should be able to earn most of a year's sponsorship income."

"I see," he said. Because he did see. For the next ten weeks, he could limp around the tour circuit, staying in even shittier motels to save what little income he had left. And because there was no such thing as a secret when it came to the sharp elbows of the athletic world, he would get nothing but pitying looks all around.

The next ten weeks would be pure torture.

Bear stood up and went for the door.

"Chin up, Bear," Lacy said as Bear clenched the doorknob. "This feels like a shock right now, but this isn't the end of the world."

Spoken like a man who did not just lose his job. Bear left without saying another word.

He did not, for what it was worth, stoop to thanking the man.

Three

STELLA WASN'T ONE TO be wowed by luxury. Her father built custom ski homes for a living. So she'd seen her fair share of beautiful rooms. And Stella was the sort of girl who cared much more about which mountain slope was outside a hotel room than what sort of furnishings were found inside.

She was, however, in the mood to celebrate. And the hotel room her brother had left for her was a fine place to do that.

In fact, the words "hotel room" could not accurately capture the amazing space she found when the door clicked open. For a moment, she could only stand there admiring it. The room was long and low, which made it feel cozy. A thick rug underfoot was set off by dark wooden beams on the ceiling. Separating the room into two halves was a sleek stone fireplace, the fire visible from both sides. On one side, a leather sofa waited patiently for a guest to sit in front of the fire. On the other, a king-sized platform bed beckoned with a heap of pillows and a furry blanket at its foot.

Wow. It was the most romantic place she'd ever seen.

Stella crossed through to the bathroom and her breath was stolen again. There was a giant Jacuzzi tub in the corner, with two champagne flutes waiting on its edge. Hank had scribbled a note on the hotel stationery, propping it up in front of the soap dish. *You're welcome*, it read, with a winking smiley face.

She did a turn all the way around, taking in three hundred and sixty degrees of luxury. This was not typical digs for a pro snowboarder. Even the successful guys were usually just scraping by. They drank cheap beer and they crashed on each other's motel-room floors. You didn't become a pro snowboarder to live the cushy life. You did it because you couldn't imagine anything better than chucking yourself off a fifteen-foot cliff while the Aspen twigs scraped your jacket, and the frigid air infiltrated your lungs.

But her brother had something special, and the whole world had noticed. The result was that companies from car manufacturers to sports drinks to wristwatch designers cut him fat checks for representing their products.

In contrast, Stella's sponsors provided her with gear — like boards, boots and helmets — and a tiny stipend for entry fees. Her big dream was to pick up a new sponsor to help with travel costs.

But this? This was just a fairy tale. Though if Hank's stardust rubbed off on her every once in a while, she'd take it.

It was tempting to just shed all her clothing and slip into that tub. But Bear would knock at any moment. So she didn't do it. Instead, Stella swept her hair off her neck into a French knot and took the world's quickest shower. Then she donned a pair of jeans that hugged her butt to maximum effect and put on the only slinky top that she carried with her when she traveled to competitions.

By the time she slicked on her lipstick, Bear had still not arrived. When she checked her phone, she discovered why. *Saving you a seat at the bar*, Bear had texted. *Meet me down here?*

On my way, she replied. *Order me a drink?*

His reply came seconds later. *Done. Margarita on the rocks no salt.*

On her way into the elevator she tapped out: *I love you desperately*. Her finger hovered over the "send" button. That statement was quite literally true. But since Bear had never taken her seriously about anything, it was perfectly safe to send it. In fact, she could have the sentiment sky-written over Lake Tahoe by a pair of crop dusters, and Bear would assume it was all in jest. She could even have the words I LOVE YOU BEAR tattooed across her boobs and flash him. If she thought she had a prayer of getting him to see her as a woman and not the kid sister of his best friend, she might actually try it. But Bear would probably just roll his eyes and grab a couple of cocktail napkins off the bar to help preserve her modesty. *Funny little Stella. Such a kidder.*

She'd been friend-zoned since childhood. It wasn't exactly news.

Stella had been in love with Bear since the year she was eight and he was ten. That had been the unfortunate year when she'd had to spend too much time indoors. She'd been ill a lot that fall with a fever that never seemed to go away. Her frantic mother had taken her from one doctor to another asking for tests.

Stella was a brave girl even then. So the blood tests didn't scare her as much as they inconvenienced her. Winter had just arrived, and she ought to have been playing with Hank and Bear on the snowy slope between their homes, not sitting in waiting rooms.

But one awful afternoon her father came home from work early. From behind their bedroom door, she heard her parents' anguished voices. A chill settled over Stella, and she went into her bedroom, climbing on the bed and pulling her favorite stuffy into her lap. Eventually, her tearful parents came in to tell her that the doctor had figured out what was wrong with Stella. It was something called leukemia, and she was going to have to get very strong medicine that might make her sick.

"Everything is going to be *fine*," her mother had promised, dabbing the corners of her eyes.

Of course it was. Stella wasn't a worrier. And at eight, she didn't know anybody who'd died, especially not a child. Her mother told her that she was going to miss some school, and that her hair might fall out. "But it will grow back," she promised.

It was all very confusing, and Stella began to get a bad feeling about what winter held. She was supposed to compete for the very first time in a juniors snowboarding contest in December. The way her mother fussed, it sounded as if she'd never be allowed outside again.

The Lazarus home became horribly quiet. There were more whispered discussions behind closed doors, and Stella had the sinking feeling that they were talking about her. Even Hank had acted weird. He was too nice to her, bringing her things and watching her in a funny way that made Stella uncomfortable. So she did the obvious thing. She punched him.

"Ow!" Hank yelled. He gave her a firm pinch in return.

"Stop!" their mother wailed. "She'll bruise easily!" The ever-present tears appeared in her eyes, and Hank looked stricken, slipping away, hanging his head.

Sheepishly, Stella retreated to her bedroom, taking up a position in the middle of her big purple bedspread. She was bored, and everyone was acting freakishly. But twenty minutes later, Bear turned up, banging into Stella's room with a frown. "It's *raining*," he complained.

Stella shared his disgust with this development. He and Hank had been building a jump from the early snow in the yard, eager to have their own practice spot for aerials. Rain would melt their efforts.

"Where is everybody?" Bear asked. And by "everybody" she knew he meant Hank.

Stella just shrugged.

Bear looked around for a second. Then he went over to Stella's bookshelf and grabbed the Uno cards. "Play you for a quarter a game."

Her heart lifted then. *Finally*. Here was someone who wasn't acting strangely. "Fifty cents," she'd countered. (She'd loved risk, even at age eight.)

"Fine." He dropped his coat on her bedroom floor and climbed onto the bed. "But no whining when I win."

That winter, they played a lot of cards, in part because it wasn't a good year for snow. "You're not missing much," Hank would say after a Saturday spent at the hill while Stella was bedridden. "The gladed trails aren't even open."

But Stella knew a white lie when she heard one. Even *bad* snowboarding was better than no snowboarding, and Hank knew it. Most everything stunk for Stella that winter. There were long hours spent at the hospital. She threw up into a weird little plastic tray they provided during her chemotherapy treatments. When her hair finally did fall out, in terrifying chunks onto the shower drain, her mother's sobs echoed against the bathroom tiles.

Stella did not dare look in the mirror. Instead, she put her favorite ski hat on her head, pulling it down to cover her embarrassingly bald scalp. When Bear thumped into the room that afternoon, chucking a wooden case down on the bed, he didn't give her head a second glance. "Have you played this?" he asked.

The box read *Backgammon* on its side. "I can figure it out," was her reply.

"Okay." He flipped open the latch and began to explain how the little pieces were supposed to move around the board. While they played, Stella studied the furrow between his brows when he was trying to decide something. Sometimes he ran a hand absently through his thick hair. Even at ten years old, there was something irresistibly sturdy about Bear. That ugly year, he was her favorite person. Even when she was cranky and nauseous, she always looked forward to the afternoons he turned up for dinner or a quick game. Some days they didn't get to play, because Hank and Bear would be in the middle of some epic video game battle in the den. But Stella felt calmer when Bear was around.

It had only taken Stella two rounds of chemo to beat back her childhood cancer. So the next winter found her back on the ski hill, frustrated that she couldn't get as much air off the jumps as Hank and Bear. *Yet*.

But she'd never stopped loving Bear. It would be years before she would begin to look at Bear *that* way. But when he was in eighth grade, and she was in sixth, the girls began to swarm around Bear. Stella was instantly jealous. She just knew in her gut that he was meant to be hers.

Bear, unfortunately, *didn't* know it. There had been a steady stream of girlfriends, and Stella had been gritting her teeth for fifteen years now.

Worse, after Hank left to compete out west, Bear had taken over the big brother role, spending a great deal of effort ruining teen-aged Stella's fun. He threw away the joint that she'd managed to score at a gravel pit party. "You are too young for that," he'd said. And Stella's cheeks had burned with embarrassment.

And then? When she finally had a boyfriend of her own (one not quite as hot as Bear, because nobody was) he took the boy's car keys away from him at parties. When the boyfriend complained, Bear would just stare him down. "I don't trust you," he'd say. Once he'd added, "She's precious cargo."

Not only was it totally infuriating to be treated like a baby, it was confusing, too. Stella loved Bear precisely because he *hadn't* babied her when everyone else had. Their relationship changed during her teen years, and not for the better. The competitive part of their friendship was still alive and well. They'd put away the Uno deck long ago in favor of poker. They were well matched at the card table. But they'd found it was possible to be competitive about many things: Snowboarding (Bear could outdo her in the terrain park, but Stella now ruled the steeps and the glades.) Rock climbing (Stella could climb faster, and Bear insisted that her smaller frame was the reason. He was probably right, but she never admitted it.)

So at least they still had that. But Stella lost to Bear sometimes out of sheer distraction. He'd only grown more attractive every year she knew him. He'd always been a fairly big boy, but at seventeen he shot up. At eighteen, his shoulders grew deliciously broad. Stella wanted to lay her head in the crook of his neck and feel all that solid mass beneath her cheek.

She stared and stared, and he never seemed to notice.

Only once had Stella gone a little crazy and actually thrown herself at him. It was more than ten years ago now, on the night of Bear's high school graduation. She'd been so proud of him, and so sad that he'd leave in the fall to follow Hank out west. To mark the occasion, she'd stolen a bottle of champagne out of her father's wine cellar and chilled it in the stream which ran downhill from the Lazarus home to Bear's house.

God, she'd tried so hard to impress him. She'd even bought wine glasses at a store in town, because her mother was much more observant than her father, and the temporary theft of stemware would have been noticed. And she'd needed *nice* glasses, because this was meant to be a special moment.

She'd cornered him that evening after the ceremony, before he was ready to leave for a night's worth of partying with his friends. At sixteen, Stella already knew how to uncork champagne. And when she'd heard that satisfying pop, and then carefully poured two flutes full of bubbly, everything had been going perfectly. They'd sipped and joked their way through a glass each.

That's when Stella had made her move. She'd set her glass down on the flat rock behind Bear's little log cabin. Then she'd gotten up and proceeded to sit on his lap.

Bear's chin had snapped up, and his eyebrows flew upwards. She should have stopped to read the signs. But Stella had always been a fearless girl, even in the face of probable defeat. At sixteen, she'd already figured out that the only way to get what you wanted was to take a few risks. So she'd put her hands on his shoulders and kissed him.

For a few golden moments, everything had been glorious. His lips were softer than she'd expected. And from the back of his throat came a startled little sound. *Yes,* her heart chanted. *Finally*. He'd taken control of the kiss, and the slow slide of his tongue had taken her breath away. High on her own bravery, Stella had leaned into him, wrapping her arms around his broad body.

That's when everything stopped.

The second Stella had connected with Bear's warm chest, he seemed to freeze as solid as the slabs of granite that her father used on his building projects. Then Bear had lifted Stella off of his lap, and stood up. When he'd spoken, his voice had been a rough whisper. "You shouldn't do that, Stella-Bell."

And with that, he'd walked away, into the house that he shared with his dad.

She'd been absolutely mortified.

That night, she'd finished the bottle of champagne by herself. She'd kicked off the dainty shoes she'd worn for the occasion (they weren't very comfortable anyway) and polished off the wine straight from the bottle. As a result, she'd puked in the woods before she went inside to bed, and woke up with a nasty headache the next morning.

But it did not compare with the ache in her heart, or the shame of rejection burning under her skin.

For ten days afterwards, she'd ducked Bear. Then her brother came home for the summer, which meant that Bear was around, too. The three of them had always hung out together, and if Stella had gone on avoiding Bear, everyone in town would have wondered why. So she had to show her face the first time he came over for dinner.

That night she'd taken extra care in selecting her outfit. She'd even gone so far as to smear a little lipstick on, which for Stella was quite an extraordinary effort. Dinner had seemed to last forever, too.

But then afterwards, Bear had come up to her in the family room at a moment when Hank had ducked into the bathroom, damn him. And she'd braced herself for an awkward conversation.

"Hey," Bear had said. "Do you want to play some ping pong?"

It had taken her a half second to decide that ping pong with Bear was better than nothing. "Okay. Loser cranks the ice cream. Winner picks the flavor."

"Deal," he'd agreed.

That night she'd won all three of the games they'd played, and Stella had come away with the suspicion that he'd let her win, so that at least she could win at something. She'd chosen peach ice cream just to spite him because Bear was a chocolate man.

The past ten years hadn't changed much. It was as if they'd been playing one very long game of ping pong, with Stella's heart as the ball.

He'd moved out west, anyway. So her heartache was the long-distance kind, which helped. He had a little condo in Utah near Hank's. And during the winter, the two guys traveled together on the Freestyle Tour. Stella graduated eventually, too. Then she spent winters traveling to whichever big mountain events she could afford to string together. During the warmer months she took college courses and worked for her father.

These days, it took a rare coincidence to bring Stella and Bear to the same corner of California for competitions a mere forty miles apart on the same weekend. So Stella approached the hotel lobby with a spring in her step. She found Bear at a corner of the long, hammered-copper bar in the Birch Room. Another snowboarder from the tour — his nickname was Duku, and she didn't think she'd ever heard him called anything else — had his elbows on the bar. He and Bear had their heads bowed in quiet conversation. In front of Duku was a frosty looking margarita on the rocks, and Stella hoped that it was meant for her.

Both men stopped talking when Stella arrived. Duku's narrow face broke open into a smile. "Hey, girl! I hear congratulations are in order. Nicely done!" He grabbed her into a bony hug.

"Thanks. It still doesn't seem real."

Duku had the toothiest grin in North America. He wasn't traditionally handsome, but there was something lively in his face that fans always found irresistible. "The first big win is an awesome feeling. It makes you say, 'so *that's* why I busted my ass all those years.'"

"Something like that," Stella agreed.

"I'm proud of you, girl. I'm going to make some calls and find some food. Maybe I'll hook up with you two in a little while?" He gave Stella's shoulder a squeeze and gave Bear a fist bump. "Hang in there, man," he said. With a final salute, Duku disappeared through the crowd.

"What was that about?" Stella asked as she slid onto the waiting bar stool.

"Nothing," Bear said, lifting his own glass. "Congratulations, Stell. You rock. Today and always." He smiled at her then, and Stella's throat went tight. He was waiting for her to pick up her drink and toast with him. But she let the moment linger because it was a rare thing to have Bear all to herself, and to have those silver eyes shining down on her and her alone.

She'd freeze this moment in amber if she could.

"Salud," Stella said finally, lifting her glass to touch it to his. She held his eyes and took a sip as tradition required. It was all too easy to just fall into his gaze.

Or rather, it would have been, except that an up-and-coming Japanese boarder stopped beside Hank and offered his hand, which Hank shook. Then the kid actually *bowed* to Hank and walked away.

"What the fuck?" Stella asked.

"He's just friendly," Bear said. "So where's your next competition?"

"Switzerland. And then Italy and British Columbia. The last event of the season is in Austria. But if I run out of money, I'm not going to make it to that one."

Bear sighed. Then he took a slug of his Jack and Coke.

"Hey!" Stella teased, pointing at his glass. "I thought I got to pick the drinks?" Bear seemed a little tired, actually. She'd need to pour a few more drinks down him so they could celebrate her victory properly.

"You can choose 'em, buddy." He gave her a small smile. "Anything you want."

Anything you want. Not hardly. And why was Bear such a pushover all of a sudden? Bear was a bossy guy, especially to her. You'd think that someone who crushed your rebellious fun would stop being so freaking attractive to her, right? You'd think. But you'd be wrong. Even after her embarrassing and ill-fated attempt to seduce Bear went awry, she'd loved him like it was her job.

But she wasn't going to get depressed about that. Not tonight. There was a cocktail menu on the bar in front of her, and she flicked it open, looking for inspiration. "They make a Manhattan with muddled cherries and orange rind. That sounds good."

"Sounds a little too fruity," Bear complained. "How many of them do I have to drink to get muddled?"

"Hush, or I'll order you the one with mango schnapps."

"That is just plain wrong."

Stella giggled. She was just teasing him, anyway. There was a nice dirty martini on the menu that she knew he'd enjoy. "Hey, did you see this hotel room that Hank left me?"

He shook his head.

"You *have* to see it. It's nuts. There's a fireplace and a hot tub."

He chuckled. "It's too bad for Hank that Bitchy Barbie wasn't in town last night." Bear gave her a sly grin. Hank's girlfriend was the only topic on which Bear and Stella always agreed.

Stella stirred her margarita with a straw. "Bear, do you think Hank is going to marry Bitchy Barbie?" she asked. This idea had been rattling around in her brain since the last time she saw Hank and his girlfriend—whose real name was Alexis—together.

"No," Bear said firmly.

"How can you be sure?"

"Because Hank isn't stupid. That's not the kind of woman you want in your life forever."

"It's been a year," Stella said quietly.

Bear shrugged. "He's too busy right now to focus on forever. They both are, honestly." Alexis was a champion ski racer, also trying to have the season of a lifetime. The fact that she had the kind of sponsorship deals that Stella wanted had always made her hate the woman even more. "But after the dust settles in February, and they spend some more time together, Hank will wake up."

"I sure hope you're right. The idea of Alexis at every Thanksgiving dinner from now until eternity really hacks me off. And I'd like to be Auntie Stella one day. What if my nieces and nephews had her bitchy voice?" She gave a mock shudder.

Bear smiled over the rim of his cocktail glass, and the sight of it gave her a little kick to the heart. "Aw," he said.

"What?"

"*Auntie Stella*. That's sweet."

Something in his voice made her throat feel tight. "Do you like kids, Bear?" The question just slipped out before she could think better of it.

"Sure. Who doesn't?"

Stella picked up her drink and took a gulp. What an idiot she was, asking that. It's not like she needed even more proof that they weren't meant to be together. Even if Bear did return her feelings, the whole issue of children would probably be a deal breaker.

Cart before horse, much?

But it had suddenly occurred to her that they were getting to that point in life when these questions mattered. Someday Bear would meet The One, and have his own brood. He'd bring his cute family around during the holidays, and she'd have to smile and pretend not to be jealous.

Stella couldn't have children. Usually she didn't worry too much about it, though. Raising a family was incompatible with the daredevil lifestyle, anyway.

It was for the best, right?

Two lanky youths wearing beanies and baggy jackets approached the bar. The boys' look screamed "snowboarder!" at the top of its lungs. "Hey, Bear!" one of them called out. His accent was Canadian. "We heard about… you know…" The kid cleared his throat, offering Bear a fist bump. "We're not drinkin' here, because it's so fuckin' pricey."

"Yah," the other one agreed.

"But if you need to get drunk or somethin', we're just at the Powder Keg. About a block that way."

"Thanks, man," Bear said. 'But I'm good here."

"Keep it real." The youngster nodded to Bear, and then he and his friends walked away.

Stella put her glass down on the bar with a thunk. "Bear, you have to level with me. Why is everyone acting like you've only got three weeks to live?"

"Three weeks?" He gave a bitter chuckle. "It's more like ten weeks."

A cold prickle crawled down Stella's neck. "That isn't the least bit funny," she whispered. "Talk to me."

Four

AW, HELL. THE look on Stella's face right now was pure fear. Not only did it cut him, but it was entirely unnecessary. "Don't look at me like that. It's nothing, really. Just tour drama. I don't want to be a buzz kill tonight, buddy."

He really did not want to see the look of pity that would cross her face when she heard the news. Bear hated pity more than anything. The year after his mother ran off, he got that look from everyone. Teachers gave him that face at school. When his father's business struggled, he saw pity reflected in the expressions of the women at church who passed their sons' clothing down to him.

The last face he wanted to see pity on was Stella's.

"You *have* to tell me what's wrong," Stella demanded. "It's only fair."

"Fair," he muttered. What the hell did that word even mean? By any measure he'd had a good run on the pro circuit. The fact that it was over pissed him off so badly. He was greedy for more. There just wasn't any other way to look at it.

"Bear!"

He pushed his glass away. "I got cut from the tour. That's what Lacy wanted to tell me when we walked in." He braced himself.

Stella froze, her hand an inch from her glass. "*What?* That can't be."

"Sure it can, buddy. He gave me until late February. But I might not stick around that long." That last bit had just popped out of his mouth. But why not leave early? Who wants to hang around after he's been fired?

Before he knew what hit him, Bear's arms were full of Stella Lazarus.

"None of this makes any sense, Bear." She wrapped her arms around as much of him as she could manage. And when she pulled back a bit to look into his eyes, what he saw there wasn't pity. It was something much more fiery than that. "Lacy is just plain *insane!* You have a million fans."

Bear felt the tension in his chest ease by just a fraction. "My fans are getting older, I think. Their acne has cleared up, and they don't need their moms to drop them off at the snow park anymore."

Stella stepped back, but kept her hands firmly parked on his shoulders. "Don't you *dare* call yourself old," Stella argued. "Twenty-nine isn't old unless you're an unmarried Jane Austen character."

"I don't win tour events, buddy," he whispered. "I never won very many, and I haven't come close in a year."

Her eyes glittered with fury. "It's not just a contest, though! It's a *spectacle*. And you give good air, Bear. You really do. Lots of guys don't win very often. Lots of guys don't win *ever*."

"And *those* guys become car salesmen after a couple of seasons." He pushed a shiny tendril of hair out of her face. It felt satiny between his fingers. "I got ten years out of it. Somehow I fooled myself into thinking that I'd get even more."

Stella gave her head a fierce shake. "This is *not* over. I think we should call Hank. Maybe he could—"

Bear had to cut her off by holding up a hand. "Don't even finish that sentence. How do you think I lasted as long as I did?" His whole life he'd depended on the Lazarus family in one way or another. God, it was difficult to acknowledge that. But it was true. "It's no accident that Lacy gave me this news the minute Hank left town. Do *not* call him. Because it won't help and it will only embarrass me."

He hadn't wanted to say that aloud. *Ever*. But there it was.

Stella studied him at very close range. She was standing so near that he could catch the fruity scent of her shampoo. "Okay," she whispered. She reached for her drink and drained it. "You should become a coach, maybe. Or a back-country guide. That could be amazing."

"I'll figure something out," Bear said. But that was just bravado. He had no fucking clue what he was going to do.

"I need to order some more drinks now." Stella waved down the bartender. "The only thing to do is get really ripped."

Bear smiled in spite of his misery. She was so fucking cute when she got fired up. Maybe he could survive this evening, after all. "Sure. But you need to eat something," he insisted.

She tossed her hair. "Okay, *Dad*. I'll order some appetizers, too."

His grin grew in size. That was Stella, always throwing sass at him. And right now, he needed that.

The surfer-dude bartender ambled over, his yellow hair flopping in his eyes. Stella leaned over the bar in her eagerness to talk to him. "We definitely need some nachos," Stella said, pointing at the menu. "And are those artichokes good? Let's have the beet salad and… the onion flower. Also, a *pitcher* of margaritas. Can you make that happen? I'll be your new best friend." She gave him a winning smile.

Bear just watched her negotiate with the young bartender, working her Stella magic, getting what she wanted on sheer grit and personality.

It would be hours until he realized one important thing. The look of pity he'd been so worried about? Stella never gave him one.

The food came, and both he and Stella pulled out their wallets. "Let me get it," she said.

"No," he bit out. "Your brother beat you to it."

"Ah," Stella said, settling onto her bar stool again. "Still asking you to babysit me after all these years."

Bear grunted so he wouldn't have to agree or disagree. Stella had always hated the fact that he'd tried to look after her when Hank had moved away. "Don't let her do anything stupid, if you can help it," Hank had said on his last night in Vermont, a dozen years ago.

"Sure, man. I'll look out for her," Bear had promised. He should have stopped to appreciate, though, what an impossible task he'd just signed up for. At fifteen, Stella had been a wild little thing. A true Lazarus, just like her big brother. The first month after Hank had left, Bear had caught Stella doing shots of whiskey under the football bleachers with the boys of the senior class. Not only had she snarled at him while he dragged her drunk little body back to his truck, she'd thrown up on Bear's boots on the way home.

Winters had been easier because Stella spent all her time at the ski hill trying to become a world-class snowboarder like her brother. During high school, Bear worked as a lifty at the ski mountain and then as a snowboarding instructor. That bought him a free season pass and an easy way to keep track of Stella.

But summers had been trickier. Once, a bunch of kids had driven to Quechee Falls to jump off the rocks. It hadn't been enough for Stella to jump off a bunch of fifteen-foot rock ledges. Someone dared her to inch out onto the support beams underneath the covered bridge and jump from there. If she'd fallen off before reaching the open water, she would have landed on head-cracking granite. "Don't do that," he'd warned. But she hadn't been listening. So Bear had threatened to take a picture and show it to her parents.

Stella hadn't jumped. But she didn't speak to him for a week, either.

She'd always hated it when he'd waded into her business. But she always forgave him eventually. The only time he'd worried that he'd really ruined their friendship was the time she'd kissed him. Bear tried not to think about that night too often. It had taken superhuman willpower to push her away. He'd wanted to wrap his arms around her and never let go.

Don't let her do anything stupid, Hank had instructed. And kissing Bear was pretty dumb. So he'd put distance between them. "You shouldn't do that," he'd told her. Stella was the brightest, shiniest thing in all of Vermont. And Bear was not. It just wouldn't be right.

God, there was just no end to the parade of depressing things to think about tonight.

Luckily, Duku rejoined their party, filling up any lapses in conversation with his usual smack talk and bullshit. He pulled up a barstool and ordered a Scotch. "Tell us about your win, Stella. Who did you thrash, anyway?"

Bear rested an elbow on the bar and watched Stella's animated face as she spun the tale. He knew he didn't have a right to feel so devastated tonight. Fate had been very good to him over the years. If his career had run its course, that was nobody's fault but his. And the fact that he didn't have a Plan B? That was on him, too.

Tonight, he would lick his wounds and raise a glass to Stella. After all she and her brother had done for him over the years, it was really the least he could do.

He sat back, admiring her soft brown eyes, and the way she lifted her chin whenever Duku made her laugh.

Five

STELLA ORDERED A SECOND pitcher of margaritas, though she'd already had enough to drink. Now that the tequila had begun to kick in, she began to feel sad and unsettled.

Duku was lively enough, but there was no papering over the fact that Bear was hurting. It was nice of him to say he didn't want to spoil her celebration. But if he was devastated, then so was she. Not that she could admit that out loud. Bear wouldn't like it.

Stella knew the truth all too well. Being a professional athlete meant always hanging by a thread. And unless you happened to be a superstar, there were always people in your life ready to cut the thread and watch you fall. They used words like "selfish" and "impractical," to describe your lifestyle.

And there were days when it all really did feel selfish, if Stella was honest with herself. Her win today felt great. But there was no denying that there was one person it benefited most: Stella. But when you win, you're allowed to stop feeling selfish for a little while. Obviously it was all worth it, right? Because the trophy or blue ribbon collecting dust on the shelf proved it.

Ack. She was thinking too hard.

No sooner did Duku knock back another Scotch when the young bartender refilled it. Deep in his cups, he got a little sentimental. "It just won't be the same around here without you," he complained to Bear. "You and Hank? You two are legends."

A flicker of discomfort crossed Bear's face, and Stella wondered if she would have to intervene and change the subject. Duku's heart was in the right place, but it wasn't making Bear feel any better. Stella was probably the only person alive who understood how the specter of Hank's success hung over Bear's career. She got it, because she felt it, too. Her whole life, Stella had measured herself against her brother. It wasn't intentional. It was just that everything worth doing, he'd done first.

That was true for Bear too, though the two of them never said those things aloud. Hopefully leaving the tour wouldn't drive a wedge into the two men's friendship. Bear was already losing so much.

The male bartender set another little glass of scotch down beside Duku's skinny elbow. The snowboarder looked up to give the guy a slow smile. "Thanks, man."

"My *pleasure*."

Stella nudged Duku. "*Somebody's* going to hook up tonight."

"Don't you know it." He took a sip from his fresh drink. "I think we need to get Bear laid, too. That will take his mind off his troubles." Duku sat up a little taller in his seat and swiveled his head. "Ladies!" He beckoned to a pair of girls who had just entered the bar, and were scoping the place out, trying to decide where to position themselves.

"Don't," Bear pleaded.

"This is exactly what you need," Duku argued.

Bear muttered into his drink. "Because I'm feeling so fucking friendly right now."

"Some friendly fucking it is, then." Duku waved the girls over.

Stella tried not to scowl too deeply when Duku introduced her to the new arrivals. She didn't commit their names to memory, however, because she hoped their stay would not be long enough to warrant it. Duku made small talk while Stella bit her lip. Then, turning her back, she checked her phone for messages. She shouldn't be thinking about sponsorships during happy hour. There was very little chance she'd find good news in her email inbox so soon. But hope was a stubborn bitch. So Stella swiped the screen to look.

Nothing.

Figures.

When she turned around again, Duku was talking up Bear. "Do you know who this is, ladies? A legend. He's been a pro snowboarder since you were playing with Barbie dolls." He swiveled to look up at the bartender. "Could I have a couple more glasses? Thanks, man." Stella tuned out the conversation. A few feet away, it looked as though Bear had tuned it out, too. He was polite when the girls asked to take a picture with him, though. She didn't think the beleaguered expression on his face was only wishful thinking, either.

But then the more aggressive of the two girls put her boobs practically in Bear's face, which made Stella feel quite stabby.

"You can have my seat," Bear offered, standing up to get out of the woman's strike zone.

"I'm fine right here, honey," she said.

Yeah. If the girl got any closer to him, Stella was going to have to evacuate. She would *not* watch Bear hook up with some stranger on what was supposed to be her victory night.

On the other hand, the other young lady provided some comic relief to the situation. She was working it pretty hard for Duku and not getting anywhere. Stella kept an eye on them, wondering how long it would take the girl to realize she was going to crash and burn.

When the girl finally stooped to rubbing herself up and down Duku's body, like a cat in heat, he said, "You're not my type, Sweetie. It's not personal."

The young woman looked instantly offended. "Who is your type?"

"He is." Duku jerked a thumb at the surfer-dude bartender. The kid didn't make eye contact, but his expression grew smug. He was probably happy to hear all that free whiskey wasn't going to be in vain.

When the girl's eyebrows drew together in dismay, Stella felt a hit of glee, followed immediately by guilt. Stella had been shot down before, and it didn't feel good. Especially when the shooter was the person she'd loved her whole life.

It *still* stung.

Unfortunately, the flirtmonster in front of Bear was only getting more aggressive. Worse, Bear had that glassy-eyed stare of a man who might be on his way to getting too drunk to fight her off. Someone would have to stage an intervention soon. And that someone was going to have to be Stella. But how?

Luckily, the two girls took a bathroom break together. Even though it risked sounding bitchy, Stella said, "Bear, I've had enough of this place."

That woke him up a bit. "Let's go then, buddy. I'm done here, too."

"What?" Duku yelped. "You're going to leave me alone to explain it to her?"

"It was your idea, man. Good luck." He threw Hank's hundred onto the bar. "Okay, Stell-Bell. Let's go."

Victory was sweet. Stella gave Duku a kiss on the cheek. Then she grabbed Bear's hand and led him out of the bar.

Six

BY THE TIME THEY left the bar, Bear was drunk, which should have made him feel less depressed.

Should have. But didn't.

He followed Stella into the hotel lobby where the cooler air woke him up a bit. "I gotta get a taxi," he said. Driving right now was out of the question.

"No you don't," Stella said over her shoulder. "You're coming with me."

"But I have a reservation." His hotel room was the dreariest place at Lake Tahoe, though. It wouldn't help his mood.

"Not my problem. Come on." Stella turned, heading across the lobby in long, graceful strides. Bear followed her, trying not to admire the view. But he'd have to be blind not to notice the way her jeans hugged her butt. Her walk had been making him half-crazy since high school.

They got on the elevator, and Stella pushed the button for the penthouse. Ah, well. At least that meant the room would have plenty of space and probably a couch to crash on if he didn't sober up.

When the doors parted on the penthouse level, they emerged into a plush hallway. There were fresh flowers on the table beside the elevator doors and soft lighting. Because rich people demanded elegant details even before they made it into their suites.

Stella waved the key card in front of the lock, and then opened the door into an opulent room. It was a Lake Tahoe style of opulent — plush but unfussy. Everything was crafted from beautiful, natural materials with simple, rustic lines. It was the sort of look designed to make a guy want to sink down onto the nearest piece of furniture and laugh at his own good fortune.

Even though Bear didn't come from money, he'd lived at the foot of it all his life. Literally. Henry Lazarus — Stella's Dad — had built half the ski condos in Windsor County, Vermont. And John Barry — Bear's father — had done electrical work in many of them. Bear had learned the rules for being a subcontractor's kid from the very start: knock on the back door, not the front. Leave your dirty boots by the door.

Don't let the boss's daughter kiss you on graduation night, even if it practically finishes you off to say no.

Stella dropped her pocketbook on a table and marched over to the fireplace. Squinting at a control panel on the wall, she pushed a button. *Whump!* A fire jumped to life in the open-design chimney. Her face lit up more brightly than the flames. "That is so delightfully cheesy!"

Bear laughed, because it was easy to do that with Stella in the room, even if your life was crumbling around you. "You are a piece of work," he said, not bothering to rein in his smile. His mood was like an injured bird, flapping ridiculously hard to stay off the ground.

"I am a piece of work who won the American Masters Cup today," she said, stomping over to the sofa and throwing herself down onto it. "There goes the winner of the American Masters Cup, removing her boots." She toed them off. Then she curled her knees up to her chest and turned to face Bear. It was quiet again, the fireplace the only audible sound. Stella's face became very serious as she studied him. "You know you're going to be okay, right?"

Thunk. His mood hit the dirt. "I know," he said, walking over to sit beside her.

"They're *crazy* to let you go. We've already established that. But sometimes a violent disruption can be good. Maybe it will lead you to a whole new way of looking at things."

"I think I read that on a greeting card once," Bear said. He'd meant to be funny, but it came out sounding bitter.

Stella rolled her eyes. "Do you remember when those condos burned down, when I was in third grade?"

"Sure." He'd been eleven and still young enough that it was a thrill to run a half mile to see all the firetrucks arriving to douse the flames lapping at six half-built units facing the ski hill.

"That was a terrible day for my father. It cost him a fortune. The insurance settlement wasn't enough money, and it wiped out his profits for the year."

"Ouch," Bear said. Funny, but he'd entirely forgotten about that disaster. The Lazarus family he knew didn't suffer misfortunes. They made deposits at the bank, never withdrawals.

"It was a total loss. And it even cost money to have the debris hauled away. Daddy was so pissed off."

She stretched out her legs until her feet landed in Bear's lap. He grabbed one of them and pressed his thumbs into the arch of her foot. "Here's the winner of the American Masters Cup, having her feet massaged in the fancy-ass hotel suite."

Stella closed her eyes on a smile and seemed to melt into the couch. When Bear kneaded her foot, she actually moaned.

Check, please. He really did not need to hear that sound again. Rubbing her feet was meant as an innocent thing. But the sound she'd made filled him with very inappropriate ideas. "So, what's the punch line?" he asked as a distraction.

"Hmm?" She was lolling against the arm of the generous sofa.

"The fire cost your daddy a shitload of money…"

Her eyes drifted open. "Right. The punchline is that he made it all back, times ten. Because the construction delay made him reconsider his design. Instead of just rebuilding those six little apartments, he put up three standalone houses with nicer finishes. They brought in a lot more money. And then his whole business plan was shifted toward higher profit dwellings."

Bear swapped Stella's right foot for her left one and considered this idea. "He had the capital to keep building, though. That kind of disaster might have wiped some guys out. He could have ended up working behind the counter at the copy shop, asking customers whether they wanted their documents collated and stapled." *Ack.* That image was a pretty crystalline projection of his own fears. Hopefully Stella would be too blissed out by her foot massage to pick up on it.

But her eyes went soft. "You have lots of capital, sweetheart. You can do *anything*."

Bear appreciated the sentiment, and he really didn't mind the look on her face when she said it. If only it were true. Other guys his age had been to college. They had degrees in useful things. They had careers that didn't end suddenly when they were pushed aside by nineteen-year-old whippersnappers.

Stella sunk a little further down into the couch cushions and let out a sigh. Bear admired her, even though she was just one more thing in his life which was close enough to touch, but completely unavailable to him.

"I think I'll have to move back to Vermont," he heard himself say. He owned a small condo in Park City. But that meant that his savings were tied up in real-estate. He'd need to sell.

The next few days were going to work just like this — uncomfortable details of his new reality smacking him in the face like fat rain drops. For example, the lease was almost up on his Land Rover. He'd expected to purchase the car after he made his final lease payment. But now that seemed like a bad idea.

Shooting for the Stars

"You'd live with your dad?" Stella asked.

"I think I'll have to, at least until I figure out my next move." Bear stopped the foot massage to reach the stiff muscles at the back of his neck. He dug his fingers in and frowned. "My dad is going to say 'I told you so.'"

Stella sat up, removed her feet from Bear's lap, and looked him straight in the eye. "He might," she said. "But your dad has never ridden Dead Tree at Squaw Valley, or taken a helicopter into the Snake River Range. You don't have to point that out to him, but if he's giving you a lot of shit, telling you all the things you should have been doing these last ten years, I just want you to remember that."

He got stuck for a second then, watching her big brown eyes positively glittering with indignation. "You are a very smart girl, Stella," he whispered.

She lifted her chin. "I'm going to remind you that you said that next time we have one of our arguments."

"You do that," he smiled.

"Now spin around," she said, giving his arm a nudge. "Because it's your turn. I'm going to find the knot in your neck, because I'm sick of watching you paw at it like a dog with fleas."

"Nice image, buddy." But he turned around anyway. A moment later, Stella's warm hands landed on his shoulders. And when her strong fingers began kneading, the buzz of stress inside his head got quieter. He let his eyes fall closed as she thumbed around his traps, searching for the knot.

"Christ, you're tight," she whispered.

"You think?" *Losing your livelihood along with your entire identity can do that to a guy.*

He still felt a little drunk, but not just on tequila. The fireplace had warmed the room, and her hands were stroking his neck. The soothing touch of feminine fingertips on his body was a rare treat. Bear didn't have a girlfriend. Sex happened with frequency, of course. A pro snowboarder had his pick of vacationing ski bunnies whenever he was in the mood. But there was no one steady in his life. Traveling seven months out of the year made dating impractical. He'd hoped to have a real girlfriend someday, and then a wife. That had always been the plan.

But that was a logical error, wasn't it? He wouldn't be traveling all the time anymore. Yet who would want a guy who was washed up at twenty-nine? One who didn't have a Plan B?

"You're fighting me," Stella said, her voice low. "Drop your shoulders."

Shit, he was. Bear made himself relax. "Thanks, buddy."

"Shhh," she said. "Actually, lift your arms over your head for a second."

He did it without thinking. And a half second later, his t-shirt was tugged over his head and tossed aside. He opened his mouth to launch a knee-jerk protest, but then soft hands landed at the juncture of his shoulder and his neck. The friction of her skin against his own was like medicine. Instead of arguing, he let out a big sigh instead.

"That's it," Stella breathed. "Drop your head."

For once in his life, he let Stella have her way without a fight. The pain of getting squashed by fate had not been dulled by tequila. It had not been soothed by Duku's antics. Stella's touch was the strongest drug yet. And it wasn't even a close contest.

"Thanks for letting me turn your celebration into my pity party," he said. "I'm sorry about the timing."

"No, sweetie. It's not like that." She dug her thumb into his achiest muscle. "I want to be around when the big stuff happens."

"Today it's all big stuff."

"Yeah," she whispered.

"I do have some regrets. That's why it's hard to tell my father to fuck off. He's right about some things."

He felt her ruffling his hair now. "It doesn't matter, though. Everybody has regrets, because nobody can do everything, right? You can only live your life in the way that creates the fewest of them."

"How did you get so wise for someone so young?"

She delivered a quick slap to his shoulder. "First of all, I'm not that young, chump. And more importantly, it's because I have this conversation with myself all the time. You might only get the lecture from your dad twice a year. But I get it all the time."

"I'm sorry." He knew that Stella's parents weren't as supportive of her athletic career as they were of Hank's. Since she didn't make enough money on the freeriding circuit, she couldn't afford to keep a place out West, like Hank and Bear did. Every summer she lived at home. Her parents often tried to convince her to consider giving up competing. She hadn't become an overnight sensation at nineteen like her brother, so they assumed there was no point.

"Your parents want to keep you close," he said.

"That's the nicest way to look at it."

"Do you think you'll end up with regrets?" he asked.

She stilled herself for a second. "I already have some." Her hands resumed their magical healing powers, though she didn't say any more.

"Well," he cleared his throat. "Are you going to share?"

"I'm thinking about it," she murmured.

Bear wasn't sure what she meant by that. But it was hard to think too hard with Stella's competent hands massaging his body. His eyes closed again, and he drifted, seeing images of the crystalline lake and the stark mountains against the darkness of his eyelids. In spite of all that had gone wrong today, this moment was pretty close to perfect.

As the knot in his neck relaxed, Stella's hands wandered down his back. With a fist, she kneaded his lats, then rubbed her fingertips up and down his lower back. It felt divine. His body listened to her soothing touch, and it liked what it heard. So much so, in fact, that he began to tingle everywhere. He felt goosebumps break out on his chest. The low groan he heard seemed to have come from him.

Stella worked her way up his back again. Then she rose up onto her knees to make herself taller, providing leverage. But it also pancaked her lush body against his bare back. *Sweet Jesus.* The heat and pressure of her curves against his skin was a little more stimulating than he wished it to be. His dick began to feel nice and heavy as she moved against him.

Down, boy. He was trying to think of a polite way of shifting away from her when her hair swept forward, draping over his bare shoulder, brushing his chest. His nipples tightened up even as he registered the fact that Stella had lowered her mouth to his skin.

Time slid to a stop as she pressed soft, open-mouthed kisses to the side of his neck. *So fucking nice. Except...* This wasn't supposed to be happening. Even as he processed this, her sweet mouth moved to the sensitive skin just below his ear. And that would have been mind-numbing on its own, but her long hair continued to tickle his chest, setting him on fire.

He didn't even try to hold back his groan.

Hearing it, Stella did not waste time. She threw a knee around his hip, almost straddling him. Yet she began to slip down his denim-clad leg.

Bear caught her with one arm, his hand cupping her ass. For a split second, neither of them moved. The only sound was his pounding heart.

Then Stella lowered her head, and he watched the slow-motion approach of her deep brown eyes. The first touch of their lips together was tentative, as if they both needed one more second to figure out whether this was truly happening.

Hell yes, it was.

Bear crushed his mouth to hers. And then they were kissing, and Bear was eighteen again, and desperate to taste her. He felt exactly the same surge of shock and pleasure as all those years ago. The slide of her soft lips on his lit him up. Without thinking, he cupped her face in one palm, and she opened up for him. A split second later, Stella's tongue invaded his mouth. She tasted like limes and danger. And pure woman.

Stella kissed him as though she owned him. And for a few paralyzing moments, he would have willingly sold himself into slavery for even one more minute of her attention. But since the dynamic between Bear and Stella had always been an energetic power struggle, instinct kicked in. He took charge, hauling her to his chest, then flipping them both over until Stella lay on her back on the sofa.

Bear planted an elbow on the sofa's edge and kissed her again, this time on his terms.

"Oh," Stella whimpered between kisses, and the sound of her seeped through his veins like a drug. They went at it like teenagers again. He chased each kiss with another, and then another, slanting his mouth over hers, perfecting their connection. Each dive into Stella's mouth was deeper than the last.

Unbidden, his free hand skimmed under her slinky top, finding the silky skin of her stomach. Ever since teenaged Stella had begun wearing bikini bathing suits, he'd been tortured by the question of how it would feel to touch her. And now he knew the answer.

Addictive. That's how it felt.

Meanwhile, her hands slid all over his bare chest. And then her legs wrapped around him, her heels digging into his ass, suddenly yanking his groin against hers. *Jesus*. He was raring to go, and it was partly because Stella was *still* trying to assert control over him. On another girl, that would have been a turn-off. From her, it was hot as fuck.

With a growl, he grabbed both her hands, holding them over her head. Then he hiked his body up a few inches, pinning her hips in place with his own. Breaking their kiss, he stared down at her.

Beneath him, Stella's face was flushed, her dark eyes lit with lust. Their eyes locked and their chests heaved from exhilaration.

But... *Goddamn*. How did he end up here, with Stella? This wasn't part of tonight's plan.

"Let me up, Bear," she said softly.

Chastened, he released her immediately, rising to his knees on the sofa.

Her face pink, Stella scrambled to a kneeling position, too. For a second they just stared at each other. He didn't *think* he'd misread the situation. But he'd had a lot to drink tonight, and where Stella was concerned, he didn't trust himself.

What was she thinking right now?

The answer came as Stella scooted closer to him again. Surprised, Bear held his body still, watching her. Her hands went to his waist. When she slid her fingers across skin, just north of his waistband, he had to bite back a moan. Her ambitious fingers found the button of his jeans, which she popped open.

That sobered his ass up. Fast. "Stella," he breathed. "You shouldn't do that." It's what he'd told her all those years ago. And it was still true.

She threw back her head, looking up into his eyes. "Bear," she chided. "I haven't been sixteen for a long time."

"No kidding." He blew out a breath. "But we've been *friends* for a long time, and…"

"Bear?"

"Yeah?"

"Do you think you could just shut up right now?" Her questing hand found a new place to stroke, just over the bulge in his jeans.

Jesus Christ. He couldn't even answer her, he was so turned on. Slowly she eased his zipper down. Then one of her exquisite hands ventured beneath the waistband of his boxer briefs. Bear's breath stuttered in his throat.

Stella chuckled. "Now I know how to silence you."

That was a second wakeup call. Stella obviously believed she'd bested him, rendering him defenseless. He planted a foot on the floor and grabbed her with both arms. Stella squeaked with surprise as he hoisted her into the air. He stalked around the sleek fireplace, tossing her on the bed. On her back, with her mussed hair spreading out on the duvet, she looked up at him with surprise.

He stood back, holding tightly to his control for one crucial moment longer. He could *not* get this wrong. "Am I getting on this bed with you?" he asked.

She licked her lips, and the anticipation made him so hungry he forgot to breathe. "Only if you lose the rest of your clothes first," she answered.

Well then. There was no way to misinterpret that. And, as Stella had pointed out, she was an adult, capable of making her own decisions. If she wanted this, he did not have to refuse.

Apparently he wasn't moving fast enough for Stella, because she came after him. Sitting up, she tugged on the waistband of his jeans. Bear shoved the denim down his ass, his legs, and off his feet. Stella divested him of his boxer briefs next. Whisking away any remaining shreds of higher-order thinking,

Stella grabbed him by both hips, tilted her head down, and began dropping wet kisses onto his shaft.

Before he could even catch a breath, Stella took him into the wet heat of her mouth. The sensation caused his muscles to lock up tight. Lifting his eyes to the ceiling, he dropped his head back, fighting for a little self control.

"Mmm," Stella hummed.

The sound made Bear pant. All the tequila he'd drunk tonight was supposed to make him numb. Instead, his body had accelerated from a standstill to crucial velocity in a matter of minutes. If he didn't put on the breaks, the entire ride would be over before he was ready.

Bear reached down, skimming his hands over Stella's hair. He grasped her silky shirt in his fingers. With a tug, he raised the fabric, forcing Stella to release him. She relented, raising her arms. He whipped the shirt over her head and tossed it onto the floor. With a gentle shove, he tipped her back onto the bed, then climbed on with her.

She reached for him. "I wasn't finished."

"Patience," he scoffed, holding her off in a way that kept her questing hands from reaching his dick. Holding her still with a hand to her shoulder, he freed up his other hand for some very necessary work. He undid her jeans, then gave them a tug. She lifted her hips, and when the fabric fell away, he choked out a laugh. Stella wore nothing underneath.

Stella Lazarus went *commando*. That was just so *her*.

And now she was spread out on the bed before him, her skin smooth and inviting, in nothing but a sporty little black bra. Not that he could keep his eyes up there. The temptation was just too great to run his gaze down her olive-toned curves. He bent over her body, skimming his lips along her hip bone. She tasted even sweeter than he'd imagined. Kissing his way across her body, he paused to nibble the top edge of the tiny triangle of black hair between her legs.

"Ohhh," Stella moaned, her hips shifting underneath him.

Bear braced himself over her, forearms aligned outside her sleek thighs. She was more muscular than the women he usually went to bed with. *Hell.* Just the idea of how she might use those muscles on him was almost more than he could take. Drawing his elbows closer to her body, he pressed her legs together tightly. Then, lowering his head, he began dropping light kisses onto every inch that was still accessible. With his mouth, he cruised the juncture between her inner thigh and her mound, pausing to let his breath ghost over her body.

"You're... ohh..." she whimpered, flopping back onto the bed. He raised his eyes to see her chest heaving. He nosed between her legs again, the trace of a sweet, musky scent of her turning him on even further. If that was possible.

She fought his grip on her legs, but he would not budge. Smiling now, he placed a single slow kiss about an inch north of the place where she would rather have it land. Again she wriggled, trying to enhance the connection to suit her.

"You're impatient, buddy." Without releasing the hold his elbows had on her, he lifted a hand to smooth from her belly button down to the crux of her thighs. He gave her nothing else but a wicked grin. Bear was desperate to escalate the situation. But it was too much fun to tease her.

"I'm impatient?" she huffed. "You made me wait ten years."

Christ. When she put it that way, he didn't feel half so guilty about this. He turned his face to the side and chuckled.

"So freaking bossy!" she complained.

"But you like it." Even as the words came out of his mouth, he realized how true they really were. That challenge in her eye when they argued? There was something more there than simple stubbornness. He'd always known Stella enjoyed challenging him. He'd just never allowed himself to wonder whether he was one of the challenges on her to-do list. Or to dream about how *hot* their long-time rivalry would feel in bed.

Jesus, he was a goner.

Above him, Stella propped herself up on her elbows. Bear, who probably had eighty pounds on Stella, still had control over her lower body. Since there was nothing she could really do to hurry him up, he dropped his head once more to graze the triangle between her legs with soft kisses. Then he raised his head to give her his cockiest grin.

Narrowing her eyes, she reached between her breasts and unhooked the clasp on her bra. The cups sprang apart, her breasts breaking free with a bounce. Her nipples were larger and darker than he'd expected. He'd been tortured by the question of exactly what lay beneath Stella's bikini tops ever since he was a teenager. Suddenly, Stella looked *far* more naked than she had a minute before. As he stared, she dropped back on the bed, arched her ribcage, and cupped her own breasts in two hands. With a breathy little moan, she began stroking them.

Bear was not even conscious of his decision to move. It was only after he found himself scaling her body, catching those soft swells in his own hands that realized that he'd been had.

Quick as a striking serpent, Stella's legs wrapped around Bear's ass, her heels digging in to pin him close to her body. "Men," she cooed, squeezing his body with strong legs. "So predictable."

In answer, Bear said: "Hrrmhaah." Because it wasn't possible to be eloquent with a boob in his mouth. He sucked the tip into a pebbled point, his tongue swirling around the wine-dark nipple. Stella gasped and held him even more tightly.

He lifted his head, and then they were kissing again. If he could, he'd stay forever in her sweet mouth. For the first time tonight, she relaxed into the kiss, letting him take the lead. Bear tried to slow down. He made an effort to appreciate each languorous slide of his tongue against hers. But his pulse was racing, and Stella's curves underneath him were more than he could withstand. She'd parted her legs a little ways, which meant that the base of his shaft settled between her legs. The slick softness he felt there was making him half mad with desire.

Finally, Bear's self-control was dragged right to the brink as Stella slipped a hand down between their two bodies, gripping him with her fingertips.

For the second time tonight, he grabbed her hand away from his dick, pinning it over her head. Then he caught her other one and did the same. Securing both of her wrists with one of his hands, he propped himself up on the other elbow and looked down to watch her face. What he saw there did nothing for his patience. Stella's cheeks were flushed a deep red, and her swollen lips moved as she panted for him. "Bear," she groaned.

He tilted his pelvis, the tip of his dick teasing her entrance. "You want this?"

"Right now," she whimpered.

Again, he teased her with a glancing slide of his aching cock. "I don't know. Let's do rock, paper, scissors to decide."

But the joke fell flat. Because there was no way to disguise how badly he wanted her. Their desire for each other was so palpable that it was hard to believe they'd avoided doing this before. Bear dropped his mouth to hers once again, giving Stella the slowest kiss he was capable of delivering. "Give me one second, buddy. I need to gear up." He rolled off of her and grabbed his jeans from the floor. Unfortunately, his wallet felt suspiciously thin. He swore under his breath.

No condom.

"I won't get pregnant," Stella said quietly.

Bear did not look at her, because the sight of a completely naked Stella lying ready for him to…

The image was too much. He didn't ask any clarifying questions, because he was not going to take chances tonight. He was already a little awestruck that they were having this conversation. And no matter how careful Stella was with the pill or whatever, taking a risk with her was out of the question.

Bear strode over to a wooden console against the wall, where he'd noticed some miniibar items. He pushed aside a wrapped package of playing cards, a six-dollar lip balm and... found a three pack of condoms.

"Hallelujah," he grunted, ripping one open. And here he'd thought fancy hotels were overrated. With shaking hands, he sheathed himself.

Stella watched him from the bed with a gleam in her eye. "Latex covers rock," she said.

"You did *not* just make that joke." He chuckled while his heart thumped loudly against his ribcage.

"So what if I did?" she teased as he lay down again on the bed. Stella raised her arms, reaching for him. Now there was a sight to file away in his brain forever.

Bear did a horny version of the military crawl, hyper-aware of everywhere they touched. He braced himself above her. The heat of her body, the smooth brush of her breasts, the flutter of her pulse at her neck... The whole experience was something he never thought he'd see. *Don't rush*, he warned himself. There might not ever be another moment as perfect as this.

"What are you waiting for?" Stella asked. "A signal from the judges?" She moved her body a crucial inch, and Bear had to close his eyes to hold on to his control. He made her wait a few more seconds. Because if he set aside their power struggle, it would change things between them too much. He needed that distracting layer of competition to keep her at an arm's length from his heart.

She clamped a hand around the back of his neck and hauled him down for the hottest, most crazy-making kiss of his life. Stella absolutely invaded his mouth, and he let her. She wrapped first one leg and then the other around him, letting out a huff of frustration at the delay.

That's when he made his move, pumping his hips, pushing home in one smooth go.

"*Yes!*" she cried out, throwing her head back.

He'd succeeded in catching her off guard, keeping one last ounce of control over the situation. The trouble was he caught himself off guard, too. She was tight and hot and so wonderful that he needed a moment to collect himself. So he bent down to kiss her again, but that only made it worse. The slide of her tongue against his own was so hot that he had to move his hips. Stella's smooth legs gripped his ass. She was under him and around him in every possible way.

At that moment, there was nothing else in the world he needed. No sponsorship mattered. No tour mattered. There was only Stella. She held him so tightly it was possible to forget every other thing in the world.

Seven

ALL THE UNO CARDS and the backgammon set had officially been thrown off the bed.

For *years* she had been fantasizing about this, and the reality was almost more than Stella could take. She didn't want to rush, but she was incapable of slowing down. Every kiss, every flex of Bear's hips brought her closer to the brink.

The intensity of Bear's silver gaze stole her breath. Hovering over her, the man of her dreams looked into her eyes. And then he *smiled*. That smile had always made her stupid, even on the best of days. Right now it was devastating. Bear lowered his beautiful mouth onto hers, and Stella was forced to drop every pretense of attitude. This was too good. It was almost too much. All she could do was put her arms around as much of Bear as she could and hold on tight.

Meanwhile, Bear picked up the pace, growling into her mouth. She'd always wondered what it would be like with him, and reality did not disappoint. She was approaching sensory overload — the scruff of his beard, the bulk of his muscle under her hands... She wished she could slow down time and memorize everything. It was all so very very good.

This was what it felt like to get exactly what you wanted. Like bathing in sunshine and sweet friction.

Bear dropped his head to take her breast into his mouth again. And that's what ruined her. When he lapped at her nipple, she couldn't hold back anymore. Vaguely aware that she was making a lot of unintelligible sounds, she tensed every naked muscle, as if she could stretch out the moment by sheer force of will. Then sensation clobbered her, knocking her back against the sheets. Through the haze of her orgasm, she saw Bear squeeze his eyes shut. "Yeah, buddy. Fuck, that's hot. Aw, yeah," he panted. Then he gave one more masculine growl and planted himself to the hilt with a shudder.

For several long moments, nobody moved. Stella could only lie there breathing, processing the ripple effects of intense stimulation. Her skin felt flushed, and her pulse raced. With his face dropped into the curve of her neck, Bear gave a long groan of satisfaction.

Then, he rolled off of her.

A few seconds were all it took for Stella to feel a twinge of... she didn't know what. Panic was too strong a word. But her defenses notched up to high alert, guarding her heart against whatever happened next. Even though plenty of tequila had been consumed tonight, Stella now felt as sober as a stone.

There was an unfamiliar sting behind her eyelids, too.

It didn't help that Bear got up and disappeared. The room felt too cool all of a sudden. She heard a flush, and knew he'd just disappeared into the john to throw the condom away. But she was very alone in that bed for a moment, wondering if she'd just made a colossal mistake.

He returned, though. She felt the bed depress, and then the warmth of his body moved over to curve around hers. His big leg hitched between hers, and a broad hand came sliding around her waist. He made a satisfied sound. She could feel his muscles relaxing against her body. *Men.* They were such simple creatures. Give them food or sex, and they were happy.

"You okay, buddy?" he asked quietly.

Stella's heart contracted at the sound of his familiar nickname for her. "Mmm," she said. It wasn't a very definitive statement, though, so she also reached a hand back, over her head, to ruffle his thick hair through her fingers. She couldn't roll to face him, though. She didn't trust her eyes not to well with tears. She'd gotten something she always wanted. But it was terrifying to realize immediately afterwards how much she *still* wanted it.

Once would never, ever be enough.

Eight

IN THE MORNING, BEAR woke up slowly.

When you spent five or more months of the year traveling to sporting events all over the world, waking up could be a confusing adventure. With his eyes still slammed shut, he took stock. The bed beneath him was comfortable and also large. No part of him dangled off the edge. It felt great, actually. It beat the hell out of waking up in his sleeping bag on someone else's hotel room floor. (That happened, sometimes.) Much of Bear felt great, actually. There was a dull pain in his head, though. That wasn't unusual.

He was, however, naked.

Bear's eyes flew open, and the realization kicked in. *Naked. Fancy wooden beams on the ceiling. Tahoe. Tequila.*

Stella.

Oh, fuck.

Gingerly, Bear turned his head to the side. It was almost a relief to discover that he was alone in the bed. The only sound he could hear was the cycling of water from that ridiculous hot tub in the bathroom.

And it was just as well, because he needed a couple minutes alone, if only to process what had happened. Bear closed his eyes and took a steadying breath. It had been glorious, really. The intense look in Stella's eye while they made love? So hot. His whole life he'd kept a sturdy wall between desire and the wonderful creature that was Stella Lazarus. Last night, he'd dropped that wall.

Afterward, he'd fallen asleep curled around her body, but woke up again a couple of hours later. Alcohol always trashed his sleep cycle. He'd tiptoed into the bathroom for a glass of water. In the dark, he'd borrowed Stella's toothbrush and washed his face. Then he'd tiptoed back to bed, climbing in as quietly as possible.

She'd turned in toward his body immediately.

"Hi, buddy," he'd whispered, not knowing whether she was asleep or awake. In answer, warm hands skimmed his chest. That was all it took. He leaned in, giving her a deep and minty kiss. On the sound of a sigh, Stella had pressed her beautiful body up against his. Before long he was pulling her up onto his thighs while she reached for a condom on the table.

With the dark cloaked around them, there hadn't been any thinking. Just heat and craving.

But now? In the daylight, things looked different. Hank was going to *shoot* him. *Jesus Christ.* "Do you mind taking Stella out tonight to celebrate?" his friend had asked. *Yeah. Sure. No problem, Hank.*

A few short hours later, he'd... Bear clapped one hand over his eyes and held back a groan. There was no greater violation of the guy code than the sin he had just committed.

They weren't cavemen, of course. There was a version of events which might have made a Bear and Stella combination acceptable. Say, if Bear had ever sat down with Hank and asked him, man to man, if it would be okay if he asked Stella out.

Unfortunately, that scenario bore no resemblance to the events that had occurred on this bed. A tequila soaked hookup? That was just plain wrong. The worst, most childish defense popped into Bear's head. "But she started it." She had, too. It was God's honest truth. She'd kissed him, and she'd unbuttoned his fly.

Right. As if that made a difference. *Oh, well then. It's fine that you banged my baby sister after splitting a pitcher of margaritas.*

Said no one ever.

Bear's head began to throb. He was such an asshole. And the more he thought about it, the worse he felt. Stella *had* started it — quite enthusiastically, too. But for ten years, she hadn't shown any interest in him — not since that kiss when he was eighteen. Why now?

Bear did not like the idea germinating in his mind. She'd done it because he got kicked off the tour yesterday. She'd done it to cheer him up.

Stella Lazarus had thrown him a pity fuck. And he'd taken her up on it.

Now he put both hands to his face, pressing the heels into his eye sockets. And this time, he didn't bother to hold back his groan.

"Bear?" The low voice came from the direction of the bathroom.

Whoops. "Yeah?" he said, his voice husky from disuse.

"Are you okay?"

That was really debatable. "Yeah, Stella." He cleared his throat. "You?"

There was a beat of silence. "I'm fine. But you just made the sound of a dying wildebeest. And now I'm wondering why."

Because I'm dumber than a wildebeest.

"Bear, come in here, would you?"

He would have rather lain on his back a while longer, beating himself up over his poor decision-making. But the damage was already done, and the only thing to do was take the consequences like a man. Bear rolled off the bed and stood up.

His head didn't like that too much. Locating his underwear on the floor, he pulled them on, then padded into the bathroom.

Stella wasn't standing in front of the mirror where he expected to find her. Instead, she was neck deep in the Jacuzzi bath, her hair piled up and clipped on top of her head. She looked adorable, actually, and his heart gave a spastic thump at the sight of her. "Hi," he managed.

"Hi yourself," she said, her face taking on a guarded expression which was unnatural for Stella. Hiding wasn't her style. That's what he loved about her. *Liked*. He liked that about her.

Bear parked his ass against a marble counter and crossed his arms. "Look, I probably shouldn't have..."

Stella held up a hand to stop him. "Nope. We're not having any conversations that begin that way."

Bear opened his mouth and then closed it again. She didn't want to talk about what happened last night. She must be embarrassed, too. "Okay. If that's what you want."

A flash of uncertainty crossed her face. Then she lifted her chin in classic Stella style. "Don't just stand there," she said. "Get in already."

Bear shifted his weight, his eyes darting to the roiling surface of the water. Soaking in hot water with his favorite girl would be heaven on any other day. But just now, he wasn't sure it was a good idea.

Stella rolled her eyes. "Get in. I'm not going to attack you again."

Bear was confused, and also fairly sure Stella was upset about something. He had no idea what. Of course, he could have easily avoided this awkwardness if only...

Right. Too late for that.

Bear ducked into the little toilet area, which was separated by a marble partition. After a necessary moment there, he washed his hands and poured two glasses of cold water. God knew he needed one to ease the pounding in his head.

"Thanks," Stella said when he handed one to her.

Then, trying not to feel self-conscious, he dropped his boxer briefs and climbed into the churning water at the unoccupied end of the oval shaped tub. He bumped legs with Stella, so she pulled hers aside to give him space. He sat down on the ledge, and sank back against the curved wall.

The hot water was heavenly. "Okay," he said slowly. "This is good."

Stella smiled a little and splashed him. "Of course it is."

Bear relaxed his legs a little, and they tipped toward Stella's. She did the same, and so they came to a tentative truce, her smooth leg braced against his larger one. Bear put one elbow on the side and rested his achy head in his hand. From there he observed her, trying to guess what she was thinking so hard about over there. Her hair had gone curly from the steam, and her cheeks had a gorgeous flush to them from the heat. It made him want to trace his thumbs over her cheekbones the way he'd done last night.

She caught him staring and her eyes flicked away.

"What happens next?" Bear asked. He wanted her to say that they could go on being friends. He did not want to lose her over a single drunken mishap. (A mishap of *judgment*, anyway. Every minute of last night had been exquisite.)

"Next, we order breakfast," Stella said. "Coffee. Bacon. Coffee. Waffles, maybe. More coffee."

"All right." She was joking with him. That was a good sign. The throbbing in his head eased up ever so slightly. "I have no idea what time it is."

"After ten."

He laughed. "Wow." On the tip of his tongue there was a joke waiting about how Stella had tired him out. But he bit it back. "I'll climb out of here in a minute and order breakfast. What time do you have to leave for the airport?"

"Eleven-thirty."

"Okay." God, he was going to have to say goodbye to her, not knowing when he'd see her again. It could be months. And then tomorrow Hank was going to fly back out west and meet up with Bear at the gym like nothing happened.

If he asked Bear how his night out with Stella had been, what the hell was he going to say? Bear cleared his throat. "Um, about Hank…"

Stella shook her head immediately. And that guarded look was back on her face. The one that made Bear feel pretty sure he'd fucked up last night. "It's none of Hank's business," she said.

Bear kept the wince off his face. Stella was obviously embarrassed about starting something last night. That did absolutely nothing for his self-confidence.

"Anytime I've ever mentioned my sex life to Hank, he puts his hands over his ears and sings *Jingle Bells*," Stella added.

"Gotcha," Bear said.

"You're sitting over there feeling all guilty, aren't you?"

"Maybe." *Definitely*.

"Don't, okay? I don't want to be one of your *regrets*." She pronounced the word as if it tasted bad.

Tongue-tied now, Bear sank a little lower in the water. He didn't know what to say to make everything okay. It was a familiar problem. He'd never been good with words, especially when they really mattered. Once in awhile he caught himself replaying in his mind all the moments in his life when words had failed him. It wasn't a pretty collection. The morning that his mother had left forever, she'd sat him down to try to explain. "I can't stay here anymore. It's too quiet. I'm no good in the country. If I just go, it will be better for you. No more fights between your father and I."

Privately, Bear had not agreed. He knew that the months between winter's snowy peak and when the trees budded out were the hardest on her. And if she could just hang on a little longer, she'd feel better again. But he hadn't said it. He'd just sat tongue-tied and angry while the hot press of tears threatened the back of his throat.

A half-hour later she was gone for good. And he hadn't said a word.

That moment was probably his biggest personal failure. But there had also been that eerie winter when Stella was sick, and had to stay in her room while he and Hank ran around in the snow. He didn't even know the word "chemotherapy" at the time, but he knew Stella was hurting. He was mighty sorry about the whole thing, and he'd wanted to tell her just how *unfair* it was. But did he say that? Nope. As best he could remember, all he'd done was deal out another hand of cards.

Bear had a near perfect record for never having the necessary words. And now it was happening again. He had no clue what to say. Frustrated, Bear shifted one of his long legs around, grabbing Stella's ankle between his two. He gave it a friendly squeeze.

At first, Stella only gave him a mistrustful lift of her eyebrow. Then, with a big sigh, she shifted her free foot against his. And even though so much in Bear's life was up in the air, including his future, his friendship with Stella, and a guilty secret he would have to keep from Hank, an ankle snuggle was somehow helpful. He drained the water in his glass, set it aside, and dropped his head back against the tub's rim.

They soaked awhile. At one point Stella's phone began to vibrate on the bathroom counter. Stella looked over at the phone, and then ignored it again. Over the next ten minutes, though, the phone rattled and chimed and practically danced the macarena. She looked more agitated each time.

"Maybe you should get that," he said eventually.

"I'm considering it," she said with a wry smile. "But if I *don't* check it, then it's still possible all those calls are from Chad, who's calling about a generous new sponsorship he's secured for me."

Bear glanced toward the phone. "Maybe it *is* Chad, though. Who else is going to call you five times on a Sunday morning?"

Stella crossed her arms, which were gleaming from the water, over her chest. The gesture made her breasts rise above the water line. Bear tried like hell to ignore them. But the vivid memory of putting his mouth...

Stop, asshole. The memory of their time together was going to torture him, wasn't it? Seemed like a fair punishment now that he thought about it. But it was probably going to be a years-long sentence. Every time he and Stella and Hank found themselves in the same city, they'd sit down at some restaurant somewhere, and Bear's mind would head *straight* into the gutter.

Awesome. That's what he got for thinking with his dick.

The phone buzzed again. "One of us should check that. Or else turn it off. Who's it gonna be?" he asked.

"Rock, paper, scissors?" Stella lifted her eyes to his, and Bear saw heat there.

Oh, fuck. He was never going to be able to think of that game again without remembering the moment he was rolling on a condom to...

Without warning, Stella rose from the water, sleek and beautiful. Bear's heart practically stopped beating as the curve of her perfect ass swung in his direction. He swallowed with difficulty as she stepped out of the tub. And it wasn't until she'd wrapped herself in a towel that he began to breathe normally.

Stella lifted the phone and swiped at the screen. He watched her face carefully, hoping for a smile. Instead her mouth formed a grim line. She wandered out of the bathroom. A moment later, he heard her say, "Hello, Mom?"

Bear took the opportunity to get up, too. Feeling warm and loose, he stepped into the glass shower stall for a quick shampoo. His subconscious was still feeling frisky, apparently. Because he spent a brief moment imagining how nice it would be if Stella joined him in there...

Not happening, he reminded himself. *She was only trying to cheer you up.*

It had worked, too.

Bear rinsed his hair quickly, shut off the spray and dried off. The towels were plush and wonderful, and of a quality never found in any hotel room Bear would book any time soon.

He pulled his underwear back on, then walked out into the bedroom. He didn't hear Stella on the phone any longer. "Stella?" he called, grabbing his jeans off the floor and jumping into them. "Should I order some breakfast?" He zipped up and then looked around for his shirt. But she'd pulled that off of him when they were sitting on the sofa...

Bear walked around the groovy fireplace. He found Stella sitting on the sofa, her phone forgotten in her hand, her towel sagging. She didn't look up when he approached. And her face had gone pale.

"Stella?" he asked quietly. "Is something wrong?"

"Hank," she whispered. "He crashed."

"What?" A chill crawled up the back of his neck. "What do you mean, *crashed?*" An awful idea leaped into his brain. Bear last saw him when he was on the way to the *airport*.

Stella was silent and still, while Bear grew more frightened by the second. He sat down beside her and took the phone out of her hand. The screen showed her mother had called several times and left a voicemail twice. Bear touched one of the voicemails in the list. He put Stella's phone to his ear. A moment later he heard the sound of Mrs. Lazarus's hysterical voice, trying to tell her daughter what had happened. "Half-pipe," he heard. "Accident." And, "unconscious," and "hospital." Worst of all, "head or back injury."

Suppressing a shudder, Bear ended the playback, tossing the phone aside. Then he hauled Stella onto his lap, towel and all, and wrapped his arms around her. It just didn't seem possible that Hank could be seriously injured. Nobody ruled the halfpipe like Hank. Nobody. He'd flown into the air off that thing every wintry day since they were boys. Hank was invincible.

"Did you speak to her?" he asked suddenly. Maybe the voicemail was just a panicked call made in the heat of the moment. Maybe Hank was thinking about ordering his first beer of the day right now.

Stella shivered in his arms, and her voice was scratchy. "She's at the hospital. They're doing a whole bunch of scans," she whispered. "He hasn't woken up."

He couldn't hold back his shudder this time.

"I need to get home," Stella said, her voice panicked now.

"Okay," Bear said. He would take her home to Vermont himself. He shifted her gently to the sofa. "Get dressed, buddy. Let's go to the airport."

"You have an event in two hours," Stella said.

"No I don't." Last night he'd been feeling so sorry for himself. It had seemed as if losing his spot on the tour was an actual tragedy.

It wasn't. Not anymore.

Nine

BEAR STOOD OUTSIDE THE hotel's front doors, waiting for the valet parking service to bring Stella's rental around. The temperature outdoors was in the teens. The hotel had mounted warming lights on the awning overhead. It was just the sort of detail a swank resort like this one would provide. Even on your ski trip, they wanted you fat and happy.

He shivered anyway. A cold prickle had crept up his neck the moment he'd learned of Hank's accident and would not leave. With his best friend unconscious at a hospital somewhere, he wondered if he'd ever feel warm again.

Through the glass doors, Bear could see Stella standing at the check-out desk, taking care of business. She looked pale, her face drawn as she spoke to the woman behind the desk. He couldn't hear their conversation, but he could imagine it. The agent at a fine hotel would be unfailingly cordial. "How was your stay with us, Ms. Lazarus?" she would ask. And then, "Did you enjoy any items from the mini bar?"

Holy fuck.

For a second, Bear experienced an ordinary wave of panic. Hank was going to see that bill, and know exactly what Bear and Stella had done last night. But then reality smacked him again, and he realized Hank's anger was now the very least of his problems.

Bear took a deep breath against the nausea that attacked him. The resentment he'd felt against Hank yesterday was unconscionable. Hank had only ever been good to him. As long as Hank woke up, though, Bear would get another chance to be a better friend. He needed Hank to wake up from his surgery, read the hotel bill, and then deck him.

Don't you dare *die*, he ordered Hank.

Stella's rental car appeared in the hotel's turnaround. Bear stepped up to the car when it stopped, taking the keys from the valet, and tipping him with three of Hank's dollars. He dropped Stella's luggage into the back seat. Then he climbed behind the wheel, idling until Stella came out. She climbed wordlessly into the passenger seat, her purse on her lap, her mouth in a grim line.

After a quick stop at the lodge where Bear collected his luggage, they were on their way.

Neither of them spoke on the drive to the Reno airport. Bear's heart was swamped with memories of he and Hank as kids together. He spooled through them as the miles went by.

When they were probably six and eight years old, the two of them had tried to build a tree fort in the woods between their houses, using nothing but fallen branches and some rope. They'd worked on it for days, tying sticks together with inexpert knots. Nothing ever came of it, but it didn't matter. Just farting around together was the whole point.

It seemed wrong to remember Hank this way right now, as if he were already gone. Bear owed Hank *everything*. And it didn't seem possible to imagine a world where there was no more Hank.

One memory in particular was the hardest to take. Christmas, the year that Bear was nine. That had been the first year that Bear's mother was gone, and the first time there'd been no Christmas tree at his house. His father had spent the entire month of December sulking with a bottle of cheap Scotch. Even now Bear associated whiskey with loss.

There had been Christmas presents, sort of. His mother mailed him a cheap package of die-cast sports cars, probably because they were easy to ship. Bear had been too big for little toy cars, though, and her insensitivity had made Bear's stomach burn.

On Christmas morning, his father gave Bear three gifts: a basketball, a new pair of waterproof gloves, and a knit Bruins hat.

"Thanks," Bear had told his dad. "This is great." He gave his dad the candles he'd made at school, and the biggest smile he could. Because Dad had tried. Even though Bear had not been given the expensive gift he'd been hoping for. Even though nothing had been wrapped, and their house was about as cheery as a tomb, it wasn't really Dad's fault that Christmas sucked.

So he put on his new hat and new gloves (which he'd needed, anyway). And he tucked the basketball under his arm and trudged up the hill to see what Hank had gotten for Christmas.

Even before Bear's mom had left, it was an accepted fact that holidays at the Lazarus house were better. For one thing, they had Hanukkah *and* Christmas, because Mr. Lazarus was Jewish but Mrs. Lazarus was not. The Hanukkah presents were small little things, but still. A wrapped present beside your plate for eight days in a row was nothing to sneeze at. And on Christmas Hank always got the very best presents. So Bear was curious to see what "Santa" (at that point, only Stella still believed) had provided that year.

When he knocked on the big back door, it opened immediately. Hank was right on the other side, suiting up already to try out his newest gift on the snow. "Look!" his friend said by way of a greeting. He held up a brand new Burton snowboard, a little bigger than the one he'd been riding last year. "Santa upgraded me."

"Cool," Bear said as an uncomfortable feeling settled into his stomach. He'd known he wouldn't receive a snowboard. But he'd hoped, anyway.

"Let's try it out," Hank said. Then his forehead wrinkled, as he did the math on how that would work. He looked down at

Bear's feet. You couldn't share a snowboard unless you also swapped the boots. "MOMMMM!" Hank yelled.

Mrs. Lazarus appeared in the vestibule a few seconds later. "Happy Christmas, sweetie," she said to Bear.

"Hey, Mom? Do we still have last year's snowboarding boots? I think they'd fit Bear."

A flicker of hope lit inside Bear's chest.

"Ah," she said. "I was saving them for him. Just a moment."

Not two minutes later, Bear found himself strapping snowboarding boots onto his feet for the first time ever. Just like that, Bear's entire winter improved by a factor of about a million. If Hank gave him a turn on the snowboard in the yard sometimes, it would almost be as good as having a board for himself.

"Be careful," Mrs. Lazarus said when they went outside. (She always said that when they went outside.)

They carried the board to the lip of the cleared part of the hill between their homes. Hank dropped the board onto the snow, bending down to strap himself in. "The maiden voyage," he announced. He popped up and leaned down the fall line, riding the snowy hill with the beautifully carved turns of a boy who would someday rule the sport.

Then — and this was a theme of their childhood — Hank had to climb the hill again. Panting, Hank set the board down in the snow and helped Bear strap it on. "Can you do this?" he asked.

"Sure," Bear had said, even though he'd never been on a board in his life. The previous winter he'd ridden a plastic disc sled while Hank used the board. Sometimes he'd stood up on it to mimic his friend, but that had always ended badly.

"Let's see you."

He hopped forward a foot or so, copying Hank. Gravity began to pull him downhill. Since turning looked tricky, Bear let the board lie flat on the snow. He picked up speed much faster than he wanted to.

"TURN!" Hank yelled from above.

Too late. Bear's windmilling arms wrecked his balance, sending him careening onto his butt. Hard. The wet December snow began to seep into his jeans, and he could hear Hank laughing somewhere above him.

In spite of the indignity — and the pain in his tail bone — Bear just sat there and grinned. Because he was nine, and made of rubber. And snowboarding was *awesome*, just like he knew it would be.

It took him a few minutes to unclip and climb the hill again. He was wet and sweating by the time he made it to the top. Hank wasn't there, but Bear spotted movement over by their equipment shed (an outbuilding that was probably half the size of Bear's entire house).

Hank reappeared, carrying the snowboard he'd ridden the two previous years. "If we go at the same time, I can show you how to turn," he said.

Bear handed Hank the new board and clipped himself onto Hank's old one.

They stood side by side on the hill. "First, rock like this," Hank instructed, showing Bear how to find his edges.

It was Bear's first snowboarding lesson ever, the first of many given to him by an eleven-year-old kid who would someday be a three-time world champion and silver medal Olympian.

When the lesson was over, Hank frowned at the old board in Bear's hands. "You should just keep that one," he said. "We'll do this again tomorrow."

And just like that, Bear had become the owner of a snowboard. The *exact* thing he'd wanted for Christmas.

Hank had handed Bear his entire life that wet December day.

Almost two decades later, behind the wheel of a rental car headed toward the Reno airport, Bear pinched his thumb and forefinger into the corners of his eyes, because the road had become curiously blurry.

Stella rode silently beside him, the citrus scent of her shampoo drifting through the small space. Last night Bear had his face buried in that hair when he should have been with Hank in Vermont.

What had he done?

October, Ten Months Later

Ten

BEAR AND HIS FATHER stood together in their little kitchen holding identical mugs of coffee. Bear spooned bites from a bowl of granola on the countertop. His father held a piece of buttered toast in his free hand.

If you Googled "bachelors eating breakfast," an image of the two of them would probably pop up.

"What are you doing today?" Bear's father asked.

Bear considered the question, which wasn't nearly as simple as it sounded. What his father meant was, "are you going to take any of my advice today?" Or, "will today be the day you figure out how to get on with your life?"

"Well…" He cleared his throat. "Today is Saturday." That too was code, for *get off my back old man*. "Later, I'm driving over to Hank's. He got some bad news, I think."

His father's eyebrows furrowed together over his coffee mug. "Is it serious?"

Bear set down his spoon. "Not medical news, Dad." Ten months after his accident, Hank's health was no longer touch and go. In fact, he was doing about as well as a guy could be doing who'd lost everything, including the use of both legs.

It's just that he was stuck in a wheelchair forever. And he was big-time depressed about it.

"What, then?"

Bear sighed. "His ex-girlfriend just got engaged, and it's all over the news."

"You never liked her, though," his father said.

Bear grunted at the stupidity of that statement. "But *he* did, Dad. Jesus."

His father ignored the protest. "So you're free until when, then? Because there's a message on my machine from the ski hill. But I was supposed to take a run over to Rutland to pick up a tire for the truck."

Okay. So his father's *what are you doing today* had really been the prelude to asking for a favor. Bear could work with that. "I'll listen to the message. If they need something today, I'll run over and take a look."

His father set his mug in the sink. "Thank you. Need anything from Rutland?"

Bear shook his head. The things he needed could not be found in stores. He needed to figure out what the fuck he was going to do with the next chapter of his life. And he needed Hank to do the same — and to get that scary, defeated look off his face. The one that suggested life wasn't worth living anymore.

After his dad left, Bear listened to the message on his father's business line. Barry Electrical kept business hours, more or less, but weekend emergencies were not uncommon. And in a small town, an electrician couldn't afford to ignore any business, no matter how ill-timed. Especially a call from the ski mountain, which was easily the biggest business in town.

"Hello, Barry men!" a voice sang into the machine. It was Anya, who worked in operations on the hill. "We need one of you to take a look at our snow cams, if you would. We might want to move one of them this year. I'm working Saturday, of course. So swing by if you get a chance. Or you can call and we'll pick another day to work on this. Toodles!"

Now he understood now why his father had asked him to handle the call, which was certainly not urgent. Cameras were Bear's thing. He was good with them. Although his father would never give praise aloud, he knew Bear was good with cameras, too.

Bear would just as soon head over there now. It was good weather for an outdoor job, and it was Saturday. That reduced his chances of running into Stella in the office. He felt the same little thud of pain in his chest that occurred every time he thought of her.

It was Stella who preferred it that he keep his distance. She'd been avoiding him since the dark days of last December.

Bear took a basic electrical toolbox from the equipment shed and carried it to the driveway. It was a gorgeous October day, sunny with a bit of a nip in the air. He put the tools in the back of Hank's old 4Runner.

It wasn't until the third time Bear had borrowed Hank's old SUV to run some errand or another for Hank that his friend had said, "Just keep that thing for awhile, okay? You gave up your Utah wheels. So you should drive my Toyota. In case you haven't noticed, I sure as hell can't drive it."

Nine months later, Bear was still driving it. And he didn't know what to do about that. Hank now drove a brand new sports car outfitted with a set of hand controls, which the 4Runner did not have. But this wasn't Bear's car, although he'd now made some repairs, and had changed the oil twice.

He could just add Hank's truck to the long list of confusing, half-decided things in his life. It wouldn't even make the top ten.

Before walking into the corporate offices at the ski hill, Bear braced himself, just in case. Seeing Stella always hurt. Whenever she caught sight of him, a look of irritation crossed her pretty face. Stella's discomfort was one of the thornier problems in his life. He had no idea how to get their friendship back to a more normal place. Every time he walked into the office building, he was reminded of how badly he'd failed his friends. Both of them.

He pushed the door open and went inside, glancing around. Half the cubicles had bodies in them, even on a Saturday. Autumn was the busy season at a ski resort. Because, as Anya always put it, the seven thousand seasonal workers they needed each winter didn't hire and manage themselves.

A quick glance into the corner of the room revealed that Stella's chair was empty. *Thank you, Jesus.*

"Hi, handsome."

Bear turned to find Anya watching him. "Hey, lady. I got your message."

She tipped her chin toward Stella's desk. "She's not here today. So you can relax."

He opened his mouth, but then shut it again. Arguing with her would only make it more obvious she'd caught him worrying.

"I don't know what's the deal with you two. But maybe you should figure out how to get past it, preferably while I'm still young." She batted her eyelashes at him in an exaggerated, comical way.

Again, Bear had no answer. He'd love to know how Anya knew he was uncomfortable. And what Stella had ever said about their unfortunate encounter at Lake Tahoe. Though he didn't really deserve to know unless he could somehow find a way to discuss it with Stella himself.

Then again, they were never having that conversation unless she stopped sprinting out of rooms when he walked into them.

"Where's this camera you want to move?" he asked.

"It's time to take a hike," Anya said, leaving her desk.

"That's what all the girls tell me," he said, and Anya laughed.

THREE HOURS LATER, Bear descended the Blue Spruce ski trail for the second time, while the sun beat down on his back. He dropped his tool box outside the office door, then went inside to find Anya.

"How did it go?" she asked, hanging up her phone.

"Fine, I think. But now we have to check the video feed to see if I'm right."

"Pull up a chair, hottie."

Ignoring her cheeky compliment, Bear dragged an office chair over from an empty cubicle. Anya passed him the keyboard. He logged into the video website, where camera number two was now showing video of an empty grassy slope.

"Hey!" She clapped her hands. "It looks good, right? Viewers will be able to see skiers as they jump that cornice."

"Yeah. The camera angle looks good. But if it slips or something, just give me a call."

"This is great! I'm glad we moved it. In the old spot, we just saw a bunch of people getting off the chairlift on Upper Hazardous. That's not nearly as interesting, except when they fall off. It was like the blooper cam."

Bear chuckled. "That could be fun, though. You know, when you're training lifties, you should show them some of that footage. There are plenty of ways to fall off a chair lift. You could show them all of 'em in a ten-minute period."

Anya sat back in her chair. "Holy crap. That's a good idea."

Bear shrugged. "Only if you still have the footage."

But Anya was already punching buttons on her phone. "Hey, Toby! Yeah, I know it's Saturday. You know Bear, right?"

They knew each other. The older man was the head of the ski patrol, and Bear had worked for him a couple of seasons when he was a teenager.

"In the staff meeting last week, you asked if we could make you a training video. Bear is going to help you with that, okay? And he has some great ideas. Yeah! I'll check. Bye!" She hung up the phone and beamed a smile at him. "You do know how to edit video, right?"

"Who doesn't?"

"Um, lots of people? But I guess the better question is whether you're okay with taking on an extra job for the mountain. Do you have the free hours?"

Free hours were just about the only things that Bear had plenty of. "I think I can fit it in," he said, giving Anya a wave goodbye.

A training video. Bear's head was full of ideas before he even reached the parking lot. He'd been shooting footage on the snow for years, but it had never occurred to him to charge for his services. It had always been a hobby.

But video was probably something the mountain needed more of, right? In fact... Bear turned around and went back inside. "Hey, Anya?" he called, striding toward her desk.

"Back already?"

"Just one last thing. Those marketing clips on your website are pretty old, right? Has there been any talk of replacing them?"

"Sure." She shrugged. "But we were going to talk about it after we get the whole website redesigned next month."

"All right." Bear cleared his throat. "I'd like a chance to pitch you guys on any new footage before you hire someone else."

"Okay," she said, grabbing a pen. "I'll add it to the agenda of our next staff meeting."

"You're the best."

She waved a hand dismissively. "I know."

BEAR WENT HOME feeling happier than he had in weeks. In the alcove which his father referred to as his "office," he entered his hours at the mountain onto a time sheet. Working part time for his father was currently his only income. His condo in Utah had been on the market for more than half a year, but there hadn't been any nibbles. If it didn't sell soon, he'd have to lower the price, wiping out the nest egg he thought he'd accumulated there. Another tricky decision to add to his list.

It was a pretty long list. And numero uno was a doozy: find something else to do with your life.

Today, he might be one step closer.

When dinnertime arrived, Bear looked into the refrigerator, pulling out some deli meat and a jar of mustard. He was a twenty-nine year-old guy living with his father like a loser. But it was the only way to keep expenses down.

"You're whistling," his father pointed out when Bear walked into the kitchen. "Got a date?"

"Nope. Got something better."

"What's that?"

"An idea."

"Uh oh." His father chuckled. "I'd better brace. That's what you said when you wanted to enter your first snowboarding competition."

The subtext of that statement was: *and look how that turned out.* But Bear was in too good a mood to let his father's jab take him down.

"So are you going to tell me what it is?" his father pressed.

"I want to make a film. Several films, actually." Some of them would be practical things, like the videos for the resort. But there was really no reason to stop there. He'd always enjoyed photography and camera work. "I'd be good at it."

His father gave a dry chuckle. "You need a *job*, son. That's a hobby."

Bear said absolutely nothing. It wouldn't matter if Martin Scorsese himself asked Bear to work on a film, his father would never see it as legit. It would be a waste of breath to try to convince him. Bear spread mustard on two slices of bread and promised himself that he wouldn't engage with his father on the topic of the future.

"I requested another application for that accounting course. It came in the mail today."

Bear kept the flinch off his face. "I still have the last one you got me."

"Fill it out, kid. The semester starts in January."

Never in his life had Bear exhibited an interest in accounting. But his father had latched on to this idea a few years ago because the accountant who did his business taxes every year charged a lot of money. "You definitely want some of that," was how he always put it.

"You can fill out the application and still make your movie," his dad added. "Movies are expensive, by the way."

True. But that didn't mean Bear couldn't make them. He layered his sandwich together and cut it in half with the mustard knife. "I'll take it under advisement."

"I know it's hard to change gears," his father said.

Seriously? When have you ever tried? His father had not left Vermont as long as Bear could remember. The man did not know shit about changing gears.

"But you got to find your feet, kid. Stop relying on the Lazarus family to plan your life. I hope you're not going to ask Hank for movie money."

Bear felt his blood pressure escalate even before his father finished his bitter little statement. He knew he shouldn't react, but it was fucking impossible not to. "I don't take his money," he bit out.

"Really? Whose car is that outside?"

And there it was. Bear picked up his plate and strode out of the room. He walked through the modest log home his father had built with his own two hands, and out onto the little porch. There weren't any chairs outside, because when his mother had still been around, there wasn't money for extra furniture. Eventually Barry Electrical came into its own and paid all the bills. But there still wasn't anyplace to sit, because a single dad with his own business didn't have free time to think about deck chairs.

Bear sat down on the wooden planks, his feet dangling off the front, his plate in his lap. But his appetite had left him. It was a shitty thing to accuse him of — trying to depend on Hank. His father had it exactly backwards. The whole reason he stayed in central Vermont, where the job market was crap, was because Hank was not okay. His best friend was in terrible distress, and

Bear had spent many hours of each day — and more than a few nights — worrying about him.

He'd started worrying that morning in Tahoe with Stella. And he'd never really stopped.

By the evening of Hank's accident, he and Stella had reached the hospital. The meager phone calls Stella and her parents had traded between flights had provided no clarity. So Bear had lead-footed it all the way down highway 89 from Burlington.

But at the hospital, there still weren't answers. The next few weeks had been a gauntlet of small milestones which only brought new questions. Would Hank wake up? Yes, he finally did. But he could not move his legs.

At first, Hank had seemed to take the devastating news with a stiff upper lip. (Later Bear realized that shock had numbed Hank's early reaction.) When Hank began an aggressive course of physical therapy to try to maximize his muscle control, Bear had sat with him in the rehab hospital while trainers buzzed around, making optimistic noises about "giving it time" and "retraining the nervous system."

But the more time that passed, the less optimistic everyone became. Especially Hank. As the one-year anniversary of his crash loomed, he could only manage a few hard-won steps at a time, and only on a set of parallel bars, with leg braces that rivaled the The Terminator's metalwork.

Bear picked up his sandwich and took a bite. It was the same turkey and cheddar on wheat that he ate every night because it was cheap. Bear only spent money on restaurants or bars when he could convince Hank to get out of his house for a beer somewhere. Even after ten months, that wasn't getting any easier. Bear didn't know what to do about it, either. It stressed him out. His father's misplaced disapproval of their friendship only added insult to injury.

The irony was that Bear *did* have a job offer. A good one.

A coach he'd known for a decade wanted Bear to join his back-country outfit outside of Aspen, Colorado. If Bear took the job, he'd leave after Thanksgiving to lead snowboarding clinics for whoever could fork over ten thousand bucks for an intense week of star-studded coaching. He would teach lessons, and also mix with the paying guests at meals, probably telling stories of his glory days as a pro.

The pay was good, and the food would be spectacular. As opportunities went, it was a pretty good one. He hadn't told his dad, though. Because he wasn't sure yet what he was going to do about the offer.

On the one hand, it would be easy to board a jet to Denver and forget every tense detail of these past few months. But it wouldn't feel right to walk away with Hank still looking so miserable. Bear's work here wasn't done.

So it smarted that his father had accused him of leeching off of Hank, when the easiest choice would be to turn his back and flee the state.

Bear's father's discomfort with the Lazarus family was his own life-long hang-up. Bear knew this. Still, he'd always had trouble shaking off his father's disapproval. Tonight was a perfect example. It had taken all of five minutes for his father to flatten Bear's optimism over his film idea.

Don't let him get to you, Bear ordered himself.

Besides, the more he thought about filmmaking, the better the idea got. Winter sports were a big business, with big money involved. And if they wouldn't pay Bear to snowboard anymore, they could pay him to *film* snowboarding.

Who else knew as much as he did about the sport *and* about cameras? He had as many industry contacts as a guy could have.

And so did Hank.

Now, his friend couldn't take a job coaching, like Bear could. But that didn't mean he had to sit indoors for the rest of his life. Maybe he could get Hank to think big. If they made a film *together*, Hank could get back into the swing of things.

It wouldn't be an easy conversation. But maybe Hank would see the possibilities, eventually. He'd have to. Because with every passing minute, the idea grew greater in Bear's mind.

He left his sandwich plate on the front porch. He got into Hank's SUV and cranked the engine. Bear drove down the private drive to the main road, carefully ignoring the steep turn-off to the Lazarus estate. Stella still lived up there in the guest house over her parents' garage. But it had been a good ten years since she'd come sliding down the hill that connected their properties to visit him.

Thirty minutes, and thirty dollars later, Bear was in possession of a fancy bottle of tequila and the absolute certainty that his big idea was a keeper. He steered the Toyota up South Hill toward Hank's renovated, handicapped-accessible bachelor pad. The engine growled at the effort. And Bear wondered what he'd find at the top of the hill. He just assumed that Alexis' marriage announcement meant that Hank was having a rough day.

Hank never spoke about his ex, Alexis. Never.

The ugly, early days of Hank's recovery were a blur to Bear, which meant that they were probably a blur to Hank, too. He hoped so, anyway.

Bear had spent the first week sitting around at the hospital, waiting for news. He'd spent the second one running errands for the Lazarus family and keeping track of the truckloads of notes and gifts that arrived for Hank. There had been balloons and flowers, T-shirts and stuffed animals. Most of them read "Get Well Soon!" Never had an English phrase been more inadequate.

Hank had spent those same weeks recovering from major back surgery, trying to wrap his head around the idea that he could no longer move his legs.

Even from the beginning, Bear had worried more about the dead expression in Hank's eyes than about his limbs. The Hank he knew had left the building, leaving behind a silent, angry shell. Bear's only hope had been that Hank would do better once he left the hospital for the rehab place.

On the eve of Hank's transfer, Bear had paid a visit, hoping to show him a video he'd edited that afternoon. He'd asked all the people Hank knew in Park City to send him a five second greeting. Many had done even better. The guys at Hank's favorite bar had an on-screen oyster-eating competition in his honor, and threatened to drink all the Guinness if Hank didn't come back soon. It was juvenile humor, especially after Bear edited it over the theme music to Rocky. He'd have done anything to get Hank to crack a smile, though.

But when Bear reached the corridor outside Hank's room, he heard Alexis's voice inside. She was easy to identify. Stella wasn't wrong when she said that Alexis had one of the more annoying voices God ever gave a woman. "I've been doing a lot of thinking," Alexis whined.

Bear halted outside the door so as not to intrude.

"Hank, I'm going to Utah tonight because I have a race tomorrow."

Hank's answer was almost too low to hear. "I know."

"But..." Alexis heaved a sigh. "Baby, I'm not coming back."

What? Bear thought, his phone halfway out of his pocket.

"What are you trying to say?" Hank rumbled.

"Look, I know you'll hate me for this," Alexis whimpered. "But the next eight weeks could be the most important of my career." Alexis, a moguls skier, had already been named to the

Olympic freestyle team. "And I need to focus on the skiing. And only on the skiing. You *know* how it is, Hank. I'm sorry. I just don't have the… space for this right now."

Bear didn't breathe at all during the silence that followed. What Alexis had just done was unconscionably cruel. He wanted to go in there and *shake* her.

When Hank finally spoke, his voice was as rough as Bear had ever heard it. "Better not miss your flight then."

"I'm sorry. I'm really sorry," Alexis babbled.

"Just go already."

A few seconds later, Alexis trotted out of the room, face red, head down. She practically sprinted for the exit.

Bear made himself wait there for a minute before he went in to check on Hank. Poking his head into the room, he looked at his friend's pale face. "Hey," he said stupidly. What did you say to a guy who'd lost everything, and then a little bit more?

Hank turned his face toward the window. "Hey."

"So…" Bear cleared his throat. "I brought you something to watch."

Hank did not even turn his head.

Bear decided to drop the illusion that he hadn't just heard what Alexis had done. "Look, maybe she's just really freaked out right now."

"She won't be back." The words were almost too soft to hear.

"Well…"

"I don't want company right now."

Of course he didn't. Because sometimes a man just needed to suffer his latest indignity in peace. "You need anything…?"

"*No.*"

At that, Bear turned and left the room, closing Hank's door softly behind him. He briefly considered putting a fist through the hallway wall. Not that it would help. But his frustration was off the charts. Hank could not catch a break. And all Bear could do for him was to leave him be, or offer him a cookie from the god-awful cafeteria.

He needed some air. Badly. So he marched down the corridor and out the back door.

Unfortunately, when he stepped outside, there stood freaking Alexis, jabbing a manicured finger at her phone.

That's when Bear kind of lost it.

"What the *hell* was that?" he spat without a preamble. "Jesus Christ! It's only been a week since he realized he's fucking *paralyzed*, and you drop him like a brick?"

Alexis whirled on him. "Where do *you* get off? For a *year* you've wished I'd disappear. You and his sister *and* his mother! All of you are so sure that I'm not good enough for the amazing Hank. Are you going to stand here and pretend that's not true?"

Bear's fury rose up in his throat, nearly choking him. He would never scream at a woman. But it took all his effort not to. "I think you just proved it."

Her eyes glittered with anger. "You don't know a goddamned thing. I had two choices. I can be cruel right now, or call him every night from the *fucking Olympic village*. Is *that* what you want? You want me to give him hourly updates on everything he's about to miss? Gosh, Bear, if I make it onto the podium, I can fly home and let him hold my *medal*."

"You could have just *stayed*," Bear said. But even as he spoke the words, he realized he was in no position to suggest it.

"And miss the Olympics. That's what you mean, right?"

He nodded.

"I'm not that girl, okay?" Alexis heaved a giant sigh. "Racing is all I have. Even without his accident, Hank and I wouldn't have lasted a year."

"You don't know that," Bear argued. He did, though. He'd suggested the same thing to Stella in Tahoe.

"I *do* know that. So I ask you — what was I supposed to do? Be a giant bitch right now? Or throw away my only chance to be an Olympic medalist just so that I could hold his hand for a year until we both remember we're not all that compatible. All my choices are bad ones, Bear. All of them." A taxi wound its way toward the two of them, and Alexis picked her bag up off the ground. "Whatever you're thinking about me, just go ahead and think it, okay? Because if Hank and I stay together just because he had an accident, he'll just be *settling* for me. And we both know it."

Alexis shot him one more glare and then climbed into her taxi.

Bear watched the tail lights disappear into the December darkness. Then he sat down on the freezing bench beside the hospital door. Until ten days ago, there were laws of nature which had always held up in his life: Hank was destined for greatness. Stella was untouchable. Bear would muddle along.

Now everything was turned on its fucking head.

The December chill seeped through his jeans, and Bear considered heading home. But then he spotted Stella coming up the hospital walkway. Her dark hair blew in the breeze, and her eyes were cast down toward the sidewalk. At the last second, she lifted them, finding Bear on the bench before she reached the doors. "Hi," she said, coming over. She sat beside him.

"Hi." Another brilliant greeting. But these days there were *two* people he didn't know how to talk to anymore.

"Are you okay?"

Not hardly. "Yeah," he said. Because that was the answer a man gave, whether it was true or not.

"I'm worried about you."

He looked up fast. "Why?"

She shrugged. "You're avoiding me."

"Not true." But *Christ*, he was. Because Stella was yet another uncertain thing in his life. He didn't know what to do with the way she made him feel. Hot and cold at the same time. As if he'd been taken apart that night they'd slept together, and the reassembly had gone just a little wrong.

Stella crossed her arms in front of her chest, probably because she was cold. "We should talk, Bear."

Oh, hell. "About what?"

He expected her to roll her eyes. That would be typical Stella. But instead, she looked worried. "Something happened in Tahoe, and you're trying to pretend that it didn't."

Busted. Pretending was just the right word. It allowed him to carry on as if she hadn't taken pity on him. "I don't see what there is to talk about."

Her eyes dipped. "I knew you would say that."

Bear had no idea how to respond. He'd assumed Stella would be embarrassed about their night together. But if that assumption was wrong, then he was even *more* confused.

Stella's dark eyes studied him for a long time. "I think... *hell.* If I tell you right now that it meant a lot to me, you're going to argue, aren't you?"

Oh, boy. Was there any answer to that question that would not get him in a world of trouble?

She lifted her perfectly kissable chin. "Maybe if our timing hadn't been so awful, you wouldn't be freaking out right now."

"I'm not freaking out," he argued. *Yeah, you so totally are*.

"Really? Then why do you avoid me? Whenever I show up at the hospital, you suddenly think of some errand that needs doing."

Ouch.

"I think…" She hesitated. "You don't want to hear that I think we could be good together. I can see it on your face." Her eyes got a little shiny. "But I had to bring it up. Because I'd regret it if I never did."

Whoa. Bear had to be very careful with whatever he said next. There was nothing in the world he wouldn't do for the girl sitting a cautious few feet away. In fact, he'd happily gather her up right here on the hospital bench and hold on tight.

But that wouldn't help Stella, not really. She was under a shitload of stress right now, and obviously seeking comfort from him. And he couldn't allow her to do that. Making Stella a part of his life—and a fixture in his bed—wasn't something he'd take lightly. It was *definitely* a bad idea when emotions were running high. Neither of them had gotten a solid night's sleep since…

Since Tahoe.

Nobody was thinking straight. And if Stella had convinced herself that being with him would make her happy, that was just the tragedy talking. When the bad shit happened, people clung to what was safe and familiar. Bear knew this firsthand, because he'd clung to the Lazarus family after his mother left.

And they weren't his to keep.

If Stella, in her sorrow, took Bear as her personal security blanket, her parents sure wouldn't approve. Not to mention Hank…

Bear swallowed hard, just imagining that conversation. *Even though you think your life is over, and your girlfriend just dumped you, I'm shacking up with your baby sister, because pain has clouded her judgment. Kay?*

He wouldn't do that to Hank.

Anyway, a year from now, Stella would be back out in the world, kicking ass and taking names. She wouldn't need him anymore. And what would *that* blow feel like? Bear didn't want to know. Shutting down Stella's misguided attraction to him was the only thing to do.

Beside him, wearing a very guarded expression on her pretty face, Stella was waiting for him to say something. Even now she wasn't acting like herself. The Stella he knew didn't wear a pining expression for anyone.

What was it that Alexis had said less than a half hour ago? *All my choices are bad ones. All of them.*

Yeah. That was eerily familiar.

He turned his chin and looked right into Stella's eyes. "It was just sex, Stell." And it was. Sex that shouldn't have happened.

"I see," Stella whispered. She stood up suddenly. "Thank you for clearing that up."

"Stell…!" He hesitated. An expression filled with hurt crossed her face. *Shit.* It didn't mean that he didn't care about her. Was there any way to explain?

That's when she'd turned and walked away.

Now, as he steered into Hank's driveway and killed the engine, he thought about all the times Stella had avoided him since that ugly day ten months ago. It was probably as many times as he'd spent wondering if what he'd said had been a total fuck-up, or exactly the right thing.

Hopefully, Stella was over whatever temporary feelings she thought she had for him. She probably snubbed him just for pride's sake, and he would have to live with that.

Meanwhile, Hank had barely mentioned Alexis, even when she won a silver medal at the Olympics. But he must have seen her big news, or heard about it from a friend. Just because her name never came up didn't mean that Hank had forgotten his ex, or the awful way they'd parted.

Tonight, he hoped he could get Hank's mind off those old troubles, and try to get him to think about filmmaking. They were going to have good tequila. And they were going to have a little talk.

He hopped up onto Hank's porch and let himself in after a quick tap on the front door. "'Sup, Hazardous?" he called. His eyes did a quick sweep of the room. Since Hank had a housekeeper who dropped by a couple of times a week, the condition of the room didn't always tell him what he needed to know.

His eyes landed on the man himself, sitting on the sofa in front of the football game. Bear gave him a quick once-over. Jeans. A T-shirt reading "Jackson Hole." And a freshly shaved face.

Bear had expected worse, given the news Hank had just received. There were days when he showed up to find Hank hunched over in his wheelchair, staring at the TV in his underwear. And that was on days without ugly news about his ex-girlfriend.

Now, Hank muted the football game and tossed the remote aside. "Why do football pundits exist?" he asked. "They're never right, anyway."

Bear didn't want to talk football. He passed Hank by and walked over to the bar dividing the kitchen from the living room.

With a quick press of his arms, Hank transferred himself from the couch to the wheelchair and followed Bear. He lifted the bottle of tequila and examined it. "Conmemorativo. That's the good shit. Are we celebrating something?"

"Maybe." Bear reached for a couple of shot glasses in the drawer. The kitchen had been completely rebuilt to accommodate Hank — with clever storage in reach of a seated person and a tiered countertop surface. "Hazardous, let's do this right. Do you have any limes?" There was a single plate in the sink and a whiff of supper in the air. Hank seemed to be doing okay today, even if his expression was flat.

That was encouraging, right? Bear allowed himself to hope that maybe today was the day when they both turned the corner. He cut limes and rehearsed the speech he wanted to give Hank in his head. For once he'd hit upon a project which had the potential to pull both of them out of the swan-dive that was their lives. Finally.

Once they were set up, drinks in hand, Bear took a breath. Leaning forward, he tried to tamp down the excitement in his voice while he told Hank his plan. "I want to make a feature-length snowboarding film," he told Hank.

The inevitable silence followed, during which he tried to read Hank's face.

His friend's first response was a thoughtful one. "Hasn't that been done before?"

"Not by us," Bear said. "You're going to be the face of the project. I can make a great film, but I need your cred." It was perfect, really. He and Hank could stay close to a sport they both loved, without having to be the center of attention.

But Hank began to look bitter. "I don't have any cred. I'm a cripple. I have cripple cred." He reached for the tequila.

That was exactly the attitude Bear needed to correct. "Listen, asshole." He held the bottle out of his friend's reach. "You'll narrate it, and I *guarantee* we'll have a blast. Guys want to hear what you have to say about the amped-up shit I'm going to film. And the ladies would throw their panties at the screen. You and I would get a couple of free heli trips out west. What's not to love?"

Hank set down his shot glass with a thunk. "Let me get this straight. You would drag my ass to the top of some sick peak, and then wave goodbye on your board? Why would I bother, if I'm only taking the heli back down?"

Bear shook his head. "I'd be filming, not riding. And you don't have to come up in the copter if you don't want to. In fact, you can just do the post-production, if that's how you want to play it. But the partying is better in Alaska than in an editing room."

"I don't think I'm interested."

Bear set the bottle on the table and tried not to feel too discouraged. He understood Hank's pain, and maybe it was too soon to suggest the film. But winter was coming. Fast.

There wasn't any manual for this. He didn't know the proper mourning period for one's entire career. But Hank hadn't shown interest in *anything* for so long, and Bear knew this idea was a good one. He'd spent the whole summer and fall trying to come up with the right Plan B for the two of them. He'd spent hours thinking through different possibilities — opening a restaurant, designing snowboarding gear.

But this idea? This was *it*.

"Hazardous," he said, his voice low and serious. "I need you on this. I want to film it this season, and the first snowfall is only six weeks out. We'll edit next summer and tour it a year from now. We can hit the college campuses and enter part of the film in the Banff festival. It will be awesome."

But Hank had no reply. Furthermore, he tipped the bottle toward his glass. And the night began its downward spiral.

Eleven

STELLA HAD ALREADY FINISHED her first beer by the time Anya showed up at the bar.

"Sorry I'm late!" Anya called. "You know how the work days go in October. There's always some fire to put out."

"You're just coming from work now?" Stella checked her watch. It was seven already.

Anya handed Stella the sweater lying over the adjacent bar stool and hopped onto the seat. "Thanks for saving me a spot."

"I fended off about twenty people for you," Stella said. "Travis is pissed at me."

Anya watched their friend scoop ice into five glasses in a row, then use two soda guns at once to fill them. "He doesn't look pissed, he looks stressed out. This place is mobbed."

"The new girl quit last week to go work on a cruise ship. Travis is short-handed." Stella tossed a pretzel into her mouth. "I almost volunteered to go back there and help out. It makes me tired just watching him."

"You can't be tired. I'm the one who worked ten hours on a Saturday."

Stella pointed a pretzel at her friend. "That's your own fault. Nobody asked you to work quite that much."

"Wave down Travis, and I'll tell you what I was working on."

Stella glanced down the bar at their friend, who was blending a frozen margarita with one hand and uncapping beers with his other. "What are you drinking?"

"Something on tap. Switchback, I guess."

"Save my seat." Stella slid off her stool. She ducked under the bar, grabbed a pint glass and dispensed a draft for her friend.

"Can I get a Bud?" a white-bearded guy inquired just as Anya's pint was filled to the top.

"Um... sure." She glanced at Travis. He was still busy at the other end of the bar.

"Lady, where is my beer?" Anya hollered theatrically. "I've been waiting hours."

Stella gave her the stink eye. "Very funny." She dispensed a beer for Santa Claus and then ducked back to her seat before anyone else mistook her for the help.

"Thanks," Travis said on a drive-by. "I'm getting my ass kicked."

"So this morning..." Anya began. She was bouncing on the barstool, clearly bursting to tell Stella a story. "You'll never guess who I spent a few hours with."

Uh oh. "I have no idea." She had a hunch, though. She and Anya had been friends since high school. These days their desks at the ski mountain were twenty feet apart, and for months Anya had been trying to figure out why Stella was avoiding a certain ex-pro-snowboarder.

"*Bear*," Anya said with a catty grin. "He was looking *especially* fine today in a dark blue thermal shirt and jeans that just hugged his..."

"Is there a story here?" Stella interrupted. She was already familiar with all the ways that Bear filled out a pair of jeans.

"I'm just trying to set the scene," Anya said, sipping her beer. "Anyway, we hiked up Upper Hazardous to reposition one of the snow cams, and I fell behind a little, so I could admire his ass..."

Stella took a long pull of her beer to keep herself from commenting.

"...And then afterwards I had the brilliant idea of asking him to make two training videos for the mountain. One for the lifties and one for the new ski instructors. For the next six weeks, he's going to be working with the ops guys and the education department."

"That's nice," Stella said carefully. But inside, she was yelling, *fuck, no!* Her job was painful enough without having the man who rejected her wandering in and out of the office all week.

"I asked him out, too," Anya added. "And he said 'oh, Anya, you beat me to it. I was thinking that we should have dinner together.'"

Stella tried to keep the wince off her face. She was probably at least fifty-percent successful.

"He said that he liked blue in a girl's hair especially, and that it probably meant we should get married next week and have four children."

Stella's heart finally restarted when she understood Anya was teasing her. "You are such a bitch."

"Gotcha!" Her friend giggled. "I wouldn't have to pull these stunts if you would just level with me. Something happened with Bear, and you won't tell me what it was. But you are *not* over it."

Wasn't that the truth?. "You can ask him all about it when the two of you have dinner," Stella teased, reaching for the pretzels.

Anya grabbed the basket and held them up out of Stella's reach. "You believed me for a minute, didn't you? The pretzels are held hostage until you spill your guts."

"Keep them. I'm only going to get fat anyway since I'm not an athlete anymore."

She'd dropped out of all the rest of the freeriding competitions last winter in order to be near Hank. The result was that even the modest sponsorships she'd won had quickly evaporated. So she was back to zero again, and her parents wouldn't help finance her. "We'd really like to have you around again this season," was one of their standard lines. "The foundation needs you," was their other one. Stella didn't actually for the Windsor Resort itself, even though her desk was in the administrative office. Stella was employed by the Lazarus Family Foundation, a charitable organization that funded her mother's favorite causes.

"I don't get why you can't compete," Anya said, setting the pretzels down on the counter. "Why don't you just nick some foundation money into your own bank account?"

"Gosh, I don't know. Maybe because embezzlement is a crime?"

"Ask for a raise?" Anya suggested.

"I can't even work during the winter if I'm competing. There wouldn't be a paycheck to raise. I think the only thing that will get the point across is if I go for the nuclear option."

"What's that?"

"Quitting," she heard herself say.

"That will fix the cash problem," Anya teased.

"But I'm just so stuck! My parents have me tethered to the desk so I won't go off and maim myself like Hank did. They're trying to smoke me out, basically. Tie me down until I say 'uncle' and go back to school full time."

"They mean well," Anya said softly. "They think they know what's best for your future."

"Just like Hitler."

Anya snorted. "Enough about them, then. Let's talk about Bear. The way he walks into the office lately is interesting."

"Why?"

"Well, you know that shed behind my house? In the summertime, there's a snake living underneath it. Every time I go in there to get my bike, I'm freaking out a little bit, hoping it doesn't dart out and touch me. That's how Bear looks when he checks your desk chair."

"I'm not going to slither up and bite him. And your snake can't hurt you, either. Rattlers are rare in Vermont."

Anya planted an elbow on the bar and leaned in closely. "Honey, what *happened?* Did you guys have a thing?"

Stella sighed. "If by a 'thing' you mean an eight-hour sex marathon, then yes. We had a thing. But he obviously did not enjoy it as much as I did. He made it pretty clear that we're never doing that again."

Anya's eyes became dreamy. "Oh, damn. I can see why that would be hard to get over. But… eight hours?" She picked up the cardboard coaster her beer had rested on, and fanned herself with it. "Doesn't that pretty much guarantee he was into it? Who wouldn't want a repeat?"

"Him. That's who." Stella drained her beer. "He said, 'it was just sex.'"

Her friend's eyebrows disappeared behind her bangs. "That's *cold.*"

Stella had thought so too, at the time. But there was something about Bear's brush-off that just hadn't rung true. Except… Maybe that was just a lifetime's worth of foolish optimism talking.

Last winter had been awful, and Stella would just as soon forget everything that had happened then. Stella remembered feeling hollow for three weeks straight. As if someone could push her over with a proverbial feather. Before her depressing conversation with Bear on the hospital bench, they'd spent a lot of time at the hospital together. And Bear had looked absolutely *shattered* sitting there under the ugly hospital lighting. Every time Stella moved closer to him, he seemed to shut down a little further. Sure, he'd put an arm around her shoulders, and make sure she got something to eat every few hours.

But when he looked at her, it was with guilty eyes. And that had frightened her almost as much as her brother's terrifying medical condition. Her whole life, they'd been there for each other when things got rough.

Eventually, they were able stop worrying about whether Hank would survive, and move on to the long-term questions: things like which rehab facility he'd go to, and which wheelchair he needed. That's when Stella had finally brought it up. "We should talk," she'd said.

From the look on his face, she knew that the conversation wouldn't go well. And she wasn't wrong. When he finally said, "it was just sex," she wanted to die right there outside the parking lot entrance.

But even as his words shredded her with their callousness, the expression on his face didn't match. And every time she'd accidentally met his eyes since, there was something else there. Something pained. And it hurt her to see it.

She hadn't brought it up again, though. How many times could a girl throw herself at the same guy? She was pretty sure she'd already hit the limit. And Stella was smart enough to know that you couldn't *convince* someone to love you.

The last ten months had been horribly lonely. She'd hung around her brother a lot at the beginning. The trouble was that Bear had the same idea. He'd practically pasted himself to Hank, especially after Hank moved into the house on South Hill that their father renovated for him.

During the past few months, Stella had aborted quite a few missions to visit Hank, because Bear had beat her to it.

"Stella?"

She looked up, focusing on Anya's face again. "Sorry. What did you say?"

Her friend smiled. "I asked if your brother knows. Did you tell Hank about your tryst?"

"God no. And I never will."

"Maybe that's the problem, sweetie. It's against the guy code, you know? Thou shalt not have a sex marathon why thy best friend's little sister. And those two are really close. Your dad is always saying what a great friend Bear has been since the accident."

Stella groaned. "It's not like I haven't considered that. Bear has appointed himself my brother's personal servant and savior. And sure — our extracurricular activities would make for one very awkward conversation. But that excuse only works up to a point, you know? If he actually cared about me, it wouldn't matter what Hank thought."

Anya's face fell. "Ow."

"Exactly."

"So what's your plan? Maybe you should just break into his house, strip yourself naked and wait for him to show up. He's a guy, after all."

Stella only sighed. "That's what I did the first time. The rush was great. The hangover has been a bitch."

Anya put an arm around her. "That sucks, honey."

"It does. But I have nobody to blame but myself. If I hadn't spent so many years pinning my hopes on him, it wouldn't be so bad. I just thought..." Stella peered into her empty glass and fought for the words. "See, I'm not cut out to be somebody's little wife." *Or mother.* But she wouldn't bore Anya with the medical details. "I'm not convinced there's someone out there who'd want a daredevil like me. But Bear is an adventurer, too. I thought if we were together, he wouldn't expect me to sit at home and keep dinner waiting. He's *fun*, Anya. We could have a good time together. It's just that he doesn't see it that way."

"Can I at least offer you another beer?"

"Can't. I'm driving. I should go, anyway. I have a big workout planned for tomorrow morning." She needed to stay fit. The first snowfall was probably only forty-five days away. Fewer in the Rockies. She had to find a way to jump start her career this winter. Even if her parents did their best to stymie her, Stella would find a way.

"You know," Anya said over the rim of her beer, "I never start sentences with: 'I have a big workout planned.'"

"You could start now," Stella suggested, hopping off her barstool.

"Nope!" Anya grinned. "Be well, sweetie. And thanks for sharing."

"Eh, it needed to be done." She gave Anya a hug. "Goodnight." On that note, Stella left the bar.

Outside the air was crisp with autumn's chill. The air smelled like leaves, but soon it would smell like snow.

Soon, she promised herself. *Somehow*.

She got into her little old car and steered toward home. Toward her *parents'* home. Like the loser that she was.

* * *

Several hours later, Stella's phone woke her from a deep sleep. As she came to, it stopped ringing. When it started up again, she grabbed it and peered sleepily at the screen. Bear. Now *that* was unusual. "Hello?"

"Stella," he said immediately, his voice a rasp. "I fucked up."

Later, she would be angry with herself over the conclusion that her feeble heart had leapt to. She heard the words *I fucked up* and hoped, for one golden second, that Bear was calling with the wee-hours epiphany that they should be together. "What's the matter, honey?"

"It's all my fault, Stella. I need you to pick me up from Hank's house and take me to the E.R."

"What?" She shook herself awake. *"Who's hurt?"*

There was a deep sigh on the end of the line. "He's fine, okay? Hank got really drunk tonight on tequila. He started vomiting, and he wasn't responding to me. So I called an ambulance. He'll probably kill me in the morning."

It took a few seconds for Stella's brain to catch up with the roller coaster ride her heart had just taken. "Are you sure he's okay?" she had to ask.

"Yeah. I probably overreacted. But his health isn't the same as it used to be. I was afraid to make the judgment call by myself on whether he could just sleep it off."

Though Bear sounded stressed out, Stella felt a wave of prickly anger. "What do you need me for, then?"

"I need to get to the hospital, buddy. Can't drive myself."

"Oh. You're drunk, too."

Another deep sigh could be heard on the other end of the line.

"You know it's two in the morning, right?"

"I know." His voice was low and miserable.

"I could just leave your ass there and go to the hospital myself."

"You could. But I fucked up, and I like to clean up my own messes."

Not all of them. Bear had infinite patience for her brother's needs. And none for hers. "Never fear," she snapped. "The Cheerful Drunk Man's Taxi Service is on its way." Then she hung up on him.

Twelve

BEAR STOOD UNDER Hank's shower head for only a minute or so. Given his druthers, he would have spent an hour in there, letting the hot water beat down on his stupid self. But there wasn't time. Shutting the water off, he grabbed one of the perfectly folded towels that had been placed on the handicapped-accessible rack by Hank's housekeeper.

The shower had helped to sober him up, at least. After toweling off, he was able to step into his jeans without swaying. In Hank's bedroom, he checked once more for any mess he may have missed.

The night had gotten ugly, and fast.

Bear walked out of Hank's bedroom, startled to find Stella already standing in the living room looking pissed. Just the sight of her, cheeks flushed, arms crossed under her breasts, caused a hitch in his breath. She was so fucking beautiful that he honestly needed, like, prep time before seeing her. "Hi," he said stupidly.

"What happened here tonight?" she asked without preamble.

Bear noticed he didn't even get a "hi." Not that he deserved one. "I brought over a bottle of tequila, and Hank drank too much of it. He was pretty upset."

"Because of Bitchy Barbie, right?"

Bear nodded. "He took it even harder than I thought he would."

Stella flinched. "He's better off without her."

"I know that, and you know that," Bear said. This was actually the longest conversation they'd had in many months.

"But Hank would have preferred to come to that conclusion himself."

Bear hadn't expected his friend to take it quite so hard, though. It wasn't until after Hank got truly sloppy that Bear began to understand why. "I'm never finding someone," Hank had slurred, face in his hands.

"That is not true," Bear had said immediately. Hank had been a total babe magnet his whole life. Even *before* he'd become a pro snowboarder. Women would always find him attractive. Wheels or no wheels.

"Yeah, it is true," he'd said. "I'm never having sex again."

Bear had just snorted. "Me neither, apparently."

Hank had looked up from his hands, a horribly serious look in his eye. "You don't get it. No woman will want me this way. My *last time* was with that bitch."

For a moment, they just stared at each other. Bear had risen abruptly and gone to the sink to fetch a couple of glasses of water, because it was his job to stay upbeat. Tonight, however, he didn't think he could keep the look of devastation off his own face. Hank thought his life was over. That no woman would ever see past the chair.

And Bear didn't have the right words to tell his friend to hang in there. Bear had never felt so fucking helpless than he had this past year. He hadn't known what to say last winter, when Hank woke up unable to move his body. *If only I was a better friend, then I'd know what to say*. If he had a dollar for every time he'd thought that, he could buy the his own car in one easy payment.

Helplessness had had been the theme of his spring and summer. And now it was fall already, and he was *still* flailing.

The only thing he knew for sure was that he could not go to Colorado. Not when Hank was still like this. There was only one thing he knew how to do: show up. He'd shown up at the rehab facility during visiting hours, when Hank was stuck in that joint for eight weeks. He showed up when Hank moved into this house, to move books and shit around, and bring the first six pack for the empty fridge. He showed up for Patriot's games on TV, and to drag Hank out of the house for happy hour.

He showed up. And it never seemed to help. But still, he had to keep trying, until one of these days Hank rejoined the living. Every time he pulled up in front of Hank's house, he hoped that today would be the day Hank said, "Sorry, I can't hang out tonight, man, I've got a date." But months had passed, and Bear was terrified that it would never happen.

That gave him the cold sweats.

When he'd returned to his seat, Hank had the bottle of tequila in his hand, and the level of the liquid had decreased dramatically.

"Hank?" he'd asked, looking around for the spill. *Please let there be a spill.*

His friend's head had sagged on his neck. And then the real fun began. It was a good thing that Hank's bachelor motif favored sleek wooden floors. It had made the cleanup a whole lot easier.

Standing in front of him, Stella cleared her throat. "Is there a mess?" she asked. "I'll clean it up before we go."

"Already did that," Bear said. "Took care of it. Started a laundry."

Her eyes flashed. "Of course you did," she muttered. "Let's go then." Stella turned and stomped out of the house.

Bear grabbed a bottle of water out of Hank's fridge and followed her. Stella's car was already running when he folded himself into the passenger seat. It was an awfully tight fit. Stella did a three-point turn on the gravel in front of Hank's woodsy house and headed down the driveway.

On Vermont's deserted roads, the trip to the hospital took the same fifteen minutes whether driven at two-thirty a.m. or at nine in the morning. Almost all of those minutes dripped by without Stella saying a word. "How've you been?" Bear finally asked into the uncomfortable silence.

"Just peachy."

Bear was still woozy from his portion of tequila, but he wasn't too drunk to pick up how she felt about him right now. And he knew he deserved it. "I hope that's really true, buddy."

She gave a little snort. "Let's see... I'm chained to a desk. My sponsors dumped me after I disappeared last year. I don't have the money to compete. There's a first-descent trip to Alaska that I'm not invited on, because I don't have any backing, and therefore any visibility. And I don't see my brother as often as I used to, because your car is in his fucking driveway all the time."

Whoa. Bear flinched. "I didn't know that. What if..." Bear rubbed his forehead with a fist. "You could take certain days of the week, and I'll stay away."

"What a great idea!" she said with too much zeal. "We could be like divorced people who were never married." Stella made the turn into a hospital parking space a little quicker than absolutely necessary.

Shit. His head was too fuzzy to figure out what to say. "I'm really sorry that you don't want to see me, Stella."

She yanked the parking brake into place and leveled him with a stare. "I think that's my line, you *ass*." Yanking the door open, she hopped out of the car and then slammed the door again.

Bear leaned back against the headrest of her little car and closed his eyes. Stella's anger confused him. Their drunken fling would have sorted itself out had it happened at any other time. Without the tragedy of Hank's accident, she would have realized by the time her plane's wheel's lifted off from Reno that Bear wasn't good boyfriend material. She would have moved on.

Instead, nobody had moved on.

He had to admit that Hank's drink-yourself-to-oblivion plan didn't seem quite so crazy just then.

Thirteen

"OH MY GOD!" Anya squealed.

Bear couldn't see the computer screen, because there were too many heads clustered in front of it. But since he'd spent a dozen hours editing this footage, he knew precisely what had set her off. It was the awesomely comical clip of the little kids falling down like bowling pins and then the chairlift scraping them forward, like the pin return at the end of the alley.

Since the safety team had begun screening Bear's training video two minutes ago, there had been grunts of appreciation and chuckles of amusement.

That was good. Very good.

Because he couldn't help it, Bear risked one more glance into the corner where Stella's desk was. There was still nobody over there. And the computer screen was dark.

It had been three weeks since that grisly night when he'd had to call her for a ride to the ER. He'd been to the ski mountain office five times since then and had only managed to glimpse her once. He'd given her a friendly smile but she had not returned it.

Big surprise.

His audience of five *oohed* and *ahhed* through the video, while Bear stood there worrying. His favorite pastime.

"This is awesome," Anya said finally.

"It's great," Toby agreed. "Can I tweak a couple of words in the narration?"

"Sure," Bear agreed. "Watch it a few more times and email me your changes."

Anya clapped her hands. "Does this mean we get to talk about the marketing video now? If you can make a training video entertaining, then I can't wait to see what happens when we turn you loose on the fun stuff."

"But no pressure, right?"

She grinned. "It's going to rock."

Bear thought so, too. In fact, this gig was just about the only shiny thing in his life right now. His eyes flicked once more to Stella's empty corner. When he looked back at Anya, she was studying him.

Busted.

Bear cleared his throat. "Is she here today?" Anya would know exactly whom he meant. She wasn't slow.

The girl shook her head, making a blue lock of her hair wag back and forth. "Nope. And she isn't coming back."

"What?" His heart sank as a reflex, but then lifted again. Maybe Stella had gone off somewhere exciting. She'd mentioned an Alaska trip. It was only October, though...

"She quit," Anya shrugged. "Told her dad she was through."

Quit? Bear wanted to pry, but anything he said to Anya would go directly back to Stella, as soon as the airwaves could carry it. Curiosity won out. "She got a better offer?" he asked hopefully.

"Depends how you define better," Anya said. "She's working for Travis."

"Doing what?"

Anya spread her hands. "Tapping beers, of course. It's not like Travis made her the chef."

"Oh. That's probably a good thing, though."

A smile began at one corner of Anya's mouth and spread slowly across her face. Stella's inability to cook was widely known. "Yeah."

Bear realized he'd shown way too much interest in the topic already. "I'll show you a few ideas for the marketing video. Maybe... next week?"

"I can't wait."

Bear got into Hank's SUV and warmed up the engine. Before the meeting at the office, he'd spent much of the day hanging lighting fixtures at a new McMansion on the ski mountain. Now that it was quitting time, he reviewed his choices. He could drag Hank out for a burger or a pizza — those being the two most prevalent food groups in a ski town — or he could go home and make himself yet another lonely bachelor sandwich.

For once, he chose a third option.

Bear reversed out of his parking spot and headed into town. Idling past Rupert's Bar & Grill, he saw Stella's car parked out front. Bear nabbed another of the parking spots on Main Street, but decided to take care of some business before he went inside.

He pulled out his phone and checked the signal. He did the Vermont Two Step — holding the phone in the air and pacing around until his phone showed four bars — which was about as good as it ever got in Vermont.

Bear needed to work some magic before the guys who worked on Rocky Mountain time went off for their own cocktail hour. He dialed, tapping a foot until he got an answer.

"Hey! How are you?" was the greeting Bear received from Christian, the rep for his favorite ex-sponsor.

"I'm doing great," Bear lied. "And you?"

"Couldn't be better. We got our first flurries last night. Three more weeks until we're skiing on it."

"Awesome."

"How's Hazardous doing these days?"

Funny, but Bear used to hear Hank's nickname all the time and think nothing of it. Now it hit way too close to home. "He's coming along," Bear said, his second lie in fifteen seconds. "I lost some money to him on the football game last weekend."

"Sorry to hear that." Christian chuckled.

"Me too," Bear said, keeping it light. "So I got this new gig I want to tell you about. I'm making films for a living."

That was a pretty good stretch of the truth. He was making films for a tiny part of his living, but on the other end of the line, some several thousand miles away, Christian made a small noise of interest. And that was enough to boost Bear's confidence. Because the company Christian worked for made video cameras.

"I have contracts with a couple of ski mountains in Vermont," he began. Another stretch of the truth. But a necessary one. "Those are for small films. But I'm putting together a big one — a feature-length film. And I wanted to offer you the chance to get involved."

"That is interesting, dude. How do you envision our role?"

"It really depends," Bear said, in as casual a voice as he could muster. "I've been using your equipment since it first came to market." This was true. Bear and Christian had once gotten into an hours-long barstool conversation one night after a tour event. The line of OverSight helmet cameras had recently launched, and their mutual love for photography had won Bear one of the first sponsorships OverSight had ever given to an athlete.

It was the business arrangement Bear was most proud of, actually. Because it had never had a thing to do with Hank.

"I could make this movie the way most snowboarding pics are filmed," Bear went on. "Mostly big cameras and heli aerials. But I think it would be really neat to do something different, you know? You've got those drone cameras now, and I don't see much marketing of drone cameras to the sporting crowd. If you were a major investor in the film, I could really show off your product. People need to know that drone cams aren't just a gimmick. They're more useful than people think. I want to feature them."

There was a silence on the end of the line, and Bear held his breath.

"That is the most interesting idea anybody has brought me lately," Christian murmured.

Bear waited for the "but."

"When did you want to make this thing?"

"I want to shoot it this year and edit over the summer."

Christian whistled into the phone. "That's aggressive."

"So am I."

"Well..." Christian cleared his throat. "You'll have to send me something, like, yesterday if you want me to take this to the board."

"I'll do that," Bear promised.

"Before the end of the week, okay?"

"No problem," Bear said. Even if it meant he wouldn't sleep the next three nights.

He said his goodbyes and shoved the phone in his pocket. *Damn.* He took a moment to just stand there grinning. He should have made that call three weeks ago, immediately after he got the idea. It had been foolish to wait. But after Hank had shot down the idea, Bear hadn't felt ready to try to sell it to anyone else.

Maybe, just maybe, this would break his way.

Tucking his phone away, Bear braced himself for the evening's next tricky conversation. When he pushed open the door to Travis Rupert's bar and grill, Stella was the first person he spotted. She was busy washing glasses behind the bar. As she worked, Bear couldn't help but notice how the clingy black top she wore exposed a whole lot of cleavage. He averted his eyes, wondering if her other customers would be as gentlemanly. *They'd better be.*

Damn. He'd better get over any proprietary feelings he had over those. Over *her*, he meant. *God.* He felt like slapping himself.

Bear took a stool at the end of the bar. Stella didn't make eye contact with him, but still, he was certain she'd clocked him the moment he came in the door. If she wanted to make him wait, he guessed there wasn't anything he could do about it.

"Excuse me!" someone piped up from a few seats down the bar. Bear turned his head to see the speaker was a frat boy wearing a polo shirt and a big frown. "I asked for a Bud Light and a Coors. You brought us a Coors Light and a Bud."

"But I wrote down…" Stella pulled a pad from her apron and squinted at it. She flinched. "Oh. Sorry. Give me one second." Stella turned her back on him to grab a couple of glasses off the overhead racks.

The grumpy customer elbowed his buddy and then shook his head, saying something under his breath that Bear could not hear. The other guy chuckled in a way that Bear did not like.

"Hey," Bear said to them before stopping to think it through. "You got a problem?"

"*No.*" The kid's tone was belligerent. "Do you?"

Stella finally looked at him, one eyebrow raised. She put two fresh beers down in front of the frat boys. Then she slid down to stand in front of him.

"Hi," he tried, hoping she'd be friendly.

"Hi," she repeated. "Can I get you a beer? Otherwise…" she drummed her fingers on the bar.

"I'd like a Switchback, please," he said, watching as she bit her lip.

"Coming right up," Stella sighed.

She turned away to get his beer, delivering it a minute later without a word. Bear drank it slowly. His budget didn't allow for lingering at the bar. He'd called his Park City realtor this morning, hoping for good news. "We'll snag a buyer come winter," the realtor said. Meanwhile, he wrote checks once a month to cover the taxes, the maintenance fees and the electricity. If he took that job in Colorado, none of that would even be a hardship.

And yet...

Bear watched Stella work. She wasn't the best waitress, and he had to bite back a smile when she spilled a beer onto the bar. Eventually, the rush of customers slowed, leaving Stella to studiously ignore him by scrubbing invisible dirt off the bar.

"Stella," he said when she wandered past him. "Talk to me."

She turned to him with a glare. "What about?"

"I'm just wondering why you're here."

"I don't know?" She gave an exaggerated shrug. "To earn a paycheck? Why do *you* work?

He sighed. "I meant, why did you leave your dad's foundation?"

"Ah. That's everyone's new favorite topic. I should just print up an outline and pass out copies."

"Look, I'm not trying to bust your balls," he tried.

Stella threw the rag on the bar. "Good thing, because I don't own a pair. And you verified that first hand."

Bear winced. "Look, did you quit because of me? I don't have to show up there so often..."

Her eyes popped wide. "Vain much?"

"No!" Now he'd really stepped in it. "I just..." *Can't be in the same zip code as you without putting my foot in my mouth.*

"Lady, can I get a beer sometime tonight?"

Bear turned his head to verify that the rude customer was the same frat boy from before. "I'm going to kill him."

"That's really going to improve my tips." Stella left to serve the dick who was drinking the cheapest beer Rupert's served.

Bear put a ten dollar bill on the bar, and shrugged on his jacket. He assumed their conversation was over. But Stella walked back over to face him one more time. "I quit because my parents weren't getting the message," she said quietly.

"What message?"

She rolled her eyes. "That they don't own me. Okay?"

Bear wanted to ask more questions, but something about Stella's defiant stance stopped him. Her arms were crossed, her hair tossed to the side. But there was a whole lot of frustration burning in those big brown eyes, and a dollop of pain, too. He wished there was something he could do about that. But he knew there wasn't. They were stuck like this — both frustrated by circumstances, unable to get what they needed.

And unable to have their easy friendship back.

"I'm sorry, buddy," he said.

"You've said that before."

Christ, he had. "Goodnight, then."

"Goodnight."

She was busy pulling another beer for someone before he made it out the door.

Fourteen

THE NEXT NIGHT, RETURNING from another electrical job for his father, Bear clocked Stella's car behind Rupert's again. But this time, he kept on driving.

The 4Runner climbed the hill where Hank lived without too much effort. He let himself into Hank's house in the usual fashion. He didn't like what he saw. There was a half-filled whiskey bottle on the table. *Uh oh.* He heard the sound of a toilet flushing from the direction of the master suite, and felt a prickle of unease.

"Hey man!" he called out. "Are you back there?"

Hank rolled into view a minute later. "Hey," he said as Bear looked him up and down. Sweatpants. No socks. The T-shirt said "Bob's Sno-Cat Lodge," this time. Hank transferred to the sofa, hiking his useless legs into place with one arm before looking up at Bear.

His gaze was steady, and Bear felt himself relax. "What's shakin'?"

Hank lifted an eyebrow to indicate the ridiculousness of the question. Then he spread both heavily-tattooed arms wide. "The usual nada. Why?"

So Hank was ornery, but not wasted. Things could be worse. Bear toed off his shoes and took a seat on the other side of the L-shaped sectional. He propped his feet on the coffee table, nudging the empty glass with his toe.

"The parents were here earlier," Hank said. "I treated myself to a little nip after they left."

"Ah. How are the 'rents these days?"

"Exhausting. My mother is all fired up about this new mobility study at the hospital. I've had exactly two hours' worth of the new therapy, and she's already looking for a progress update. I pity the people in charge."

Bear chuckled. Hank might be ornery, but he had his mother pegged. Mrs. Lazarus was a tough cookie. "Maybe the doctor running the study needs the scotch worse than you."

"Have you met her? Callie Anders?" Hank asked.

Bear shook his head. "You mentioned her a couple of times before, though." He watched Hank carefully.

Sure enough, Hank twisted his head to the side, hiding a smile. "She's a hottie. It's one of the only things I don't hate about the program. She's easy on the eyes. And I'm going to be there seven hours a week for a year."

"I can get you out of it," Bear offered.

"How? Kidnapping?"

"Sort of. Come out west. Make a film with me."

Hank didn't meet Bear's eyes. "I thought about it."

This was progress. Bear held his breath.

"I heard what you said, okay? That both of us have to figure out something to do now. I heard you loud and clear, and you are not wrong. And I have no fucking clue what my act two looks like. It's just that I don't think I can… face that. Not right now."

"Okay," Bear whispered. His throat felt thick. He'd needed Hank to hear him out, and consider the movie, and his friend had done it. The answer wasn't what he wanted to hear, but, hey, a little more bad news wasn't exactly a surprise, was it? "So can I ask you about something else?" Bear prompted.

"Anything," Hank said.

"The blue-book value on your 4Runner is about nine thousand dollars. Do you want to sell it to me? I could pay you two grand now, and a couple hundred a month going forward."

Hank was so indifferent that he could only be bothered to lift one shoulder. "Keep it, man. In case you didn't notice, I can't drive it anymore."

"Dude, I can't just *keep* it. It's not the same as passing me a used snowboard, you know?"

Hank looked him in the eye finally. "You need the money for your movie, right? Consider this my contribution."

Bear's pulse jumped in his temple. "I didn't *ask* you for money. I'm going to convince OverSight to fund it."

Hank held up two hands in submission. "That's cool. And I know you didn't ask me for money. But you need that truck and I don't. And even though I didn't ask *them* for it, my parents gave me a house worth more than half a million dollars with a roll-in shower and speakers in every room. I'm giving you a rusty truck with a broken speedometer. People do shit for each other sometimes. Someday we'll be dead, Bear, and arguing about this is wasted breath."

Bear was uncomfortable again, emotions rolling through his chest he couldn't express. "I fixed the speedometer," he said, stupidly.

Hank raised his arms and then dropped them into his lap. "See? She belongs to you already."

Bear sighed. His conversations with Hank never went in the direction he'd planned. "Look, I'm going to pay you nine grand for the truck, and maybe you should think about giving the money to Stella."

Hank's eyebrows shot up. "Why?"

"She needs the money for travel."

"Seriously?"

"Yeah. Your parents don't want her competing this year. So they won't help her."

Hank scrubbed his forehead. "That's insane. Why didn't she tell me?"

Bear did not answer that question. He just folded his arms and waited.

His friend sighed. "Nobody tells me shit anymore."

"They don't think they can, man."

"My ears aren't broken."

No, just your attitude. "Stella quit her job, too. Did she tell you that?"

Hank's chin snapped up. "No, she did not. What the fuck?"

"She's pouring beers for Travis now, but I think the pay sucks. I think she's trying to tell your parents that she won't be bossed."

At that, Hank threw his head back and laughed. "That's my girl. You can't make her do *anything*."

Bear smiled, because that was easy to do whenever he thought of Stella. "You should call her. Or just drop by Rupert's to see her in action."

Hank grabbed a Nerf football wedged between his body and the armrest and threw it to Bear. "I haven't been paying enough attention to my sister, have I?"

Bear tossed the ball to Hank without weighing in on the question. It was obvious Hank had not paid enough attention to *anyone* lately.

Hank tossed the ball back. "I can't see Stella being very good at waitressing. She can be kind of a klutz when she's not on a snowboard."

True. Bear had been watching Stella his whole life. All he had to do was close his eyes and call her up the image of her smooth hands fumbling with the cork on the bubbly she'd poured him that night when they were teenagers. He could visualize her walk, and the way she tossed her hair to get it out of her face.

His lot in life was to admire her from afar. And there was really no way around it.

Hank gave up on the football. He transferred to his wheelchair, rolled into the kitchen and opened the under-counter refrigerator. When he returned, he held two beers. Hank had perfected a method of holding a long neck with the fingers of each hand, while propelling his wheelchair forward with the heels of his hands. It didn't look comfortable, but Bear had learned months ago not to offer help unless it was blatantly necessary. Hank didn't want to be babied, and Bear totally got that.

"That's who you need in your movie," Hank said.

"Sorry?" Bear took one of the beers.

"Stella. A film could do her a lot of good. I heard her asking that useless agent of hers whether Nike was going to make another snowboarding movie. She needs the visibility."

"I thought about asking Stella," Bear said, in a whopping understatement. He'd thought about it plenty. But without Hank involved, it would be so awkward.

"If you don't ask her, she'll never speak to you again." Hank chuckled. "Besides. If you want big mountain shots, who's better than her?"

"Nobody," Bear admitted. Hank didn't seem to have noticed Stella was avoiding him.

Hank took a sip of his beer. "My parents really won't give her the money? Seriously?"

"Well..." Bear cleared his throat. "I don't have all the details. I don't know how hard she pressed her case. I think she hates that she has to ask for help. She hates that she's twenty-seven and still not earning enough to cover the travel. You made snowboarding pay the bills before you could legally drink. She's pissed it hasn't worked like that for her." It didn't matter that Stella hadn't spelled all of that out to him lately. It was his own life story, too. He had that fucker memorized.

Hank traced the lip of his beer bottle with one finger. "It's not her fault that freeriding doesn't pay that well."

"Or that the women never get paid like the men."

Hank looked up to meet Bear's eyes, a smirk on his face. "Bear, I never took you for a feminist."

"Very funny." Bear took a slug of his beer, paranoid about Hank's scrutiny. He'd always been tuned into Stella, even before he'd stepped over the line with her.

"You're right, though." Hank ran his hand across the overgrown whiskers on his chin. "Poor kid. She must be so frustrated. I'll go find her tomorrow, and see if there's anything I can do."

Bear chuckled in spite of himself. "Just don't be surprised if she won't take your help. Trying to talk her into something is like trying to talk *you* into something. Impossible, really."

Hank grinned. "We're just here to give the whole world a hard time."

Wasn't that the truth.

Fifteen

OCTOBER SLID INTO NOVEMBER while Bear became even more frustrated by all the things in his life which could not be resolved — big and small.

Hank wasn't returning his calls, and Bear didn't know why. He could only hope the new therapy regime taking up more of Hank's time. And Bear had his fingers crossed that Hank had started spending time with that hot doctor he admired.

There was, however, no evidence that had happened.

Meanwhile, he'd sent Hank a check in the mail for two grand, which had gone uncashed. Which could mean that Hank didn't open his mail. Or that he'd opened it, and shredded the check.

Most pressing, Bear was still waiting to hear from OverSight. He'd sent in a detailed proposal and cost estimates, and had been promised an answer within "a few days." Days had turned to weeks, and Bear had taken to checking his cell phone every half hour during the work day to be sure that he hadn't missed anything. But all that turned up on his voicemail were pleas from his Colorado friend who wanted him to commit to the Aspen job.

The call he'd been waiting for finally came at about ten o'clock on a Monday night. Bear had just finished showering the sawdust from one of his father's job sites out of his hair. As he pulled on a pair of jeans, the phone rang.

"Working late?" he asked Christian when he picked up the call.

"Yeah, man. You know how it is in the fall."

Bear did know. Everyone who worked with the snowsports industry put in overtime to set up for the season. As soon as that crisp, leafy smell hit the air, it was time to book flights, work the kinks out of the equipment and spend a whole lot of time getting into shape.

Now that snowboarding was no longer his life, Bear didn't know what to do with autumn anymore.

"So, we think your proposal has legs," Christian said. Bear's heart skipped a beat. "We want to do it. There's just one stipulation."

"What's that?" Bear asked, while mentally jumping up and down.

"We need Hank Lazarus to sign on with the project before we'll fund it."

Crash. His private celebration suffered a hard landing. Bear took a few seconds before answering, because he needed to make himself clear without losing his temper. But it wouldn't be easy. "I hear you," he said slowly. "But that's not the way this works. Hank is going to do this project with me, but he's doing it on his own time frame. And I will not rush that man. It's only been a *year*, Christian."

There was a silence on the other end of the line then. "I get it. But maybe this project works better next year, then."

Bear felt like screaming. Another year like this past one would kill him. "I don't have a year. And there's no better investment than a film made by me."

Christian sighed. "It's a lot of money, Bear. And I own a camera company. I've got a dozen guys who can make a film. If I'm going to spend this much cake on *your* film, I need to know that people will go out to see it. Hank isn't just a face. He's newsworthy. Viewers will want to see how he's doing."

And now Bear felt sick. "It's not that kind of film. He'll be the expert, not the *subject*."

"I read your proposal," the rep said quietly. "The slant you're taking is a good one. But Hank will draw curious eyeballs. He must know that. If he doesn't want the attention, he won't do the film. And if he won't do the film it doesn't have the same audience. I'm sorry, but that's just true."

Shit. "Listen. I'm not giving up on Hank. But I can't promise him. And I won't use him as a bargaining chip."

Now it was Christian's turn to choose his words carefully. Bear could hear the man's gears turning in the silence before he spoke. "It's in your hands, Bear. My board needs to see me committing money to projects that will pay off. So let me know if you think you can meet our specs."

Specs. That's how you'd refer to a piece of equipment you were building. But his relationship with Hank was not a mechanical object that could be disassembled and rebuilt at someone else's convenience.

Fuck you, he thought.

"I'll let you know if there's a change on my end," Bear said aloud.

"Thanks, man," Christian said. "Best of luck, too."

I'll need it, Bear thought as he disconnected the call.

After that unpleasantness, Bear bumped around their little house feeling empty. The TV was on in their small living room, but he didn't think he could sit calmly beside his father and watch a football game tonight.

What he needed was a glass of scotch — just a couple of fingers of the well-aged single malt he used to order once in a while when he needed cheering up.

But that cost money. Which he did not currently have.

Instead, he swiped one of his father's cans of cheap light beer out of the refrigerator, something he usually avoided because, one, it was crappy beer and, two, he didn't want to give his father more ammunition on the topic of Bear not pulling his weight.

Desperate times, though.

Back in his bedroom, he sat on his twin bed and opened the file where he'd kept all his notes about the film. Without OverSight, he couldn't do ninety percent of what he'd planned. The best he could hope for was to make a short little film and leverage the results to fund a longer one next year.

He tipped his head back against the wall and tried to imagine another year in his childhood room. There were dusty trophies on the top of the bookshelf from the juniors competitions he used to enter. He hadn't started winning until after Hank went west. After that, Bear won them all.

Not that it counted for anything now.

With a sigh, he turned back to his movie notes, wondering which bits he'd be able to pull off without traveling too far, or hiring much help. If he did something nearby, it would be that much easier to get Hank involved at the last minute.

Distracted, Bear didn't immediately pay attention to the sound of someone pounding on the front door. It stopped, anyway. But it was followed by the sound of two feet stomping through the house.

Even as Bear wondered who had come by at ten o'clock on a Sunday night, an unexpected face appeared in the doorway to his bedroom.

"You're making a film?" Stella yelped. "A *feature length snowboarding movie?*"

Oh, shit. "I hope to," he said. "Someday."

Stella's dark eyes flashed with fury. "My brother dropped this bomb on me today. And I thought, 'that can't be true, because Bear would have *told me that.*'"

The force of her gaze made him squirm. "Maybe if you didn't run out of every room I walked into, I would have had the chance."

"Oh, hell no!" She crossed her arms and glared. "You don't get to lay this whole thing at my feet. You want the awkwardness to go away? Then you actually have to *look me in the eye*." She was yelling at him now. At full volume.

"Stella." He dropped his voice. "Calm down." His father was just a room away. Because that's all the further you could be from one another inside their little house.

"Calm down? I don't think I can calm down right now, Bear. That is not how I feel when I'm standing in front of you." Her chin dipped as she said this, her dark lashes fluttering over red cheeks. "Look. It's bad enough that once every decade I throw myself at you. But can you stop looking *guilty* every time we run into each other?"

Christ. He hadn't known he was so easy to read. But there was really no point in denying it. "Stella, I *am* guilty." In Tahoe, he'd taken advantage of her kindness, and nothing good had come of it. He'd never make that mistake again. In the meantime, he felt like a heel every time he saw her sweet face.

"God, *why?*" she asked. "It was *just sex*, right? Those were your words. And once was enough for you. Fine. But don't make me feel like I'm a bad person over it."

"Stella," he practically growled. "I don't want *you* to feel guilty. That's ridiculous. *Christ*. It's me who's guilty."

She gave her glossy hair a single shake. "Get over yourself, already. We're both adults."

A quick glance around Bear's room provided no evidence that was true. "Sit down, buddy," he said quietly.

For a second he thought she might turn around and march out of the house. But she pressed her lips together in a straight line and took a seat at the foot of his bed.

Bear closed the bedroom door, then sat down in his desk chair, turning to face her. The little space made for a more intimate conversation than he was ready for. Bear was conscious of the fact that he didn't have a shirt on.

There was a heavy silence between them, and he hated the uncertainty in her brown eyes. "I'm sorry if I ever made you feel bad," he said quietly. "You never did anything wrong."

"Why are you so sure that anybody did, then?" she asked.

The answer was obvious to him, but he didn't know if he could explain himself without hurting her worse. The night they'd had together had been amazing. But it had allowed her to imagine that there was something bigger there. *Christ*. The way she'd looked at him that night? It scared him senseless. Nobody should look at him like that — as if Bear could be trusted with that kind of love.

"I make a mess of things," he said, hoping she'd take it at face value. "My movie thing? It's a mess. And I made a mess of our friendship. *Hank* is a mess."

Stella sighed. "What does Hank have to do with it? Our timing sucked, Bear. But leave him out of it."

He reached for the T-shirt he'd left on the desk and shrugged it over his head. Of all the places Stella could choose to chew him a new one, it had to be here, in the cramped little prison of his failure. There was a reason that they'd always hung out up the hill at the Lazarus house. His room was not even ten-feet square. And the red-and-white checked curtains on the windows predated his mother's departure.

Maybe this was for the best, though. If, for even a moment, Stella had imagined she wanted him, this glimpse of him would surely squash her fantasy flat.

"Look," he said. "There's a lot that's broken right now, and most of it I can't fix. I thought I had a shot at helping Hank."

What he left unsaid was that he didn't have a clue how to repair his friendship with Stella.

"Is that why you want to make a movie?" she asked. "He said you wanted him involved."

Slowly, Bear nodded. "It wasn't *just* for him. I think I'd be good at it." He might not have had the balls to try it, though, if he didn't think he had a shot of dragging Hank out of his funk.

"You *would* be good at it," Stella said. "I love the footage you take."

Her cheeks pinked up again when she said that, and Bear had to look away. "It wasn't just about the shots, though. Hank's whole life was out west, you know? He has a thousand friends. And I thought I could get him talking to people again if he had a project. Distraction, and all that."

"And he turned you down?"

Bear shrugged. "For now. But I was going ahead with it anyway, as soon as my funding came through. I thought I could pull him in at the last minute. Ask for his help. But now it's all for shit."

"Why?" her eyes got wide.

"Can't fund it," he said simply. "I thought OverSight was going to come through. But they had a stipulation…" He let the sentence die.

"What?"

He shook his head.

Stella made two fists and struck them against her knees. "Just tell me, okay? For once, just level with me."

Bear grunted with irritation. "The sponsor insists that Hank sign on, or they won't give me the green light. So I'm going to have to drop most of the project."

"Why?"

"Because I won't pressure him to do something he's not ready for, just to further my project. *Jesus*."

Stella winced. "Okay."

"It was supposed to help both of us."

"But not me." Stella sighed. "Because that would be taking things too far."

"Buddy, don't." He leaned over and yanked a file folder off the bed. Flipping through the itinerary to the back, he handed her a page.

She read it. He could tell the moment she found her name on the page, because her chin snapped up. "You want to shoot in Bella Coola? With me? And Duku?"

"I know you wanted to go to Alaska. But there are too many bad-weather days in the Chugach. I was afraid we'd get all the gear and the crew there and get nothing. So I chose British Columbia. And I knew you'd be awesome."

Her face softened. "Wow. I would have really loved to go."

"I know, buddy. I wasn't going to talk to you about it until I was sure it would happen." That was almost the whole truth. He didn't reveal that he still hadn't figured out how he could take Stella to a remote mountainside in the wildest part of Canada and not make a fool of himself again.

Her gaze dropped to her lap. "I'm sorry I yelled at you."

"It's okay." There was a long moment of silence, but it was an easier one than they'd shared in a long time. "Can I offer you a really shitty brand of beer? It's the house special here at the Barry Bachelor Pad."

A smile flared in Stella's glassy eyes. She tipped her chin and laughed. "Thanks, but no. I get enough shitty beer at work these days."

"I'll bet."

Stella's eyes traced the wood beams over her head. "I always liked this house."

"Jesus, why?" He'd never been ashamed of their little house, but the place didn't have the magic of the Lazarus home, with its soaring stone fireplace and floor-to-ceiling windows.

"Your house always reminded me of storybooks. I had a picture book about a family of bears who lived in a log home."

"Did someone named Goldilocks come along and drink the good beer?"

Stella laughed, and the low, rough sound of it touched something inside his chest. "I think she did."

"What a bitch."

She gave him one more smile, and Bear wondered if maybe one little part of tonight had gone okay.

After he walked Stella out, Bear put his beer can in the recycling bin, and poured himself a cup of many-hours-old coffee. He'd need to spend tonight cyber-stalking alternative sponsors for his film. But it was probably hopeless. It was snowing out west already, and time was short.

While his coffee spun around in the microwave, his father walked into the kitchen with his own empties. "Why was she here?" he asked without preamble.

Bear bit back the urge to give his father a teenager's answer. *None of your business.* "We had a misunderstanding," he said instead. "It's sorted out now."

"Whatever you did to that girl, apologize. And stay the hell away. You cannot get involved with her."

Bear just stood there, choking on his anger. He didn't know which was worse — the fact that the man would tell his own son to his face he wasn't good enough for Stella Lazarus, or the fact that it was true. "I am not involved with her," he said through a tight jaw. "We're not kids though. So I don't see why anyone but the two of us would care."

He couldn't even look at the old man right now. His dad didn't actually give a crap about Bear's feelings for Stella. He only cared that Barry Electrical might be passed over for a contract if his wayward son was boinking the boss's daughter.

He removed his mug from the nuker and stalked past his father.

Sixteen

SEVERAL DAYS LATER, STELLA received a six a.m. call from the manager at the ski hill asking her to sell season passes behind the desk that day.

Stella didn't bother arguing. When your family owned a ski hill, it was all hands on deck for the first powder day of the season. When the mountain needed to open two weeks ahead of schedule, there was no point in arguing you were no longer an employee. If it snowed on November eighth, you *were* an employee, whether you wanted to be or not.

November eighth was early for skiable snow in Vermont. Very early.

For most people in the world, the weather was just a backdrop. Skiable snow in November meant children got an unexpected day off from school. And Vermonters without garages spent an unexpected hour or two digging out their cars. Merchants in town probably felt a little less guilty about sneaking Christmas decorations into the store windows before everyone's Halloween candy was eaten.

For Stella the snow wasn't a distraction or an inconvenience. It was a harbinger of the competition season. As she stood behind the counter of the Members Services Desk at the ski lodge all day, she felt her first wave of optimism in months. Each time the doors opened to admit another customer, Stella got a whiff of snowy air. That smell — like pine needles and ice — was the scent of her whole life.

She'd been on her feet for seven hours when quitting time finally arrived. Thankfully she wasn't on the schedule at Rupert's tonight.

She locked the cash drawer and waved to Mary, the manager. Her jacket under one arm, she stepped out into the white. It was four o'clock, and the sun was low over the ridge. Gently-falling flurries stuck to her eyelashes. She shook them off, hurrying toward the Red Barn, the on-mountain bar. Her brother had texted her an hour ago, urging her to join him over there when she could.

As she pulled the door open, the sound of après ski revelry greeted her ears. The Red Barn was packed full of skiers and snowboarders, all of them still wearing snowpants (and, in many cases, unfortunate helmet hair.) Stella scanned the place, looking for Hank. Naturally her gaze snagged on Bear's broad shoulders first.

Stella's heart tripped over itself, the way it always did when she spotted him across the room.

Steady, she coached herself. After their chat last week she'd promised herself she would put on her big girl panties and stop hiding from him. Stella wove through the crowd towards the table Bear and Hank had somehow snagged in a prime spot right up against the window.

Closing in on them, Stella noticed a couple of important details. First, Callie Anders was sitting with Hank and Bear. Though he hadn't really confided in her about it, Stella knew Hank had been pining after the doctor for the last month or so. From the looks of things, it seemed Hank had won her over. The two of them were smiling at each other like a couple of lovesick teenagers.

Instinctively, Stella's eyes flicked to Bear's. Since the two of them had quietly endured Hank's last relationship, they'd become very good at exchanging silent information.

Look who's here, Bear's eyes said.

This is good, right? Stella replied silently.

Bear smiled at her, and Stella felt a rush of love for him. It was a knee-melting smile, for sure. But it was also good to have back even a narrow edge of their old friendship.

"Stell-Bell!" her brother called. "They let you out of the salt mines already? Somebody get this girl a drink!"

"Hi, Stella," Callie greeted her.

"Hi guys. How was opening day? Tell me everything."

"It was awesome," Hank said immediately.

Hell. Stella couldn't even guess how long it had been since Hank had last used that word. Maybe a year.

"...My new toy works great," Hank went on. "You should see me go."

He'd been given a sit-ski by one of his sponsors after the accident. Stella had been shocked this morning to hear he'd planned to try it out on the first snow day of the year. But her brother was a hardcore athlete and a hardcore personality. Always had been.

"I wish I could have seen you ride it," she said. Although the sight of Hank taking a run down the hill would probably only have made her cry.

Bear took out his phone, tapped the screen a few times and handed it over. Stella touched the "play" icon on the video he'd queued up, and squinted at the whiteness on the screen. She was about to say she couldn't see anything when a figure came into view at the upper left-hand corner of the screen. Moving fast, Hank's seated form made gorgeous s-turns down the hill, alternately extending a pair of odd, ski-footed poles to either side as he curved through the snow.

It looked effortless.

"Oh, damn," Stella whispered, blinking back tears.

Her brother reached across the table and punched her in the arm.

"Ow! What was that for?"

"Lighten up already. Life is good." Hank lifted his beer and drained it.

Stella glanced at Bear again, because it would have been impossible not to. *Lighten up?* She telegraphed. It was the very thing Hank had been unable to do for the past eleven months.

I know, Bear's eyebrow lift replied. *Be happy,* his smile suggested.

Good point.

"So." Stella cleared her throat. "How did the skiing go today, Callie? Was it really your first time?"

The pretty doctor beamed. "I was on my backside just as often as my feet. But I'm still counting it as a success."

"Who did Hank find to teach you?" The mountain had dozens of ski instructors on staff.

Callie pointed one index finger at Hank and another one at Bear.

"What?" Stella gasped. "You know they haven't worn skis in fifteen years, right? That, and they're terrible teachers."

Hank clutched his heart in mock distress. "Little girl, we taught you everything you know."

"That's where you're wrong," Stella said, trying to flag down a passing waitress, but the poor overworked soul did not spot her. "See, all those times you said, 'just jump off of it, Stella. Don't be a baby,' did not actually teach me much about technique. It only taught me that bruises heal, and I'd better grow up quick and kick both your asses."

Hank and Bear both burst out laughing, and again, Stella marveled. She hadn't heard unrestrained glee from her brother in far too long. And the fact that everyone was smiling made it just a little easier to be near Bear today.

Stella smiled back at them, feeling lighter than she had in a long time. Outside the window, snow was still falling in pretty, little flakes. If she could only get a drink, this afternoon would be perfect. "I'm going to go over to the bar. Anyone need anything?" She slid off her stool.

"I'll come with you," Bear said.

Stella maneuvered through the crowd, parking herself at the only available corner of the bar. Seconds later, she felt Bear slide in behind her, grazing the backs of her legs with his own. He was so close that she could feel the heat of his body at her back.

"What do you think?" he whispered.

Who could think at all with him so close? Stella took a steadying breath, and fingered the twenty dollar bill in her hand. "I can't believe how happy he looks," she said.

"I know, right? Listening to them making plans today… It sounds like the real deal."

"Basically," Stella taunted him, "you've spent months trying to cheer him up. And all he needed was a little nookie."

Bear laughed, and his nearness meant she could feel the rumble in her chest. *God*. What she wouldn't give to feel the scruff of his beard again as he kissed her neck…

Enough, she coached herself. *You're only making yourself crazy.*

"You know it hurts me to agree with you about anything, but it seems that a little lovin' has made Hank into a brand new man," Bear said.

She tipped her chin back, catching an oblique view of his face. "Shame it didn't work on you, though."

His eyes went wide. "*Stella.*"

"What — I can't even make a little joke?" The bartender materialized in front of her, and she had to turn her attention to him. "I'd like a Heady Topper, and whatever this guy wants." She jerked her thumb toward Bear, who ordered a beer and two sodas.

Bear cleared his throat. "You'll never guess what Hank told me this morning."

"What?"

"He wants to do my movie."

Stella was so surprised she spun around to see him properly. "Seriously?"

Bear swallowed — something Stella noticed because they were full frontal now. Stella's girlie parts quivered from the proximity. "That's what he said." Bear's voice was gruff.

Stella reached up to put a hand on his chest. "That's great. Does that mean you get to call OverSight and tell them to cut you a check?"

Bear didn't answer right away. He seemed distracted, his eyes flicking down to where her hand rested on his shirt. "Probably," he whispered. They stared at each other for a long second. The nearness of Bear's mouth was making Stella's brain short circuit. Finally, Bear's gaze lifted, catching on something over Stella's shoulder. "The drinks are ready."

Right.

Stella turned around and plucked two glasses off the bar. Bear reached around her to grab the other two. For one glorious second, he was wrapped around her, the way she'd always wanted.

Then he put his credit card down on the bar, lifted the glasses, and disappeared into the crowd.

Stella stood there a moment longer, gathering her wits. She was just going to have to get better at covering up her reactions to him. She closed her hands around the two drinks she was meant to carry, and steered herself back to their table.

When she sat back down, Stella gave Callie a smile. She tried to make it a friendly one. But it may have also implied, *if you break my brother's heart, I will kill you in your sleep.*

"So, back to this movie…" her brother said.

Bear grinned over the rim of his glass. "For two months I can't get you to talk about it. Now it's your only topic."

"Wait, you're complaining?" Hank winked at his new girlfriend.

"*No.*" Bear's eyes were dancing. Stella couldn't remember the last time she'd seen *him* so happy, either. There must be something in the water.

"Did OverSight fund you yet?"

"Not quite." Bear picked up his drink. "Honestly, I'd use somebody else if I could. I got pissed at them last week."

"Why?"

Bear's expression darkened. "They wanted me to pressure you into signing on."

Hank's eyebrows shot up. "You didn't tell me that."

"No kidding. It was a D.M. on their part. And sharing that with you about it would be a D.M. on my part."

"What's a D.M.?" Callie broke in.

Hank, Bear and Stella answered in unison. "A *dick move.*"

Callie laughed. "I can't always follow the smack talk. I didn't grow up in Vermont."

"I don't think it's a Vermont thing," Stella explained. "It's a big brother thing. Did you have one?"

"I'm an only child."

"Ah." What a pity. Even when he was infuriating, Stella would never wish Hank away. A life as Hank's little sister wasn't easy, but it was still great. Even if it meant a lifetime of pining for his hunky best friend.

"I'm tempted to shop the film around to other sponsors," Bear was saying. "But I've run out of time."

"And it's not like OverSight is *perfect* or anything," Stella said, focusing her attention on the conversation once again. "A *camera* company funding a film…"

Hank reached up to give Stella's ponytail a tug. It was a move he'd perfected at about age seven. "It's just the usual sponsor bullshit, Bear. Go on. Take the money."

"Are you sure, man? I'm offended for both of us."

Hank chuckled. "Take the money and run. Do I need to *sing* the Steve Miller Band song? People will point and stare."

Bear held up a hand. "Not necessary."

Hank started humming anyway, and Stella decided he was only moments away from breaking out the air guitar.

"Are you really sure, Hank?" Bear asked suddenly. "Now I feel like I pushed you into it."

Hank broke off from humming and looked at each of them in turn. "I think I can do it. See…" He broke off for a second, looking thoughtful. "It might suck to be out there shooting stuff that I can no longer do. But the alternative is to sit at home and mope. And I already proved that it isn't any way to live."

Bear's gaze shifted into his beer.

"Besides," Hank said roughly, "if this winter is just fucking awful for me, at least I'll get to be near you guys."

Stella's throat felt rough then. She grabbed Hank's hand and squeezed it. Callie put a hand on his other arm. And Bear gave Hank a sad grin.

Outside the window, snow continued to fall. Winter was coming whether the people at this table were ready for it or not.

Stella chanced a glance at Bear, wondering how it would all play out. Were they really going to work on a film together? And pretend like nothing had happened last year? Could she do that?

She'd have to. Because she would *always* feel stuck on him. That was just a fact she'd have to live with. The same way some people lived with partial deafness, or bunions.

If only there was an orthotic which corrected for yearning.

It was quite possible that Stella was better off this way — loving someone who did not love her back. It saved her the heartache of wading deep into a relationship, only to find out later that her partner needed her to be something she couldn't become.

Stella took another sip of her beer and tried to wrap the day's victories around herself like a blanket against the cold.

March

Seventeen

BEAR PUSHED "PLAY" on another video file, and felt his friends lean in behind him. The screen dissolved to a shot of Duku standing on top of an abandoned train station outside of Ketchum, Idaho. The on-screen Duku clipped into his board, while, behind Bear, the real-life Duku flicked the catch on his cigarette lighter.

"No smoking in here," Bear said automatically.

"You're killing me," the snowboarder groused over his shoulder.

"The *cigarettes* are killing you," Stella argued from against the wall. "And the rest of us, too."

"I'll kill you both if you don't stop arguing," Hank countered from Bear's other side.

They'd spent a whole lot of time in tight quarters lately, and the strain was beginning to show.

But the crazy shots they'd gotten earlier would keep everyone on the right side of agreeable. Viewing video in a skeevy little room in the basement of their cheap hotel had become a nightly ritual. Before dinner, Bear, Hank and whichever snowboarders they'd corralled into appearing in the film would review the day's raw footage together.

On the screen in front of them, the digital Duku balanced his snowboard on top of a brick chimney. The five feet of snow

Idaho had just received had made a ramp of snow down the chimney and onto the roof. With a hop, Duku launched himself into action. The board skidded across the flat portion of the roof, then down the pitched roof line. Bear had composed the shot in a way which made the viewer uncertain about just how far Duku would fall from the rooftop. But then his board landed on another angled pitch, and he leaped across a yawning gap to *another* roof.

"Sick," Hank whispered.

The shot did not end until after Duku skated over a shed and down a ramp of piled-up snow to the parking lot below.

"Wait. Back that one up," Hank insisted. "To the jump." When Bear complied, Hank pointed at the screen. "Check it out. Duku, did you lose your hat between the buildings?"

Bear backed up, and they all saw that Hank was right. "Good eye, Hazardous. He's wearing it here… and then it's gone. It must have landed *there*. Right about where my corpse would be found if I attempted that run."

Stella laughed but Duku swore. "I always liked that hat. I shoplifted it from a snooty store in Aspen when I was a teenager."

"See? Karma is real," Stella teased.

"Yeah?" Duku muttered. "Then the hat is the least of my troubles."

Bear rolled his head, trying to stretch out his neck. It had been an incredibly long day, and it wasn't over yet. "Okay. Let's review Stella's footage."

"I can't wait to see this," Duku said. "It's going to be awesome."

Bear only grunted. This shot had better be spectacular. Because getting it had taken a year off his life.

"I'll ride switch through that chute," Stella had proposed that afternoon as they were setting up the shot, "to hook an aerial off that rock."

"Which rock?" Bear had asked. All he'd seen was a fifteen-foot cliff.

"Um, that one right in front of your face?"

Bear had shaken his head immediately. "How are you going to spot the landing?"

"With my eyes?" she'd returned, her tone full of sass. "I've ridden this face before, Bear. Two years ago, the Iron Ore Invitational was right on this spot."

But two years ago the surface of the snow would have been completely different, and they both knew it. "Did you backflip it in competition?"

"No," Stella scoffed. "But what difference does it make? You just set up a shot where Duku jumped off a *building*."

Fuck me, I did, Bear had growled to himself. But Duku was a rangy, surly-faced trickster. That dude couldn't even make it through the day without risking his life in some way or another. Whereas Stella was... *Stella*. He'd brought her out to Idaho to make great footage. The trouble was that great footage meant risk-taking. And watching Stella fling herself upside-down over a cliff would probably shatter him.

Bear had lost the argument, though, when Stella had promised to take it easy on her first run down the face. "I'll just feel it out," she'd promised.

Apparently, "feeling it out" meant she'd rip the flip anyway, without warning, and then take the rest of the run at nearly supersonic speed. She'd kicked up a small avalanche, too, and Bear had nearly turned blue from holding his breath until she'd popped out of the moving powder, still making turns on her board.

When she'd finally come to a stop in front of him, he hadn't known whether to hug her or strangle her. (He'd settled for yelling, and she hadn't appreciated it.)

Now, in the tight confines of their pre-dinner replay session, Bear muted the volume on his laptop. He didn't want the others to hear the string of curses he'd sputtered when Stella practically stopped his heart from beating.

He pressed "play," and the onscreen Stella dropped onto the steep slope, her ponytail flying out from behind her helmet. Much of the Sun Valley resort was above the tree line, giving the shot a dramatic, surface-of-the-moon effect. Watching Stella rip down those steeps was a breathtaking thing.

This week he'd spent hours peering at her through the lens of his cameras. On the one hand, it made staring at her completely legal. Yet it had also torn him apart, little by little. He felt battered by the strain of being so close to her. It was torture.

"Shiiiiiit!" Duku exclaimed when Stella flipped off the cliff.

Bear only sighed.

"I think you're going to like the angle I got on the drone cam," Hank said. It turned out Hank was good at flying OverSight's toy. The shots he took gave Bear a choice of takes when editing film.

"Cool," Bear mumbled. "We'll watch that one next."

Hank had enjoyed himself today. Hazardous had traveled to every shoot for the film except for one. The fact that Hank liked camera work made Bear's job easier.

Not much else did.

It was exhausting to be both producer and director. Every detail was his to arrange — their travel plans, their schedule, the local people they hired to help get permission for their shoots. It was all on him. And he was afraid to delegate the work because the budget was excruciatingly tight. No one else cared as much about saving every last dollar, so nobody else could be put in charge of the details.

Bear cued up Hank's shot of Stella and played it through. "Nice shot, Hank," he complimented his friend. He cleared his throat. "All that terrain behind her is striking." Every time he spoke about Stella, he felt utterly transparent. It seemed impossible to conceal how she made him feel.

"I know, right?" Hank chuckled easily. "Can we eat now? I'm dying."

"Good plan," Stella said, standing. "I don't need to watch any more. I saw it earlier in the flesh."

In the flesh. Bear felt a little prickle of awareness on the back of his neck as she stood up behind him.

Hank reversed his wheelchair and steered himself around to face the door. "Coming, Bear?"

"Um, I'm going to try on a couple of edits for a few minutes," he said. "Order me a burger or something?"

"Sure," Duku agreed, following the others out. "But don't forget to come upstairs to eat it."

Alone, Bear watched the footage from Stella's helmet cam. The run she'd chosen was so steep her on-board camera gave the illusion she'd been standing on the edge of the world. He made a couple of splices, sewing Hank's shots together with Stella's and his own. He replayed this new cut, sitting back in his seat to watch. Moments like this, he could feel the intersection between sport and art. He was watching Stella do something incredibly athletic, but the arc of her body leaning hard toward the surface of the snow was also graceful and gorgeous.

Whether it was right or wrong, when he watched Stella's footage, it was with a lover's eyes.

Until last week, he hadn't seen much of her. Back in Vermont, she'd worked her butt off until just after New Year's, slinging beers at Travis Rupert's bar and saving up her money. Then, she'd bought a ticket to a big mountain competition in the Swiss Alps and told her parents she would hitchhike across Europe if she had to in order to make her way around the competition circuit.

They relented and funded her trip. Stella won two out of the three events she'd entered. She'd even picked up a couple of modest sponsorships, which made her *almost* self-sufficient on the road. "At least in a shoe-string budget sort of way," was how she'd put it to him.

Bear was intimately familiar with shoe-string budgets. And getting more so every day. He and Hank had worked hard on the film all winter. Bear had conned nearly a dozen of their old tour pals into riding in his film. They'd done shoots in Colorado in January and in Utah in February. Those shoots had featured freestyle tricksters, so Stella hadn't been involved.

Bear had saved the big mountain shots for last because he knew they'd require the most difficult camera work. He wanted as much experience as possible before he had to drag his video equipment to a remote peak.

But he hadn't factored in his own exhaustion. Now, at the moment when he felt utterly stressed-out and emotionally depleted, Stella had waltzed back into his life. Unlike Bear, she looked livelier than ever. Her smoky laugh drifted into every room he entered. More than once he'd broken out in a sweat when she stood nearby.

He found himself avoiding her eyes when he was laying out the day's schedule or giving her instructions. Stella was a sharp girl, and she'd be able to read his discomfort.

For all these reasons, Bear sat alone while he edited the footage.

Things were going well for the film, but Bear knew he wasn't insulated against failure. He was starting to realize that making a good film wasn't going to be good enough. First, he had to make a *great* film. And even then, it was possible that nobody would care.

Filmmaking, he was learning, was not a meritocracy. As an athlete, Bear had merely entered competitions, and when his tricks were bigger than the next guy's, people noticed. There were contests for films, of course, and Bear planned to enter those. But it might not be enough. He had no contacts. He knew nothing of film festivals and distribution.

He worked a ridiculous number of hours each day, because he needed this project to light the way — to make a new path for himself and Hank, and to get Stella the exposure she needed to move up a couple of rungs on the snowboarding food chain.

If they didn't hit any snags, it was *almost* in reach. He could feel it.

Bear set the newest files to upload, and pushed back the creaky desk chair. Crap. He'd been sitting here for forty-five minutes. He got up and wandered upstairs into the hotel bar. Scanning the room, he couldn't find his friends at any of the tables. He checked the bar, seeing only a group of young guys drinking together.

Wait. There was Stella, sitting in the center of the group, a drink in her hands.

Bear crossed the room. When she saw him, she gave him a slightly tipsy wave. That was fast. "Hi," he greeted her warily. He didn't like the way the frat boy to her left had his hand on the back of her bar stool. He didn't like the way the frat boy to her right was sneaking peeks down the front of her shirt.

"Hi yourself," Stella grinned, lifting a plate off bar. "This is yours. You didn't come for it."

"Got distracted," he said. "Thank you for ordering it." Taking the plate, he looked around for somewhere to sit. The frat boys didn't offer him a chair. No surprise there. "Where'd everyone else go?" He stuck a French fry in his mouth. It was stone cold.

"Well, Callie called from the airport, saying her flight was early. So Duku took Hank to meet her at the Palmer Lodge. You know. So the sexual marathon could begin."

"Now you're speaking my language," Right-Hand Frat Boy said.

"I'll bet," Stella said, flashing him a slightly patronizing smile.

Her tone made Bear feel a little better. Stella was a party girl, but she wasn't a pushover. "Duku didn't come back?" Bear asked. He didn't really feel like leaving Stella alone with these chumps.

"He said he wanted a change of scenery."

With Duku, that meant that he hadn't found the town's gay bar yet. "Why didn't you go with him?" It was a great idea, actually. He'd rather she hung out with gay men than any other kind. Forever, probably.

Good luck with that, he chided himself.

"Because I was waiting for you to show up and eat dinner with me," she said, exasperated.

"Oh." And now he felt like an ass. "Sorry."

"But now we're heading out to two-for-one margarita night," Left-Hand Frat Boy said. He waved for the bartender. "And you can finish telling me about your movie. I want to see it."

"When it's all done, you can buy a ticket," Bear said with a little more of a growl than was probably necessary.

Stella's mouth quirked into a little smile just for him. Another good sign. If she thought these two guys were jerkwads, he could probably manage to concentrate on all the work he needed to do tonight.

"You could come with us, you know," Stella said, sliding into her jacket. "The place isn't far. Nothing in Ketchum is far."

"True," he said. "But I have to set up for our meeting tomorrow morning. Don't be late." God, he hated the sound of his own voice. Being in charge? It sucked.

"I'll bet you could have a margarita and still get that done." Stella hopped off her barstool. "I seem to remember that margaritas don't slow you down very much."

Bear tipped his head to the side, wondering what she expected him to say. Drinking margaritas with Stella was not a good idea. "You have fun. Call me if you need a ride."

"Okay, Dad," she said quickly. He couldn't decide if she looked disappointed, or if the frown he thought he'd seen was just a trick of the light.

As if it mattered. Partying with Stella was not what he'd come to Idaho to do. He'd come here to make a great film, help all of his friends, and maybe even help himself. Fun wasn't on the menu.

After they left, he slid onto Stella's abandoned barstool.

"What can I bring you?" the bartender asked, wiping away the rings of condensation — the only evidence that Stella and her pals had been here at all.

"Uh, a Coke," Bear decided. He would have loved to have a beer. But he needed the caffeine, and he needed to stay sober in case Stella did, in fact, need a ride. Also, soda was cheaper.

If he'd taken the Colorado gig, he would probably be dining on steak and truffles with hedge-fund managers right now, after a day of taking rich people into the back country.

The food sounded good. The company did not. Although, he was alone right now, которое made him zero for two.

Lamest man in Idaho, ladies and gentlemen. They could skip the preliminaries and just award him the prize right now.

Eighteen

THREE HOURS LATER, STELLA was in need of a rescue.

It wasn't a life or death situation. She wasn't at the bottom of a snowy crevasse, or stranded on a kayak in the middle of the Pacific.

Luckily, Stella's rescue would not require a helicopter's retrieval basket or the merchant marine. Instead, she required the services of a friend with a car. But who?

She drummed her fingertips on the table and glanced around the bar. The drink specials had ended an hour ago, and the place was emptying out. Unfortunately, the two lunks Stella had accompanied to this dark-paneled place didn't seem in a hurry to leave.

She was hemmed in on two sides, and they were shitfaced. The guy on her left was Tom, and the one on her right had been called "Mash" by his friend all night. Stella had not been interested enough to ask why. All they'd done these past few hours was drink and make risque jokes. They'd been joined briefly by another of their friends, but that guy was across the room, his tongue tangled with a woman wearing leather pants.

Accompanying them to the bar had been a big mistake. Stella had done it because she'd been feeling lonely. And when the night was young, it was easy to be optimistic. The bar they'd brought her to *might* have been fabulous and fun. Or she might have *met* someone fabulous and fun.

That hadn't happened. But really, when did it ever?

The other reason Stella had agreed to accompany two irritating dudes was that Bear had been watching. Now she was paying for thirty seconds of hopefully (but probably not) making him jealous with four hours of trying to laugh at jokes which only got worse after each margarita.

She did not have a car. They were too drunk to drive.

This problem was not going to fix itself.

"Excuse me," she said, nudging the one who was called Mash. "I need to go to the ladies' room."

He tipped his head back drunkenly. "I got a better idea. Our hotel is just next door. Come on over, and you can use ours."

Stella held in her sigh. "It's an emergency, big guy. Move your chair."

Instead? He tipped it back against the wall. Not even Tinkerbell could fit through the space he'd made. He grinned — probably going for catty, but succeeding only in looking sloppy.

Ugh. Stella turned the other direction. "Excuse me. Bathroom emergency."

Tom hitched his chair a couple of inches, and she crammed her body between his big frame and the wall. "Don't be a stranger," he slurred as she walked quickly across the old wide-plank floors.

Instead of heading for the ladies' room, Stella stopped at the bar. "Could you call me a cab?" she asked when she had the bartender's attention.

He winced. "I just called one for them," he pointed at the couple sucking face beside the pool table. "And was told it would be forty minutes. But when it comes, I could ask them to share with you."

Stella gave the couple another glance, and tried to picture herself sharing a seat with two slobbering Dobermans. "I'll try to come up with a better plan," she said. "But maybe that can be my backup."

"Let me know, okay? Looks like you need to pull the ripcord with Itchy and Scratchy over there."

"Should have pulled it hours ago," Stella admitted, and the man laughed.

She went into the ladies' room, which was small and a bit smelly. Ugh *again*. She pulled out her phone and scrolled to Bear's number, hitting the "call" button.

He answered on the first ring. "Hi, Stella. Where are you?"

"Hiding in the bathroom of a bar called The Cactus. I'm sorry to ask…"

"You need a lift?"

"Yeah. There aren't any taxis. Sorry."

He sighed. "I'll be there in ten."

"Thanks." She pocketed her phone and tried to use the facilities without touching anything. Then she washed her hands with ice-cold water — the only sort provided — and wiped them on her jeans.

She took out her phone one more time, and dialed Anya back in Vermont.

"You know it's two in the morning, right?" her friend answered. "Are you having an emergency?"

Stella winced. "I'm sorry. I forgot about the time difference."

"You know it's a weeknight, right? Even at midnight I was already asleep. At least I think it's a weeknight. Fuck."

"I'm sorry, Anya. I'll call you tomorrow."

"Well I'm up *now*," her friend protested. "What did you call to tell me? It must be something about Bear. You don't call to shoot the breeze about snowboarding at this hour."

"Ugh. Who knew I was so predictable?"

"I did, little lady. Now what did he do?"

Stella sighed. "Not a thing, of course. Except tonight I went out drinking with a couple of guys who think they've been cast in a remake of *Animal House*, and I just had to call Bear to come and rescue me."

"I know how much you enjoy being rescued."

"And by him! Shoot me."

Anya giggled. "I can't shoot you until you give me back the shoes you borrowed at New Year's."

"Sure you can. I'll write them into my will."

"So where are you right now?"

"In a gross bathroom, killing a few minutes so I don't have to sit with Thing One and Thing Two. This won't be good for the hero complex Bear has developed. He's become such a stressy grumpmonster."

"Wow, sorry. Isn't the movie going well?"

"I think it's going great. But he's turned into a broody artist, or something. Like it's all on him to make the Movie of the Decade, change Hank's outlook on life, relaunch his own career, and improve me, too."

Stella got the sense that featuring her in the film was Bear's way of apologizing for their… fling. Sexcapade. Whatever. And that only made her feel like an idiot. If Bear didn't want her, she wished they could just move on already. It was hard to do that when Bear wore "I'm sorry" in his eyes all the time.

"Bummer, Stella. That doesn't sound fun."

"He's okay," Stella said. "It's not that bad."

"You always do that."

"What?"

"You complain that he's bossing you around, or that he isn't treating you well. But if anyone else says a word against him, you defend him. You're a textbook case of a girl in love."

Stella pinched her eyes shut. "I'm not in love with him. Why did I call you again?"

"You told me you were."

"When?"

"In ninth grade. Duh."

"Anya! That hardly counts."

"If we're still talking about him more than ten years later, I'm pretty sure it does. And it kind of explains why you've never had a real relationship."

"Sure I have."

But that was a lie so bald that Anya didn't even bother to call her on it. The longest Stella had ever been with one guy was two months. And Anya had already disqualified that one because they'd discovered later that the two weeks during which he had not returned Stella's calls were because he was in jail.

Anya yawned loudly into the phone. "Sort it out, sweetie. For your own sanity."

"Are you going to be able to get back to sleep?"

"Yup. Take care of yourself. Later, gator."

"Later."

Stella left the icky bathroom, realizing she'd made a tactical error. Her coat was still draped over the back of her chair. That maneuver had made her bathroom emergency more believable, but required another interaction with the drunks she'd arrived with.

With a sigh, she approached their table with the friendliest smile she could muster. "Well, boys, I'm out of here. Thanks for the drink. You have fun tonight." She reached over Mash for her jacket. That seemed simpler than asking the asshole to move.

It was a miscalculation.

Mash grabbed her forearm as she leaned. Stella landed belly-first across his lap. "What have we here?" he crowed above her.

"Awesome," Tom chuckled. "Somebody needs a spanking." Stella's face flushed red from humiliation and anger. She strained to push up and off of Mash, but he put one heavy forearm across her shoulder blades. And Tom — that jerk — grabbed both her hands. "Don't leave yet, sweetheart. The night is still young."

"You ass," Stella growled. "Let me up."

"But that's not fun," Mash teased. He patted her bottom, and Stella's blood pressure went up another few degrees.

How do I get myself in these jams? She tucked her chin, curled her abs and bit Mash in the thigh.

"Arrrhg!" he yelped as the weight of his arm disappeared from her upper back.

But Tom still had her hands. He was probably stronger than Stella, but his reflexes would be slowed by bargain margaritas. And Stella had been holding her own against the boys all her life. She jerked her arms closer together, grabbing one of Tom's wrists in her hand. All she needed now was his other one…

Behind her there was a sudden movement. Mash's chair seemed to tip back suddenly, and there was a clunk which might or might not have been the sound of his skull colliding with the wood-paneled wall.

Thank you, bartender, Stella privately cheered.

But it was a more familiar voice that rasped, "I will fucking *kill* you."

Even as Stella turned her head to see him, Bear yanked her by her underarms into a standing position. He set her aside, then lifted Mash to his feet by the collar of his shirt. "You stupid little *punk*," he growled into Mash's face. Bear shook Mash, and the drunk's jaw flopped helplessly against the onslaught. "That's the kind of man you are? To get a girl to touch you, you have to trap her so she's helpless on your lap?"

"Who are you calling a helpless *girl*?" Stella couldn't stop herself from asking. At the same time, she rubbed her wrists where Tom had squeezed them.

"Let him go," the bartender said, coming to stand behind Stella. "I know he deserves a good beating, but the law won't see it that way."

Oh, great. Stella's mind churned with worry. Not only had she just humiliated herself in front of Bear, but if he didn't chill out, he could end up in the back of a police cruiser. "Let's just go," she said quietly, putting one hand on Bear's back.

But the veins were standing out on his neck, and Stella endured a long, tense moment when she had no idea which way this would go. Bear let go of Mash suddenly, and the guy toppled backward, crashing into the wall and bouncing off his chair before ending up on the floor.

"Whoops!" the bartender said cheerfully. "All right. Everybody head out now."

"Come on," Stella whispered to Bear, who was still red-faced and breathing hard. She grabbed his hand and gave it a tug.

Bear removed his hand from Stella's, turned his back on her and stalked toward the door.

Oh, boy. It was not going to be a fun little car ride back to the hotel.

The bartender reached past Mash — who was still seated on the floor and rubbing the back of his head — to fetch Stella's jacket.

"Thanks," she said.

"No problem. Glad to see you don't need a ride home anymore."

"Right. Thanks." A taxi sounded pretty good right now, actually. Stella slipped her coat on while she walked out of the bar. Just outside, she found the big ugly van that Bear had rented for hauling people and equipment around Idaho.

She opened the passenger door, climbed in and shut it behind her. Bear gripped the steering wheel as if he might break it off. "Um, thank you for picking me up."

Without a word, he pulled away from the curb. They drove in silence for a couple of minutes. Stella wasn't a fan of this cold act Bear was trying out, but she knew better than to poke the angry beast. The angry... Bear. This silly little analogy caused an inappropriate giggle to bubble from her throat before she could choke it back.

"I don't see what's so funny," Bear growled.

But this was one of those better-laugh-or-else-you'll-cry situations. She'd had to ask Bear, of all people, for a rescue. And then he'd walked in to see her splayed across the *lap* of one of those idiots, her ass in the air, flailing like Olive Oyl in a Popeye cartoon.

It didn't get much more ridiculous than that. Her stomach began to shake.

Abruptly, the van pulled over. "Nothing that happened in there is fucking funny," Bear hissed. "I'm not a fan of finding you overpowered by a couple of tools."

Stella felt her temper flare. It was high school all over again — with Bear trying to play protector, when she really only wanted his love. "You can't be serious. I wasn't in any real danger of being hurt." *Just embarrassed.*

His jaw got even tighter. "How do you figure? I know you're strong, but it was two against one—"

"In a crowded room, with the bartender watching me. I'd already had a conversation with him about needing to lose those two. You just walked in at the wrong moment. It looked worse than it was."

"The *wrong moment?*" he repeated incredulously. "Fuck. I can't even *show* them exactly how wrong it was, because getting stuck in Idaho an extra day will fuck up the schedule and torpedo the fucking *budget.*" He slapped the dashboard with two hands.

"Well, I wouldn't have called you if I knew it would endanger your precious *budget,*" Stella snapped.

Bear took a deep breath through his nose. "That is not how I meant it."

"That's what you said." She was not willing to drop it. Bear had originally described this film as a labor of love. But now he'd transformed into the grumpy CEO. She was willing to call him on it, even if nobody else would.

With a sigh, Bear pulled away from the curb again. "I shouldn't have put it like that, Stella. I'm just stressed out."

Stella collapsed back against her seat. It was hard to stay mad at Bear when he sounded so defeated. And it was hard to stay mad at him when they were alone together. The dashboard lights revealed only a cursory outline of his rugged face and broad shoulders. But she'd been conditioned since the beginning of time to appreciate those. She didn't need light to see how perfect he was. The only flaw was the way his shoulders were tensed with the weight of worry upon them.

"We're heading to Alaska tomorrow," Bear continued, "and that's the trickiest shoot. It all adds up to a lot of details to take care of, you know?"

"Who takes care of *you,* Bear?" she whispered.

He just shook his head.

"Maybe you don't have to go it alone all the time. I know I tried to apply for the position once. But my application was rejected."

Bear stared through the windshield, jaw tight. "That is not what happened."

"The hell it isn't," Stella whispered. That was as far as she was willing to push, though. If she threw herself at his feet, proclaiming her everlasting love, it would only make the next decade of their friendship even *more* awkward.

The rest of the short trip happened in silence. Soon enough, Bear pulled into the hotel's circular drive and stopped the van in front of the door.

Stella turned to face him. "You didn't have to drop me at the door, Bear. I know you're not a taxi service."

He gave her a wry half-smile.

"Okay, tonight you were kind of my taxi service. But I really appreciate it." *Grovel, grovel.* Stella wondered how long he'd stay mad at her.

"You're welcome, Stell," he said gruffly. "I'm dropping you here because I park the van beside a wall, and it's a tight fit on the passenger side."

"Oh," she said, stupidly. "Goodnight."

Nineteen

BEAR EASED THE VAN into the unholy spot where the hotel had asked him to park it. He shut her down, but did not get out right away. Instead, he listened to the tick of the cooling engine and the distant howl of coyotes.

If he thought he'd been stressed out three hours ago, it was nothing compared to seeing Stella *physically restrained* by two drunk idiots. The sight of their hands holding her down made him almost physically ill.

Hell. His blood pressure might never return to normal. If something happened to Stella while she was working on his film? He would never get over it. And Stella? She'd *laughed*. Even after everything that had happened to her brother, she still had the Lazarus deathwish.

He got out of the van and checked the locks. Though he kept the cameras in his hotel room, there was other equipment in the van. Life felt like a string of liabilities. Guard the cameras. Monitor Hank's attitude. Watch the weather. Look out for Stella. Bear's lower back was tight and painful. He hadn't really felt relaxed since he and Hank had started shooting four months ago.

Bear used his key card to enter the hotel's back door. It was late now, after one a.m., but when he got to his room, he was still feeling too strung out to sleep. He poured himself a little glass of cognac and picked up a snowboarding magazine. But the cheap hotel bed wasn't helping his stiff back.

Fidgety, he slipped his shoes onto bare feet, grabbed his key card and wandered into the quiet hallway. Each time he'd used the back door, he'd smelled chlorine. A few turns later and he found what he was looking for. A placard reading HOT TUB was affixed to a door. Bear reached for the knob, hoping this was at least a nice enough hotel to supply towels by the hot tub because he hadn't brought one.

He hadn't packed a bathing suit, either.

To his surprise, the little hot tub area was outdoors on a patio surrounded by a very high wooden fence. Also surprising? He wasn't the only one here.

"Hello," a bikini-clad Stella greeted him from the tub. "Fancy meeting you here."

"Hi," he said after a beat.

He must have done a poor job of keeping his features blank because Stella's face fell. "Don't ever play poker," she said, crossing her arms.

"I'm not bad at poker," he argued automatically. Life would be easier, actually, if card games were still the only conflict between them.

"Uh huh," she said, unconvinced. "Well, are you just going to stand there all night, or get in?"

He looked down at himself, taking stock. "I'm not exactly dressed for it. I just wondered what was out here."

Stella opened her arms wide. "It's the nicest spot in the hotel. I've been in here every night."

It's a good thing I didn't know that, Bear told himself. But now he was caught between getting in with Stella or hightailing it out of there.

"In or out?" she said, raising an eyebrow. She'd read him like a book, of course. Stella always could. "You could at least pretend I'm not the last person you hoped to find here."

"Stella." He toed off his shoes. "It's not like that." Self-conscious now, Bear removed both the shirts he was wearing. He unzipped his jeans and removed them.

"Nice tights," Stella teased, eyeing his long underwear.

"Yeah, yeah. I'm sure they'd look better on you than me." Filming in the snow all day, a guy got cold. He peeled this last layer down over his quads, stepping out of them. Naked, he turned to catch Stella watching him, a guilty look on her face.

Without comment, he grabbed a towel off the stack, dropped it beside the tub and climbed in. Now he was covered, at least. He moved a few inches so that one of the jets went to work on his achy back. It felt great, actually. *Right*. This was the reason he'd come looking for the hot tub in the first place.

"The heat is nice, don't you think?" Stella asked. "I feel a little banged up from today's shoot."

Bear opened his eyes. "Are you okay?"

Stella let out a little snort of laughter. "Yes, Dad. But a girl can't bomb through those saplings without taking a beating."

He didn't argue. What Bear felt toward Stella wasn't very fatherly, either. And if he'd looked uncomfortable to find her here, it was only because he was forced to remember the last time they'd sat in a hot tub together in Tahoe. Sitting in hot, churning water with Stella again was like inviting the elephant into the room and asking him to sit on your lap.

Bear needed a fresh topic of conversation. His gaze traveled around the small patio. Tacked to the wooden fence was a sign that read: Maximum Occupancy 8. Eight people in here? Impossible. *Two* felt awfully goddamned intimate. That could be the Stella effect, though.

He pointed up at the sign. "That would be a tight fit."

Stella pushed curling tendrils of hair from her face. "I suppose it depends on what they were doing." She gave him a naughty smile, and Bear felt it low in his groin. *Damn*. With the water swirling everywhere around his bare skin, that smile of hers had twice its usual potency.

"Why did you go off with those guys tonight?" he heard himself ask.

Stella tipped her head back to rest against the lip of the tub. "I was just bored, that's all. There was the possibility that the bar might be fun, you know? It was for a little while. I beat a college kid at darts."

"Win any money off him?" Bear smiled at the image of Stella hustling a tourist.

"It was just a friendly game, or he would have been in trouble." Under the water, Stella moved her feet to rest on top of his. It was a perfectly chaste gesture, but it sent an electrical charge up and down his spine. The warm, frothing water grazed him *everywhere*. Fighting his body's reaction pointless — he was just going to have to sit here in this decadent place feeling turned-on and tempted. There were worse problems. In fact, lounging horny in a hot tub with a beautiful woman was more fun than he'd had in days.

"I knew they were tools, you know," Stella continued. "I'm not stupid."

"I know." He tipped his head back too. It was a good night for stargazing. He didn't know the constellations very well, except for the one or two top-sellers. Orion wasn't visible tonight and that meant spring was coming. In a couple of months, all the snow would melt. His film would be finished shooting whether he was ready or not. Maybe then he could stop being such a stress case.

"What do you see up there?" Stella asked.

He chuckled, the question reminding him of something funny. "Stella, when you were little, you told me that your name meant 'star.' And you were *so* proud of that."

She groaned. "How old do I have to be before you and Hank stop reminding me of all the stupid shit I said when I was five?"

"I dunno, buddy. You were a pretty cute kid." She had been, too. Bear had a very visual memory, so he was able to picture Stella at every age. He could see her in a dress on the first day of kindergarten, clutching Hank's hand. (The hand-clutching had lasted one day. After which, if he remembered correctly, she'd practically run the elementary school.) He could picture her snowboarding behind them both a few years later. He could see the shine of the braces on her teeth in middle school.

It was such a rare thing to really grow up with someone. No wonder he had an unrealistic attachment to her. They'd been breathing the same air for so long. He didn't know how to unhook his consciousness from hers. And he wasn't at all sure he wanted to.

But appreciating Stella's company and deserving her love weren't the same thing. He'd played this little game more than he cared to admit. The game of: *What Would I Have to Do to Deserve Her?* And he always tried to see it in Hank's eyes. Or her parents'. They might like him as a companion and a neighbor. But as the life partner of their baby girl? Who would want a washed-up athlete turned wannabe filmmaker?

If he was truly successful as a filmmaker, perhaps that would be enough. But the gulf between Still-Lives-With-His-Father and industry domination was as vast as Arapaho Basin.

Funny. When they were little, Stella occasionally made him pretend to marry her. She'd hold a messy bouquet of wildflowers in her hand, and wear one of her father's handkerchiefs over her face. Stella's mother had thought it was hysterical.

Little kids are allowed to pretend anything. When you grew up, the rules changed.

Stella straightened up, removing her feet from his. She reached over the side, fishing for her towel. "Well, my nose is cold, but the rest of me is going to pickle in here," Stella declared. "I'd better call it a night."

Bear felt a stab of disappointment that she was ending this quiet little moment together. Not that he'd say so. "That's a bold move. You'd better go first. If you freeze into an icicle before you make it to the door, I'll yell for help." He sank lower into the water. In truth, he needed Stella to get out first, because that made it easier to hide the effect sitting naked in a tub with her had on his body.

Stella rose to her feet, the water sluicing down her curves, shining on her skin in the moonlight. "It will be *hours* until I'm cold. I think I understand why Norwegians like to plunge from a hot bath into the Baltic."

"You go ahead. I'll watch from the fjord."

Stella chuckled. She climbed out and began to towel off. "I wonder if the vending machine works. I feel a Snickers craving coming on." She wrapped a robe around her body and stepped into her shoes.

"Consider the Oreos. Mine didn't fall down, so you might get two."

"Some kid probably got to them already." She gave him a wave. "Good night!"

When the door shut behind her, he climbed out. The cold blast of air against his skin quickly took care of his boner. Bear wrapped himself in a couple of towels and calculated the distance to his room. It wasn't far at all. Making a run for it would be so much easier than dragging cold clothes over damp skin.

He shuffled to his room with his clothes under one arm and holding his towel closed with the other. HIs hotel key card he held in his teeth. When he reached the door to his room, he spent a moment trying to figure out how to unlock it without either dropping trow or setting his clothing onto the hotel's well-trodden hallway carpeting.

"Shorthanded, sailor?" a voice asked behind him.

Bear turned automatically toward the warmth in her voice and was walloped all over again by Stella's sparkling eyes. First she slipped two snack-sized packages of Oreos on top of the pile of clothing under his arm. Then she slipped the hotel key from his teeth and swiped it through the device on the door jam.

"Thank you," he said, feeling inadequate.

Instead of answering, Stella gave him a funny little smile. Then she rose to her tiptoes and pressed a very soft kiss to his lips.

Not just a quick peck, either. She took her time, melding her lips to his, slowly kissing him for several beats of his heart. There was something mournful about it. But the kiss stole his breath all the same. He heard her sigh as she finally retreated. "Goodnight," Stella breathed, turning away.

Still stunned, he watched her disappear around the corner, standing there with his hands full like an idiot. Wanting more. Barely holding it together. "Goodnight," he finally remembered to say.

But she was gone. And the only reply was silence.

Twenty

STELLA WAS PROUD of herself. She made it all the way into her hotel room — with the door closed — before she let herself cry. The ache in her heart erupted then, even as she got ready for bed. With tears dripping off her face, Stella changed into a roomy Aspen T-shirt and brushed her teeth.

Kissing Bear goodnight had been stupid. But she'd been trying to take just one more hit off her addiction before letting him go.

Tonight on the phone, Anya had told her to sort it out. To come to terms with a lifetime of unrequited love.

Her friend was right, too. She had to shut off that trickle of hope that kept her awake at night. For years, that steady drip of yearning had prevented her from finding someone else to love.

Habits were very hard to break, though. Tonight, when Bear had walked through that patio door, Stella's heart had leapt. Her chest had begun to flutter just because he'd shown his face. That old saw about hope springing eternal? It was one hundred percent true. Every time they came face to face, Stella couldn't stop her foolish heart from wondering if today would be the day he'd kiss her again. If he'd love her as much as she loved him.

Instead? He'd sat across the tub looking uncomfortable.

Enough is enough, Stella had finally decided. But she didn't have a clue how to stop reacting to him. If there was a course called Moving On 101, she'd take it. If there was a YouTube video, she'd watch it. If there was a pill for getting over Bear, she'd happily swallow it.

Stella climbed into bed, turned off the light and wiped her eyes one more time. It didn't help that her mind played tricks on her. When she looked into Bear's eyes, she sometimes swore she saw heat in them. But that was just a flicker, sparked by one really amazing night that they'd shared.

"A flicker isn't enough," Stella whispered into the darkness. She'd just have to learn to accept it.

Calmer now, she lay in bed thinking of Alaska. A personal pep talk was very much in order. *Alaskan footage, girl. It's all about the big mountain footage.* The sponsors she hoped to court cared about exposure. Bear's film could help a lot, especially if her shots were featured prominently. If the Alaska scenes went well, she had no doubt that he'd give her good screen time.

If she couldn't have the man, she could still have the career. It was something.

She'd been waiting years to ride the Chugach. And now it would finally happen. The mountains were waiting for her, even if Bear was not. She had a ridge all picked out, too. She'd been scoping it out on Google Earth every time she got the chance.

There came a light knock on her door.

In the dark, she opened her eyes. "Yeah?"

Bear cleared his throat. "Stella, it's me. If you're still up, can I come in?"

If Stella opened that door, Bear would want to know why her eyes were red and swollen. But he wouldn't be knocking this late unless it was important.

Here we go again. Her foolish heart couldn't help but wonder what Bear had to say to her at this hour. *Let's fly to Vegas and get married?* Stella snorted as she climbed out of bed. He probably needed more change for the vending machine.

She opened the door. When the latch gave, she retreated into the dark room, hoping that Bear would not get a chance to see her face.

"Sorry to wake you," he said immediately, closing the door behind himself.

"S'okay," Stella said. "I was just drifting off. What's the matter?"

Bear made an irritated noise. "Duku is fucking some guy in our bathroom."

That wasn't even on the menu of things she'd imagined he might say. "Oh. Sorry. So... you need to hang out here?"

"Only if it's okay. I went to the desk to try to get another room. I mean... Hank just checked out of one, right? So that he could go stay at that fancy place with Callie. But they're full up."

"Oh."

"But you're sleeping. So I'll go hang out at the bar, give them an hour..."

"No," she said quickly. "Just sleep here."

He squinted as his eyes tried to become accustomed to the dark. "Are you sure?" He didn't say it, but she knew what he was thinking. There was only one bed.

"It's fine." She could do this. She could spend a few hours in a room with him, without deceiving herself.

The bed was king-sized, anyway. There was plenty of room for Stella and Bear, plus the giant helping of awkwardness which lay between them. Stella walked around the bed to the far edge and climbed in, curling up on her side.

There was a pause while Bear tried to figure out what to do. But then she heard him kick off his shoes and sit down. The silence stretched out between them, until Bear gave a big yawn.

"Duku didn't leave a bandanna on the door, did he?" Stella asked. "I didn't see one."

Bear chuckled in the dark. "Nope. I was half dressed by the time I figured out that he wasn't alone in that shower. But then it got loud enough that I had to sing Jingle Bells while I finished getting dressed. I'll text him in an hour. Maybe the coast will be clear."

"Just sleep," Stella whispered. "We had a long day."

He didn't answer her. But some time later, she heard him get up and drop his jeans on the floor. Then the covers were pulled back, and he climbed in.

Stella listened to him settling in. Eventually, his breathing lengthened into sleep. She was never going to have this — the peaceful solace of a mate sleeping beside her in the dark. Her lifestyle was exciting, but it lacked this simple comfort.

Stella rolled over, moving just a little closer to his sleeping form. He'd always been irresistible to her, like a magnetic force. She would do anything to stop feeling the pull. Stella yearned to scoot backwards across the mattress and curl into his warmth. But she couldn't do that.

A fresh set of tears stung her eyes, and so she pressed her fingertips into the corners. It was late, and she was tired. This sadness would pass. It would have to.

Twenty-One

BEAR DID NOT WAKE up until snowy light filtered in through the drapes of Stella's hotel room. He hadn't set an alarm, so there was a possibility he was running late to the meeting he'd planned.

Even so, he did not get up right away. Because someone warm and soft was curled against his back. Hey lay there for a few minutes, appreciating the peace of Stella's sleeping form. Her breathing was slow and deep, and it seemed a crime to disturb her.

He regretted his laziness a minute later, though, when he heard a tap on the door. "Stella! You up?" Duku's voice called.

Shit.

Bear slid out of bed and grabbed his jeans off the floor. He hopped into them as if the building were on fire.

"Stella?" Duku called. "Have you seen Bear?"

"Hrmmmp," she said at first, rolling onto her back. Then her eyes snapped open and flew to Bear's. "Oh shit," she mouthed, a sparkle of humor lighting her face.

Bear shoved his feet into his unlaced boots went to the door, which he jerked open. "I'm right here," he said, his voice rough. "No thanks to your exploits."

Duku laughed. "Your meeting is starting in ten, I thought?"

"Yeah," Bear ran a hand through messy hair. "I can take a quick shower. Stella, you'll meet me in the conference room, right?"

"Yes."

Bear pulled the door closed, then turned toward his own hotel room.

He didn't make it but two steps, though, before Hank came wheeling around the corner. "You *slept* with my *sister?*"

Still half asleep, Bear stopped in his tracks. "No! Well. Yes to the *sleeping*..."

Hank laughed up at him. "Just having a little fun with you. Duku told me that he scared you away last night. Seriously, you're really rocking the I-slept-in-my-clothes look today."

Bear just shook his head, stumbling toward his own hotel room, while Hank laughed after him.

Two minutes of hot water improved him. Armed with maps and hand-outs, he hurried to the lobby, where Duku was filling a large thermos at the free coffee cart. "Dude. If you drain that thing, you'll only end up splitting it with me."

"Tough crowd here for a Wednesday morning," Duku replied, stepping out of his way. "Relax. They brought in this full urn while I was standing here."

"You're awfully cheerful this morning." Bear grabbed a paper cup and waited for Duku to step aside.

"I got laid last night. You should try it some time."

"You're not my type," Bear said, earning a snort from Duku.

Bear filled a cup and high-tailed it into the little conference room off the lobby he'd reserved for their strategy session. Hank was waiting with a camera on a tripod, so that they could record the meeting for potential use as "behind the scenes" footage.

Stella ran in two minutes later, carrying a cup identical to Bear's. "Sorry," she said.

"It's okay." Bear met her gaze and was startled by what he found there. Her eyes were red and puffy. "Are you okay?"

"I'm fine," she said stiffly.

He regarded her for a moment, wondering whether to press the issue. When she lifted her chin as if to stave off more inquiry, he passed her an itinerary. Tomorrow they were flying into Anchorage. From there, they'd drive three hours into the Chugach mountains.

"Morning, Stell-Bell," her brother said, rolling up beside her. "What's wrong with your face?"

Stella punched him in the shoulder. "I'm too polite to ask the same of you. Though I've always wondered." She looked around. "Where's Callie?"

"She dropped me off, and now she's taking a private ski lesson. I'll see her tonight."

"She didn't want to listen to us argue for an hour?" Duku asked, gulping from the world's largest coffee. "I call shotgun in Alaska."

"What?" Hank spat. "You can't call shotgun until the vehicle is in sight. That's the first rule of shotgun."

"Look, kids." Bear unrolled a map on the surface of the table. "As entertaining as you imagine you are, we have work to do."

"Yes, master," Duku grunted.

At least someone was down with the program. Stella leaned over the maps, studying the Chugach mountain range. "Devil's Spine," she said, laying her finger on the marker for one of the higher ridges in the range. "Nobody has ever ridden it before. I want to make a first descent right here."

There was a silence at the table while everyone else leaned in to take a peek at Stella's choice.

Bear's blood pressure went up three points when he saw the spot she'd chosen. "Stella, there's a *reason* that ridge hasn't had its cherry popped. Those crevasses on either side are doozies."

"I see that," Stella argued. "But the slope itself isn't too narrow. And if you put the camera down here somewhere," — she pointed to a spot beyond the crevasse — "it will look a lot more dangerous than it is."

"Pretty sneaky, sis," Hank offered.

"I know, right?"

Bear grunted. She was not going to ride that ridge. Not on his watch. "That slope is an unnecessary risk. Pick something else."

"I can handle it," she argued.

Her brother chuckled. "Time for rock, paper, scissors. Isn't that how you two settle all your disagreements?"

Bear felt his face heat. And he couldn't even *look* at Stella. The last time they'd discussed rock, paper, scissors, they'd been naked and sweaty. Head down, he went back to the map. "There are plenty of good shots to be had anywhere along here," Bear pointed out, gesturing across the mountain range. "We'll make it a game-time decision."

Across the table, Stella folded her arms. "Fine. But I have a good feeling about this."

Bear was careful to make his shrug non-committal. Because there was no way Stella was going to ride that deadly bit of snow-covered rock. "Has anyone looked at the weather report? Because it's pretty shaky. This is why I wanted to go to British Columbia. Alaska is so dicey in the spring."

"Why are we going, then?" Duku asked.

"Somebody at OverSight has a relationship with an Alaskan helicopter outfit. Supposedly we're saving some money.

But ten percent off on the choppers will be pretty meaningless if we can't fly in the first place."

"It will work out," Hank said. "Even if we only get one day's worth, it will be great footage. We'll work with it."

Bear risked a glance at Stella. She was still standing there in an ass-kicking stance, sizing him up. Their eyes locked for a second, and Bear saw determination in them. "I'm going to go and suit up," she said, turning from the table.

"The van leaves for our last shots at Sun Valley in forty-five minutes," he said, looking away. "Be ready."

"I'm *always* ready," Stella grumbled. Then she left the room.

Twenty-Two

ON THEIR FIRST DAY in Alaska, Bear captured some quality footage in a canyon.

Unfortunately, two days of snow and sleet had followed. This morning it had actually been raining, which had depressed the hell out of everyone. If they wanted to ride in the rain, they could go back to Vermont.

Trapped in the lodge, Bear watched Hank deal a hand of five-card draw. Not that Bear was able concentrate on the cards. He was going to go out of his mind very soon, unless the guide stepped into the lodge and gave him the pilots' weather forecast.

With one eye on the door, he anted up, placing a dollar bill in the center of the table. In his hand he found a pair of fours and not much else.

Figures.

Bear needed a break, and he needed it soon. And his poker hand was not the problem. They'd been stuck inside for forty-eight hours, basically. Except for trips to the lodge next door for all their meals, they'd been housebound by bad weather. And for each hour of poor visibility that passed, the odds that they'd go home with minimal footage increased.

He stole another look at the door, as if he could force it open with his mind, like some kind of weather-beating Jedi.

This afternoon was their last chance, and it was two o'clock already. It gave Bear a nauseous rush to think that he'd put his friends through five months of planning, riding, shooting and travel. One more afternoon of shooting was all he needed. Just one.

Across the table, Stella's eyes sparkled. "I'll raise a dollar!"

Bear folded, largely from lack of interest. Duku did too. But Hank raised her two dollars, and Stella threw in two more. After a flurry of betting, Duku, who had dealt, asked Stella how many cards she wanted.

"Four!" she said cheerfully.

Her brother groaned. "Seriously. You are the worst card player ever."

"Not true," Stella argued, arranging her freshly renovated hand. "I just don't mind risk. Sometimes it pays off."

"Whatever," her brother argued. "I'll raise you five bucks."

Stella slapped a five onto the table without blinking.

"This will be interesting," Hank said, opening his hand. He had a pair of aces.

She revealed her cards, too. "Tens over nines."

"You crazy little *brat...*"

The lodge door opened — finally — and Wickham, the outfit's senior guide, beckoned. "It's clear enough to fly. Can you be ready in ten?"

"Yeah!" Stella cried, jumping up from the table, her winnings forgotten. "I'm ready now."

"Whoa. Not so fast," Bear said, walking over to the guide. "Let's hear about the conditions out there."

Wickham scratched his chin. "The north-facing aspects got loaded down with most of the wet stuff. So if we pick out a sheltered, south-facing slope, we should have the most luck."

"Wait," Stella said. "I want to try Devil's Spine."

The guide frowned. "That one aint exactly sheltered. Or south-facing, for that matter."

"But we can go up there and have a look at it, right?"

"No way," Bear said. In poor conditions, he could not have Stella picking a risky slope.

"What do you mean, *no way?* How can you tell from inside this lodge what we'll find on that peak?"

Bear took a deep, calming breath before answering. Stella was working a defiant stance, hands on her hips. He was not going to let her do something stupid. "There's too much grade on that slope." He tried to sound calm and logical, but suspected that he was failing. "The rain we had will make the surface heavy. You *know* how this works." Wickham still had not offered an opinion, Bear noticed. "What do you think?" he asked the older man. *Come on, help me out here, buddy.*

Wickham frowned again. "You know what's weird? You guys aren't the only ones talking about Devil's Spine today."

"What?" Stella breathed.

The guide jerked a thumb toward the door. "The guys in the other lodge want to ride it, too."

"How could that *be?*" Stella yelped. "Since the helicopter was invented, nobody has done that peak. And today there are two teams who want the first descent?"

Bear cleared his throat. "You were talking about it at dinner last night."

Stella's eyes widened before they began to burn with fury. "Those *assholes*," she gasped. "We have to go. *Now.* I'm suiting up. I'll see you outside."

"Stella!" Bear called after her. But she did not listen. The chill in his chest thickened as he turned to Hank. "I need you to talk to your sister for me."

His friend's eyebrows arched. "No can do."

"Are you kidding me? Do you not fucking *care* that she's being an idiot?"

Hank stared up at Bear, measuring him with sharp eyes. "I care a great deal, asshole. But I can't tell Stella what to do. And for the record, she isn't being an idiot. Not yet, anyway."

"You need to talk her down from this."

Hank shook his head. "That's not how it works. She has to decide for herself."

"That is crazy! The risk out there could be off the charts."

His friend wheeled over to a hook on the wall and liberated his parka. "If it's sketchy, Stella won't ride it. She knows more about back-country conditions than either of us."

"But she wants this so bad."

Hank bent forward to get his jacket on, navigating the wheelchair's backrest. "I'd be lying if I said I wasn't worried about the risk. But me telling her not to do it? That's not my place."

"Hank, this is a bad idea." He *felt* it in his gut. It wasn't a twinge. It wasn't a tickle. It was heavy. Like dread.

"So let her go out there and poke the snow on that peak. If it's unstable, she'll feel it."

Bear didn't want her anywhere near the place. How could Stella stand there on the peak of her dreams and not give it a try? It was like taking a Golden Retriever to a meadow that may or may not be full of land mines, and throwing a tennis ball.

He would *not* be the person responsible for that.

"If you feel so strongly about it," Hank said, "why are you telling me and not her?"

Right.

Bear stomped across the big room to the narrow doorway to the littlest bunkroom, which Stella had commandeered. "You can't do this."

"Do what?"

Scare me half to death. "The pitch on that spine is off the charts. After the rain we got, there's no more dangerous slope in Alaska."

Her eyes flashed with irritation. "Possibly. But we don't know that until I get a look."

Just picturing her up on top of an avalanche hazard made bile rise in Bear's throat. "Buddy, no. I can't let you do this."

Her gaze challenged him. "Why?" she asked simply.

Because I love you. The words were choking him. He needed to get a fucking grip, and handle this professionally. But what did that even mean? What was the right thing to say to the girl you loved, when you'd fucked everything up and didn't have time to fix it? He could hear the pilots outside right now, snapping the gear basket on the side of the copter closed.

Bear put his hands on Stella's shoulders. "We have to do this safely, okay?"

Her expression was guarded. "Can you just answer one question for me?"

"Sure."

"If it was Duku who wanted this descent, would you tell him he couldn't even have a look at it?"

Bear's heart contracted. *I'm not in love with Duku.*

Unfortunately, Stella misinterpreted his hesitation. She let out an irritation-filled sigh. "Yeah. I didn't think so." She shook off his hands.

"Hey! You didn't let me answer. Stella, *nobody* dies on my movie, okay?"

Her eyes went flat. "Nobody dies on your movie," she repeated. "What on earth would the critics say?"

"Stella!" That's not what he'd meant.

"Bad PR could really crush those ticket sales," she said, zipping her jacket.

"*Stell*," he tried again.

But she pushed past him and stomped toward the door. "I'm going to take a look at that peak. And you're going to let me."

"If you're not careful, I swear to God I will…"

"Will what?" she challenged.

I will not get over it. He didn't say that, though. "Where is your transponder?" Anyone getting out of the helicopter would wear an avalanche beacon. It was standard procedure. "Show it to me." He chased her across the room.

Stella spun to face him. "Right here," she patted her chest. "And I cannot believe you just asked me that. Like I haven't done this before."

"Stella…"

"What?" she cried, exasperated with him. "You're freaking out on me like I'm some stupid little twit who can't be trusted to make the right decision. Just save it, okay?" She stomped past him, out of the bedroom, then all the way out of the lodge, slamming the door behind her.

Sick with worry, there was nothing Bear could do but don his own jacket, check his cameras, and get into the other chopper.

Twenty-Three

IT WAS IMPOSSIBLE to feel calm while flying over the Chugach mountain range. Stella's heart fluttered as the helicopter sped over the white vista. The mountain peaks seemed to stretch on forever. The only breaks in the whiteness were the black cliffs poking through the snow. It was all so beautiful and forbidding, set against a leaden sky.

The common wisdom about riding the Alaska back country was to remember: It's much bigger than you could imagine. And it's much steeper than you could imagine. *Check and check.* The steeps and cliffs were heart-stopping. The vastness of it was so impressive. Since the view was largely above the treeline, the whole span looked as inhospitable as it was wide.

Breathe, she told herself. *It's just like you've done before. Only better.*

From the seat behind her, Duku whooped with joy at the scenery. Some riders liked to psych themselves up with loud encouragements, but Stella preferred to take it all in quietly.

Although the banked turns of the helicopter had initially disoriented her, when Devil's Spine came into view, Stella recognized it right away. The slope was breathtaking. Nature wasn't always so fond of symmetry, but Devil's Spine was a perfect wedge of white, framed on either side by deep slices in the rock. If Stella rode it, the video footage would be *amazing*.

"Jesus fuck," her brother said from the seat beside her. "That's a *beast*, Stella." He laughed. "You sure know how to pick 'em."

Her heart rate kicked up another notch as the pilot brought their altitude up in order to summit the mountain, and the view became even more incredible for a few seconds. Stella's life seemed to accelerate to two or three times the normal speed, when the pilot set the helicopter down on top of Devil's Spine.

Stella unbuckled herself from the helicopter's seat as Wickham hopped out and opened the rear door. She tried to keep her patience as Hank began to set her up with some gear.

"Lean forward," he said. When she complied, he fitted a tiny video camera into the specially designed foot on her helmet. "It's running, you don't have to even think about it," he said.

"Thanks."

Hank handed Wickham a two-way radio. Then he turned to Stella, his brown eyes studying her. "Be smart, little sister."

She felt her throat thicken. "I will."

"Love you lots," he said. That was it. No pressure. No fear. And even more amazingly, no jealousy, either. These were mountains that Hank would never ride.

Her throat got even tighter. "Love you, too," she said. In fact, Stella had never loved him more than she did right here, right now.

He held up a fist, and she bumped it. "Now go perform all your stability checks."

"I'm on it," she promised. Without another word, Stella climbed over her brother's seat, jumped down and — staying low — she moved toward the nose of the helicopter so the pilot could see that she was clear. Wickham had already dragged their gear out of the basket on the side of the helicopter's body. A few seconds later, Hank's door shut and the helicopter lifted off.

The rotor noise receded as the chopper flew into the distance, delivering Duku to a south-facing slope. From the helicopter, Hank would try to get some decent aerial footage of Duku's run. Nobody had said so to her face, but Stella's insistence on a solo first descent made filming Duku harder, too. Hank wasn't maneuverable enough to get out of the copter.

She pushed those thoughts away. It was time to focus. With the copter noise gone, all she could hear was the wind whistling through her helmet. Stella turned slowly around, taking stock of the crazy, intimidating place in the world where she'd landed.

Wickham ruined her reverie by speaking. "We're going to stay well in back of the cornice while we make our first checks."

If Stella had not been so entranced by the crazy 360-degree views around her, she might have rolled her eyes. Wickham was a nice enough guy, she supposed. But even in extreme sports, there would always be men who would treat her like the Little Woman.

Of *course* they were going to stay well back of the cornice while they sampled the snow underfoot.

Stella took one pole and Wickham another, and they began testing the texture of the snow. Where Stella currently stood, it was heavy, but stable. The rain's weight made the surface feel solid, but it could be a ruse. Heavy snow on top of lighter snow could be terribly unstable, and Stella was going to need more information before she decided whether the slope was safe.

Below them, another helicopter swung into view, landing on a plateau in the near distance. Though Stella was not close enough to the peak's edge to see him alight, she knew the other helicopter was depositing Bear and a whole lot of camera equipment. Thousands of dollars were being spent right now to get this shot. There was the cost of copter fuel, the guide's time, and their stay at the remote lodge.

If Stella didn't get her descent done right now, her Alaskan adventure would be over. They couldn't linger here. Tomorrow, the lodge had a new slate of guests arriving. And their expensive flight out of Anchorage had already been scheduled.

They couldn't go on, playing at making a film. This was the last stop on the train, right here.

Stella poked at the snow, creeping closer to the peak's edge. There wasn't a noticeable difference in the snow pack. *Yet.* She lifted her head toward the opposite plateau, and saw an ant-sized Bear leaning over a speck of a tripod. His hands would be practically frozen by the time he'd set up both his big camera and his drone cam.

All this trouble to get Stella's shot. By any measure, back-country riding was an egotistical discipline, and she'd always known it. No wonder Stella didn't have a man in her life. She might be low maintenance in all the typical girly ways. But this lifestyle? It was as high-maintenance as they come.

A few yards away, Wickham was using a shovel to dig a block of snow out of the surface. He tilted the shovel thirty degrees or so then tapped the bottom of it. The snow stayed put. So he tapped harder. "Huh," he said eventually. "That's pretty solid. But how deep does it go, you know?"

"That's the million-dollar question. Let's try to push the cornice," she suggested. She and Wickham could apply force to the snow near the lip, trying to tease out its potential for avalanching.

"All right."

She moved closer to him, and together they used their feet like bulldozers, shoving the snow toward the edge. Wickham wore snowshoes, and could push more snow than she could.

Nothing budged.

Wickham picked up a pole and probed the cornice. "I don't know what to think," he said finally. "She feels steady. But the temperature is going up fast. Ten degrees in the past half hour."

Stella felt it. She was already sweating, but she'd assumed it was because of nerves. The change in the weather added another layer of complexity to Stella's calculations. "Is it warm enough to melt, you think?"

Before he could answer, Wickham's radio crackled, and Bear's voice came through. "I'm ready down here. But I don't like this weather."

Stella studied the sky. In front of them, the sun was trying its best to steam up the heavy layer of clouds, making the sky an odd gray-yellow color. But behind them, the sky was dark and angry. She took Wickham's radio and pressed the transmit button. "Good light for shooting, though," she said. There wouldn't be any nasty shadows.

Bear didn't dignify her comment with a response. "Wickham? What do you think of the conditions?"

Nice. Bear didn't think enough of her opinion to ask it. That smarted.

Wickham took the radio. "We're working through it. So far, we haven't found any weakness. But it's tricky weather, like you said. We're worried about a heavy slab on top of less stable snow."

"Should I take down my equipment?" Bear asked.

Stella grabbed the radio back. "No," she said. "We're going to try to cut a cornice."

Wickham tucked the radio into his pocket and leaned on his shovel. "I'm not sure we can cut a cornice deeply enough for a good test. This is heavy stuff."

She'd been afraid he might say that. "So we could spend an hour cutting, and still not know," she said.

"Yeah. Meanwhile, you'd lose your weather."

Stella eyed the sky once again. She had to make a decision based on the information they'd been able to gather thus far.

"Okay. I'm going to board up and take a look. You get back off the cornice, and tell Bear to get ready."

For a moment Wickham didn't move. "Are you sure?"

"No, I'm *thinking*," Stella snapped. "But I'm going to think on my snowboard." She walked to where her board lay in the snow. The beautiful thing about snowboarding was that once you'd dragged yourself (at great expense) to the top of some sick peak, gear was no longer an issue. It was just you and the board.

She carried her board over to the very roof of the cornice. The snow felt solid under her feet. But if the cornice broke right now, she'd be buried faster than you can say "look out below." A cubic meter of snow weighed in at six hundred and sixty pounds. And that was just an average. The snow she was standing on right now probably weighed more.

Stella set the board down and clipped in. She heard Wickham and Bear chatting over the radio, but did not listen to their words. Because this was the important moment right here. Stella took a deep breath of cool air in through her nose and finally looked down at the incredibly steep slope below her.

Jesus, Mary and Joseph, it was steep. Riding Devil's Spine would feel like snowboarding down a two hundred story building.

Easy, she coached herself. She couldn't afford to have a brain clouded by adrenaline right now. There were still important decisions to make. Her eyes traced the line of descent she'd chosen by studying maps and photographs. In this case, choosing a path down the face had not been all that difficult. There was really only one way down. And it was so steep that the top half of the descent would be over almost before it began.

But now Stella studied the twin crevasses at either side. They were even more forbidding in person than they'd been in pictures. Their edges were uneven, so Stella would not be able to ride very close to either side, for fear that the heavy snow disguised points of weakness.

And that was the whole problem. If the snow *did* prove unstable, there was no alternate route to safety.

For all the talk of avalanches, Stella had triggered them many times in her life. A boarder could ride moving snow as long as she kept her wits about her. Moving toward the edge of an avalanche slab would usually bring a rider out of danger.

But this? There *were* no edges. There was no Plan B. If the snow moved, she wasn't going to get out of its way. And if it pushed her sideways?

She made herself picture that. Not pretty.

Stella had always loved risk. And if she turned back now, she'd never know what might have been. It would bother her for a long time. Perhaps forever.

She felt the minutes ticking by even as she considered her choices. She was going to have to make a choice and live with the consequences. Or not, if the worst came to pass.

Stella closed her eyes for a moment, and took stock. Her whole life, she'd listened to her gut, and her gut was absolutely churning over this one. That was unusual. Stella was usually rock steady. What was different?

Bear. His unhappy expression popped into her mind. He'd left her feeling unsettled. And the fight they'd had was clouding her thinking. *Ugh.* This was absolutely the wrong moment to think about him. If she made this run, it could not be out of spite.

She opened her eyes again, and the first thing she saw was the black outline of two crevasses.

Be smart, Hank had said.

Stella took a very deep breath from her diaphragm and blew it out again. This slope was not smart. It was ballsy and beautiful. But it was *not* smart. She might ride it and get lucky, though.

Lucky. But not smart.

"Damn," Stella whispered. Then she bent over and unclipped her bindings. "Damn," she whispered again, trudging back toward Wickham. She wouldn't risk so much for her own vanity. But giving up was going to bother her for a long time.

"What's the verdict?" he asked.

Miserable, Stella just shook her head.

When the helicopter returned to pick her up, her brother was not on it. But that was okay with Stella, because she did not feel like talking to anyone. Not even him.

The radio stayed silent, another blessing. After today's fiasco, Bear was probably going to hang her picture up on the lodge dartboard and commence target practice. It was either that, or tally up the amount of money her afternoon of hubris had cost him. She should have let Wickham take them all to a more sheltered spot.

There were so, so many things she wished she'd done differently.

Stella's unhappy reverie was interrupted by a flash of yellow out the window. Another helicopter passed them, heading in the other direction. She craned her neck to watch as it headed straight for Devil's Spine. "You have *got* to be shitting me," Stella said under her breath. She couldn't see where it set down, but she had a bad feeling. An hour from now, another snowboarder might be able to call himself the first one to ever descend Devil's Spine.

The amazing scenery out the window mocked her. She sunk back into her seat and closed her eyes.

Twenty-Four

WHEN THE PILOT SET her down on the landing pad, Stella removed her board from the basket and hurried inside the lodge. She stomped into her little room and shut the door. There was no lock on it, unfortunately. She needed what little solitude there was to be had. After a while, she heard what was probably Bear's helicopter return. Luckily, there were no footsteps outside her door.

For the second time today, rain began to batter the window at the foot of her bunk. Alone in the lodge, Stella took off her snowpants and jacket. In long underwear and a sweater, she lay on her narrow little bed, feeling like the most useless person alive. She lay there a long while. It was easy to lose track of time while counting up all the ways you'd screwed up. If she'd only backed down when Bear argued for the more conservative peak, she could have gotten a run in. Maybe even two.

Instead? They got nothing. Except a bill from two helicopter pilots and a guide. And the lodge. And let's not forget the airline tickets...

Damn. Good thing they'd gotten those meager shots earlier in the week. Stella wished she had access to the footage, just to see how much was there. Maybe it wasn't as bad as she feared.

Nope. It was probably worse.

Her phone rang, and the display showed that it was her mother calling. With a sigh, Stella took the call. "Hi Mom." She tried to keep the misery out of her voice.

"Hi, sweetheart. I just spoke to Hank. He said that you were having a bad day."

"I'll live." It was an odd choice of words. But it was true.

"I'm sorry your shoot didn't go the way you'd planned."

"Thank you," Stella said, chewing on her lip. "I know you don't think I should try these things, anyway."

It was her mother's turn to sigh. "That is not exactly true," she said. "I never sowed my wild oats, Stella. And there were years when I regretted that."

Stella propped herself up on an elbow. "Really? I didn't know you had any wild oats."

Her mother laughed. "I have always been a good girl, it's true. So you scared the dickens out of me, little girl. You came out of the womb taking risks that I never could. Every day I'm proud of your spirit. But every day I worry."

Stella felt her eyes fill. "I'm sorry."

"Don't be. I just hope you can understand why I don't often turn up to watch you hurdle down the mountain. It scares me to watch. But I'm always thinking about you."

"You watched Hank, though," she said. Then she wished she could take it back. She sounded like the jealous little sister.

"I did," her mother said. "In my mind, he was tougher. Less likely to break. Maybe it's because you were sick when you were little. Or maybe it's just the sexist way I was brought up." Stella heard her mother sniff. "And look how smart that was? My boy almost killed himself while I looked on."

"Oh, Mom," Stella sighed. "I'm sorry."

"I know. But it's not your fault, okay? Hank told me you took good care of yourself today. I just wanted you to know I appreciate it."

Stella smiled a bitter smile. At least there was one person who didn't think she'd ruined the day. "Thanks, Mom."

"I love you, sweetie."

"I love you, too."

They hung up a minute later, and Stella went back to brooding. She was about to become the only top snowboarder she knew who'd made it all the way to Alaska with almost nothing to show for it.

Eventually, she heard voices in the lofty main area of the lodge, and they were animated. Stella was curious about why, but not curious enough to show her face. In fact, she might never show it again. Heavy footsteps approached her room door, and Stella braced.

"Stella?" It was Bear's voice. "Can I come in?"

"Not right now," she said, feeling like an unreasonable teenager. But if Bear came in here to talk to her right now, Stella was afraid of what she might say.

"Stella. Open the fucking door or I will break it down. And then I'll have to pay for it, too."

"That would really be quite stupid," she shot back. "Because there's no lock on it anyway."

The next second, Bear blew in like a gale force wind. He kicked the door shut. Then, crossing the room, he sat down on the bed. Stella sat up to meet her pissed-off friend on more equal terms. But before she even knew what was happening, she'd been scooped onto Bear's lap. "We are going to have a talk," he said, his voice rough.

"Okay," Stella said, because that seemed like her only option. His big arms came around to brace her, and he tucked her head onto his shoulder.

"Even though it started raining, the other team tried a descent of Devil's Spine."

Any other time, with Bear storming her room and demanding this up-close-and-personal discussion, Stella might have fought back. But with that as a lead-in, she couldn't even pretend. "They *tried?* That doesn't sound good."

"It wasn't. The rider made only a few turns before the snow started to slip. He tried to cut across, to get off the slab…"

"And fell into the crevasse?" Stella squeaked.

"Yeah. On to a ledge, though. They can see him moving around down there, and now they're rustling up a rescue team to go in and haul him out."

"Oh my God." Stella shivered involuntarily. "What if the wind keeps up until dark?"

Bear's arms tightened around her like a vice. "Those guys are good. They don't need a big window." He let out a breath, and Stella thought it sounded oddly shaky. Then he dropped his head and pressed his nose into her neck, which was awfully darned odd. But tragedy made people act strange sometimes. "So glad it isn't you down there," he said.

"I didn't go through with it," she said automatically.

"I know."

"My gut didn't like the setup."

"Your gut made the right call. I'm sorry, Stella. I'm so fucking sorry. My gut has been making all the wrong calls."

"What?" she tried to turn to face him, but his arms held on tightly. "You're the one who didn't want to try it in the first place."

Now Bear put his hands on Stella's hips and turned her bodily toward him, which wasn't easy, seeing as her legs were in the way. He yanked her closer to his chest nonetheless. "I made the right call about the snow, but the wrong call about everything else. I *love* you, buddy. So much. And I didn't tell you that.

Stupidest thing I've ever done. I could be standing at the top of a crevasse right now, wishing I'd said it already."

Stella let her forehead fall onto Bear's shoulder. Then she worked on playing back everything he'd just said in her mind. She didn't trust it. The "L" word had many different meanings. And she'd been disappointed so many times before. "Shit," she squeaked.

"*Shit?* That's all you've got?" He kissed the top of her head.

Stella was afraid to raise her eyes to his. "I'm trying to decide if there's more than one way to interpret that. I promised myself I wouldn't mope around anymore trying to figure you out."

"Aw, hell." Bear leaned back, taking Stella's chin in two gentle hands and tilting it upwards. She had no choice but to look up into his silver eyes. And what she saw there made her stop breathing. He was *serious*. And all that intensity was aimed directly at her. "I'm not a fan of making you sad, buddy."

This time, she didn't have any kind of witty comeback to offer him. She felt trapped under the weight of his gaze, so she let her own wander down until it came to rest on his mouth. Several days' worth of scruff outlined his full, kissable lips. Stella felt hungry just looking at them.

And now they were coming closer. Stella grabbed Bear's sweater in two hands and hung on tight as his mouth landed on hers. For a second, she was frozen there, trying to adjust to the idea that this was really happening. But the sensation of Bear's lips brushing against hers was all too real. Stella softened into him, and the kiss went wild immediately, as if they'd both been waiting a lifetime for this.

In a way, they had, Stella realized as Bear pulled her down on the bed. Their little escapade in Tahoe wasn't honest. Because Stella hadn't told him how she felt. And the sad kiss she'd given him in Idaho was more of a goodbye than anything else.

But this kiss made a whole new set of promises. Bear cupped her jaw and took control, telling her on no uncertain terms that he was fully invested. With his other arm, he settled Stella against his chest, while his warm mouth made a thorough assault on her ability to think. Stella fought back against his grip, if only out of habit. She jammed a leg between his, and nipped his lower lip.

Bear growled a little, shifting his body against hers in a sexy way.

Naturally, Stella moved away. If only to torture him.

"Oh, buddy." Bear chuckled. "You've never been a pushover."

"You like it that way." Stella reached for him again, running her fingers through his thick hair.

"Fuck, yeah. I always have." He lowered his mouth to the sensitive skin on her neck, and sucked.

Stella felt it *everywhere*. She clenched her thighs against a wave of arousal. Even if her brain was still a little confused by Bear's sudden turnabout, her body was on board with the program.

"You like that, don't you?" Bear whispered. "I like it too. I'll like this even better." He lifted the hem of her sweater, and began dropping open-mouthed kisses on her stomach.

Stella moaned, which earned her a big palm over her mouth. "Shhh!" Bear chuckled. "Or else I'm going to have to stop." Then he swept a single fingertip across her belly, just beneath the waistline of her leggings, and Stella's whole torso contracted with desire.

"Bear," she whispered.

"Yeah," he mumbled against her belly button. The kisses headed south, and she could barely breathe.

Her capacity for reason was about to flee the building. Before it did that, she had a question. "What are we doing?"

He raised his head to look at her. "Only what you want to. Should I stop?"

Stella shook her head. "No, I mean..." She couldn't believe she was going to ask this. It was such a girl thing to say. "What does it *mean?*" She'd been serious when she'd said she was done moping around for him. An I'm-so-glad-you're-alive hookup wasn't going to work for Stella. She'd only feel worse later.

He hitched himself up beside her on the bed. "I need you, buddy. In my bed, and in my life. And I'm an idiot for not saying so before."

Stella ran one of her palms up and down Bear's face. Because if she wasn't dreaming right now (and that seemed like a real possibility) then touching him was allowed. "I've always wanted you. Since seventh grade, okay? When you were busy trying to kiss Misty Carrera under the bleachers on the football field. So don't say that unless you mean it."

His eyes got wide, which gave Stella a moment of fear. "I'm not playing around, Stell. I had this dumb idea that I couldn't be with you unless I got my whole life figured out. But none of us knows how much time we're going to get. So I can't wait any longer."

Stella felt a slow smile begin at her lips and then take over her entire face. "I'm listening."

Bear rolled her onto her back and climbed onto her body. Holding his weight aloft by his forearms, he dropped a soft kiss onto her mouth. "I don't know how the next year plays out. I don't know if the film will be any good, or if anyone will care. But maybe none of that shit matters if I can figure out a way to come home to you every night."

There was a lump in her throat now.

"Does that sound okay to you?" His face had gone intense again. As if he really thought she might say no.

"Sounds perfect," she choked out.

His warm eyes continued to hold hers. "There's no privacy here, so I'm not sure if I can show you how happy that makes me." He kissed her again, and Stella whimpered into his mouth, it felt so good. She ran her hands up and down his sides, just feeling lucky to be able to touch him.

One of Bear's hands skimmed down her belly, past the waistband of the long underwear she was wearing. He tucked his hand between her legs and just left it there, warm and pressing. Stella squirmed under his touch, wanting more. She broke off their kiss on a gasp. "Where is everyone, anyway?"

Bear spoke against her mouth. "At the lodge across the way, waiting for news."

"It will have to do." She dropped her hands to Bear's waist, popping the button on his jeans.

He looked down at her hands. "Are you sure? I've got nothing against a good quickie. But I would rather celebrate nice and slow."

"That will be tomorrow," she said, yanking on his clothes. "This is just a preview. And I'm a fan of risk, remember?"

"God, I love you." He chuckled against her neck. Then he propped himself up and shoved his pants and long johns down.

"Not all the way," Stella whispered. "We have to be quick."

But Bear wasn't really listening. He dove in for another kiss, and she met every sweet slide of his tongue with her own. Suddenly, they were on the same team again. And it was Team Urgent. He yanked her leggings down, her panties going with them.

She dropped a hand between their bodies, cupping him. She teased him until his eyes squeezed shut with pleasure, and he made a quiet little huff of desperate anticipation. "You're killing me," he whispered, knocking her hand away.

"Come to me then," she breathed.

With a heated look in his silver eyes, Bear braced over her. But then he froze. "I don't have a condom."

She gave her head a single shake. "We're good."

His eyes raked over her face again, this time with lust, not worry. Then he lined himself up between her legs, while Stella quivered with anticipation. Finally, he took her mouth in a hard kiss, at the same moment he pushed inside her.

Stella's moan went into his mouth. "Shh," he chided, his hips in motion.

She was so turned on it was hard to be still. But she managed it. At first, the only sounds were their own heavy breathing, but footfalls began to echo in the big room outside the door. At the sound of voices, Stella looked up at Bear with wide eyes. He didn't seem worried, though. He gave her a very naughty smile, which made Stella forget everything else.

Silently, they made love. The bunk they were on was built into the wall, and thankfully creak-free. With her leggings still tangled around her knees, Stella's legs were mostly tied together, which meant that each thrust bore down on her clit. She opened her mouth to groan, and found Bear's hand suddenly pressed across it. So she sucked on his palm.

It was all such a rush. Just as amazing as flying down a mountain.

"Jesus, buddy," Bear whispered through clenched teeth. "Come for me. Right fucking now."

Stella arched against him. The hand over her mouth was replaced by an aggressive kiss. She pushed her tongue into Bear's mouth, and he began to suck on it. That's all it took. The pleasure rolled through her, but Stella remembered to stay quiet. She threw her head back against the pillow and only gasped. A second later, Bear shoved his face into her neck, his body shaking with the force of his orgasm.

Then there was only their ragged breathing and the sensation of two heartbeats in close proximity, trying to calm down. "Holy wow," Stella breathed.

Bear traced the side of her face with his lips. "You and I…" He sighed. "Damn. I'm a god damned idiot."

"You're really hot, though," Stella whispered. "So it's all good."

His stomach began to shake with silent laughter. He rolled off of her and gathered her up in his arms. Stella snuggled in close. Finally. She was allowed to do this. She could wrap herself around him, and not hold back.

They didn't speak, because there was really no need.

They were still tangled up in their half-shucked clothing when the knock came. Three sharp raps on the door. "Stella! Are you in there?" It was her brother's voice.

Frozen against Bear, Stella had no idea what to do.

But Bear spoke up, his voice clear and untroubled. "Give us a minute, okay? There are some things that need to be said."

There was a beat of silence, and Stella's blood chilled at the thought that the next sound she heard might be the latch on the door. "Okay," Hank said at last. "But there's news."

Stella held her breath until it was safe to assume that her brother had rolled away from the door. Then she grabbed her leggings and yanked them up.

Bear kissed her forehead and grinned. "That was close."

"We have to say something to him."

Easing his own clothing up around his waist, Bear flinched. "I'll take care of it. In forty-eight hours we'll be on a plane to Vermont. The night after we get home, I'll take a bottle of scotch over to his place and tell him how it is. If he's going to be pissed at me, he can do that on his own turf."

Stella chewed her lip. "I think it will be fine. Why are you worried?"

He zipped his jeans. "You don't think he'd pick someone else for you? Some guy with a good job, who wasn't crashing in his childhood bedroom, and driving *his* car? Your parents, too. *Christ*."

She watched the grimace that crossed Bear's handsome face, and she didn't like it. "You're right. I could find myself a nice real estate developer who golfs. Then I could just shoot myself."

"Aw, buddy." Bear sat down again, pulling her close. "You kill me. You really do."

"We both live with our parents, Bear. We'll be losers together."

With a sigh, he released her and stood up, looking down at his clothes, taking inventory. Stella rose to wrap her arms around him. "Are you okay?"

His embrace pulled her closer. "Absolutely. You?"

"Never better."

A kiss landed on her forehead. "I'd planned to be a little more eloquent. Not just…"

"Rip my clothes off?"

He gave a little groan. "Yeah."

"You can be eloquent later. Tonight."

Bear rubbed her back. "I'm sharing a room with your brother, buddy."

"Tomorrow then. Change the reservation in Anchorage."

The knock sounded on the door again. "Seriously," Hank said. "What are you two plotting in there?"

Bear broke off their hug without another word, went to the door and opened it. "What's up?" he asked Hank. He left, pulling the door closed behind him.

Stella stood there alone, trying to take it all in. What, really, had just happened? She still didn't know what Bear expected their relationship to be. She still hadn't told him the truth about her infertility.

Except the sound of his "I love you. So fucking much," echoed in her head. She took a deep breath and let it out again. That's all that mattered, right? She'd never been the kind of girl who got hung up on planning and definitions. Stella went to her phone and texted Anya. *You will not BELIEVE what just went down with me.*

A minute or so later, she got a reply. *Please, baby Jesus, tell me this is about Bear.*

Stella: :D

Anya: WOOT!

Stella sat there a minute, grinning at her phone. Beyond the flimsy door she could hear men's voices in discussion. She wondered if Bear had already moved on to focusing on logistics. Or if maybe his mind was still in this room with her, and the horny-teen-rabbit sex that had just occurred.

Maybe she didn't have to wonder. With an evil grin, Stella removed her shirt and lay down on the bed.

Twenty-Five

BEAR SAT AT THE lodge table feeling flushed and jumpy, trying to focus on Hank's words.

"…if the other party doesn't arrive until one, and they need an hour to clock out and refuel, that means we could get two runs, maybe even three."

"That's great," Bear said, hopefully at the right moment. He was pretty sure Hank had just told him the party of people who were coming to displace them at the lodge tomorrow had been delayed by half a day. Therefore, the pilots could give them one more morning's time. "If we, uh, don't pick too tricky a shot, that will help," he added.

"Exactly. And the weather is supposed to cooperate."

"Awesome." Across the room, Stella's door opened, and she emerged, a sly little grin on her face.

Bear felt his neck get warm. But then his phone chimed with an incoming text, and he tapped the screen as a distraction. A close-up photo of a gorgeous pair of bare breasts filled the display. *Holy…* He pressed down so hard on the MENU button that his thumb knuckle cracked.

"Hi guys," Stella said.

Hank spun his wheels to look at her. "Hey! Come here." Stella went over to her brother and leaned down so he could hug her. "You okay?" he asked.

"Yeah." She cleared her throat. "I'm good. What's the news, anyway?" She stood.

"They got the poor fool off the ledge and off to the hospital in Anchorage," Hank said, slapping Stella on the rear.

"Good."

"It gets better. Tomorrow we can have a couple more hours of copter time, first thing in the morning before the next set of people rolls in."

Bear watched Stella's eyes light up. "Wow! One more chance?"

"At a *different* location," Bear said quickly. The ridge Stella had wanted to ride felt cursed to him now. When he got a moment alone with the guide, he was going to tell him that tomorrow they weren't taking any chances.

Stella's lips quirked. "A different location," she repeated.

"Absolutely." He held her eyes, trying to convey that this was nonnegotiable. He hadn't come all this way simply to risk losing her a second time.

She crossed her arms. "We'll see about that."

His body tightened up. "Stella! The Chugach is nineteen thousand square miles. I'm sure there's a better spot for tomorrow's shoot in there somewhere."

A slow grin spread across her face. "Stand down, tiger. I was just yanking your chain a little. You can choose the peak."

Whiplashed, Bear forced himself to uncurl the fists he hadn't realized he'd made. "Okay."

"In fact," Stella said, "I think maybe you're going to have to learn to trust me a little more than you've been. Maybe it doesn't have to be your permanent mission to save us all from ourselves. Not that we don't appreciate you."

Bear felt a little sting from her words. What she said was true. "Okay," he said again. "I'll try."

Stella's eyes sparkled, as if she wanted to say more. But it wasn't really the time or the place.

"Well, I guess that's settled," Hank said, clearing his throat. Bear risked a look at his friend, who wore a bemused expression. "Is it dinnertime yet? Because I'm starved. It's hungry work watching you two drama queens duke it out all day."

"I'll grab my jacket," Stella said, turning back toward her little room.

Bear found his own jacket and pulled it on. Then he took a deep breath. He was going to have to learn not to rise to her bait every single time. There was nobody on the planet who could get Bear worked up like Stella could. With a private grin down at his boots, he gave his head a little shake. There was a *reason* Stella had such an effect on him. The best kind of reason. From now on, he was going to enjoy it, and try not to fuck it up.

His phone chimed with a text, and he pulled it out of his pocket automatically. The screen showed a profile shot this time — Stella's breast, her hand supporting the underside, fingers splayed on the soft swell precisely where he would like to put his own hand. The effect on his body was immediate. His groin warmed, his dick growing heavy with anticipation.

Check, please. Bear powered his phone all the way down for caution's sake. He would have to have a little chat with Stella later about how awkward it would be if anyone was standing nearby when one of those texts showed up. Would she listen? Probably not. Because giving him a jolt was the whole point, right?

Go with it, he coached himself. *Pick your battles*. It was a skill he'd need to learn. Stella was right.

He zipped his jacket, hoping to hide the lingering effects of Stella's sexy selfie. Then he went next door to share a meal with his friends and his girl.

Twenty-Six

THE FOLLOWING NIGHT, BEAR lay on his belly on a hotel room bed with Hank.

Sure, it wasn't the Lazarus sibling that he wanted to be next to. But until Hank turned in for the night, Bear was stuck with him. And in the meantime, they were watching today's footage on his laptop.

"That was a sweet peak," Hank enthused. "Wish I could have ridden that."

"Me too, man." He watched Hank back the cursor up to replay a sick little jump that Duku had done off a cornice. Seconds later, Stella popped off the same jump. The two of them looked gorgeous scissoring down the mountain, one after the other, in the world's most high-stakes game of tag.

Bear sneaked a look at his friend's face, finding genuine joy on it. He'd said, "Wish I could have ridden it." But he'd said it the way anyone would and not like a man who couldn't stand the reality of his own life.

On the screen, Duku wiped out in a big puff of powder. "Whoops." Hank chuckled. "Save that bit for the blooper reel."

Bear's heart swelled then. They'd racked up a hell of a blooper reel these past twenty years. But here they were, on a hotel bed in Alaska, finishing off a couple of beers from the minibar. And *happy*.

Somehow, he'd done a lot of what he'd set out to do. He was on his way to making a great film. He'd dragged Hank out of the house. *Way* out of the house. He'd brought Stella to Alaska, where she'd always wanted to go. He'd told her how he felt.

That last one mattered most.

Bear got up to brush his teeth. If Hank ever went to sleep, Bear could go down to Stella's room and tell her again.

TWO HOURS LATER, Bear let himself out of their darkened hotel room, closing the door as silently as he could. He took the elevator down one floor, then pulled a copy of Stella's key out of his pocket. (One of the perks of being in charge of absofuckinglutely everything was having access to any hotel keys he needed.) He swiped the card and opened the door. "Hi buddy," he whispered, to prevent her from worrying that a stranger had invaded.

There was only silence. She was asleep on her side, dark hair streaming over the sheet she'd pulled up to her neck. She'd left a lamp burning in the corner, probably for his sake. Bear tiptoed over to the light and extinguished it. He undressed, dropping his clothes on a chair. Lifting the covers, he climbed into bed with her.

Bear moved over until he felt the satin warmth of her skin against his. Like him, she wasn't wearing a stitch of clothing. He smiled to himself as Stella stirred in her sleep, tucking her body closer to his.

Don't touch, he ordered himself. He would not to be selfish. Even though he ached to roll her into his arms and touch her everywhere, he would just let her rest. She'd ridden several thousand feet of vertical drop this morning, carving up those snow-covered descents like a woman on a mission. It was no surprise that she was worn out.

Still. Her hair smelled like citrus, and he couldn't resist kissing her once on the temple. She was *right there*. Finally. This afternoon, he'd driven their van back to Anchorage. It had been hard to keep his eyes on the road when all he really wanted to do was sneak looks at her in the rearview mirror.

Now, he snuggled up as close as possible. He didn't want to disturb her, but she was irresistible. Carefully, he tucked an arm around her waist.

Stella shifted, finding his hand and clasping it. "Sleepy," she murmured.

He grinned in the dark. "I know. It's okay. Sleep."

Bear closed his eyes, too, although sleeping was pretty much hopeless. His body had not failed to measure his proximity to a very naked Stella. But no matter. He'd lie here awake, drinking in the scent of her hair and her clean skin. This was too good to sleep through. He could sleep tomorrow on the plane.

After a time, Stella's feet curled back, clasping his. Even though he'd stayed still, she was waking up. Finally, she rolled over, her dark eyes glinting in the dim light. "Hey there, sailor." One warm hand landed on the scruff of his cheek. He hadn't shaved earlier, because Hank might notice and wonder why.

"Hey there, yourself."

"How did the footage look?" she asked.

He pressed closer, pulling her hips toward his body. "What footage?"

Stella giggled. And then they were kissing, and it was glorious. Bear purposefully held himself back, sliding his lips across hers as lazily as he could manage. For once, they had time. He'd attacked her like such a beast yesterday. Tonight would be different.

Slowly — very slowly — he eased her onto her back. She dragged her fingernails up his spine, making him shudder. Bear dropped his face down, finding the sweet juncture of her neck and shoulder with his lips. He placed slow, open-mouthed kisses on her shoulder, and then the pulse-point fluttering at her neck. This was the girl he wanted in his bed forever. There was no one alive who challenged him the way Stella did. There was no one alive who *loved* him the way Stella did. He saw it in her eyes whenever she looked at him. It had been there his whole life, and he'd been too stupid to see it.

Gently, he traveled downward, kissing between her breasts. He nibbled the soft swells, chuckling into the skin. "You were *killing* me with those photos yesterday. You know the picture just pops up on the phone, right? For the whole world to see?"

She wiggled beneath him. "That's a setting you can change on your phone."

He snickered. "Am I going to have to change it?"

"If you know what's good for you." Stella arched, pressing more of her beautiful breast against his mouth. He opened up, taking as much of her nipple against his tongue as he could. And Stella gave a moan of approval.

It wasn't long until they were both panting with desire. *God.* To be with Stella like this was even better than his fantasies. The way she gasped his name sent shivers down his spine. It was a struggle to break off their kisses, but it had to be done. "Buddy, I need to grab a condom."

At that, Stella's voice became low and serious. "You don't, actually. Not for pregnancy, anyway."

Her tone was so serious that Bear forced his libido back a few clicks on the dial and tried to concentrate. "I'm clean," he said. "And the last person I was with was you."

Her mouth quirked into a smile. "That was yesterday, Bear. Forgive me if I'm not impressed."

He chuckled, his lips an inch off of hers. "I meant in Tahoe, dummy."

Even in the dark, he could see her eyes widen. "Oh. The same is true for me."

"What a waste, right?" He took her mouth in a bossy kiss. He'd been lonely for more than a year, and so had Stella. And all because he'd been stubborn and insecure.

"Mmm," she said. But she broke off their kiss. "Bear, I have to tell you this now. Because if it's a big deal, I need to know."

Something in her tone made him snap to attention. "What's the matter?"

She put a warm hand on the side of his face. "I can't have children. And maybe it's presumptuous of me to project so far ahead. But I know you want them. And if that's going to be an issue for you..." She broke off, sounding sad. "Maybe we shouldn't start something that's going to end badly."

"Buddy, *no*." He gave her a quick kiss. "I'm not going to feel bad about that. *Christ*. The bigger risk is that we waste more time apart. I want you, whether you can pop out babies or not." He rolled off of her and onto his side, pulling Stella into a hug.

"Think about it, though, before you say that. For some people it's a big deal."

He shook his head. "For some people I'm sure it is. But I don't have my life planned out like that. We're not planners, Stella." He gave her a squeeze. "You and I, we take it as it comes."

She burrowed into his chest. "That's true, isn't it? We're not big on writing a five-year projection."

The sexy mood was broken, but Bear didn't really mind. He wanted this too — lying side by side, hearing all the things on Stella's mind. "Boring people make plans," he said, and Stella laughed. "Buddy, I'm sorry if you feel bad about the baby thing. But there's always adoption. That could be an adventure. And we're good with adventure."

"Maybe." She yawned.

He smoothed her hair away from her face. He'd always wanted to touch her like this. They'd both been lonely. And now they didn't need to be. If a family wasn't in the cards, that only meant more time for naked affection.

They lazed together for a while, and Stella's head began to feel heavy on his chest. Holding her, Bear listened to her lengthening breaths. Then he joined her in her dreams.

Twenty-Seven

THE NEXT MORNING, STELLA woke up to the sensation of her new boyfriend reaching over her hip to stoke her tummy. As she came to, his hand slipped between her legs. While his fingers slowly teased her, she let out a sleepy sigh. "What time is it?"

"Only seven thirty," he whispered, his fingertips skimming all the right places. "Nobody will be looking for us for a while."

She shivered with pleasure as he tightened his grip on her body. Even better, he drew her knee up, fitting the length of his erection between her legs where she could reach it. She tightened her thighs around him, and he reached both arms around her, palming her breasts, his mouth on the back of her neck.

There was nothing like a little hotel room sex to heat a girl up fast.

When she took him in from behind, he groaned. After a minute, he rolled her onto her elbows and knees, his hands cupping her breasts while he rocked into her. Stella closed her eyes and enjoyed the sensation of his powerful body curled around hers.

"You could not be any sexier," he whispered as they moved together. "But I want your mouth on mine." With a lusty grunt, he pulled out and rolled onto his back. "Come here," he demanded.

It was funny how Bear's bossy tone was so much more appealing when they were both naked.

He lifted her onto his broad chest. Their eyes locked. Slowly, she slipped him inside, and his eyes squeezed shut in appreciation. "Damn, lady," he said. "Even if your brother decks me, it will be worth it."

Stella ground her hips onto his. "Hush," she said.

"Shut me up, then."

She dropped down, tilting her head, capturing his mouth in a wet kiss. Beneath her, Bear's hips jacked up. He took control, steering her hips against his. And then there was no more talking, only gasps of pleasure and the steam of skin against skin.

THEY LAY THERE afterward, holding each other as the clock ticked forward. "I don't want to get out of this bed," Stella said.

"I hear you. But we have to turn up in the lobby eventually. You can have the first shower," Bear offered.

Eventually, she talked herself into getting up. After a shower, she tossed all her belongings in her bag, straightened up the bed and combed her wet hair. Then she tapped on the bathroom door, where Bear was showering. "Yeah!" he answered.

She opened the door. "I come in search of a hair dryer," she said.

"I think I saw one somewhere."

She looked around the hotel bathroom, but then heard a knock at the door. "Room service." The voice was muffled by the sound of running water.

Stella hadn't heard Bear order anything, but she went to open the door anyway.

And there sat her brother, smiling up at her.

Stella's mouth fell open. The sound of the shower ended, and the next thing she heard was Bear's voice. "Did you find it, buddy?"

Hank pushed the door open just as Stella turned around to see, as she feared, Bear standing completely naked in the open bathroom doorway.

"Oh, I'm sure she found it," Hank said.

Never had a man moved so quickly to grab a towel than Bear did right then.

"Actually, dude, I've seen your junk before," Hank said. "And I'm guessing my baby sister has too."

Stella was still rooted to the rug, too surprised to speak. She could only watch as her brother rolled past her, flicking the door closed behind him. He crossed over to the display of mini bar items on the console. Hank chose a small can of mixed nuts and popped open the top.

"Hank," Bear said quietly, the towel around his waist. "You're up early."

Hank chuckled and put an almond into his mouth. "Just think, Bear. What if I'd been *even* earlier?"

Bear closed his eyes. "I was going to talk to you tomorrow after we got home."

"What? And spoil the surprise?" He pointed a pecan at Stella. "You two are a couple of knuckleheads. Why all the secrecy?"

"I just thought..." Bear shook his head. "Your little sister."

Hank shook the can of nuts. "Look, if you hurt her, it won't be mixed nuts that I'm cracking. It will be yours." He grinned at his own joke. "But if you're both happy, I don't have a problem with it."

Stella sat down on the edge of the bed, relieved Hank wasn't going to make a big deal about this. Although Bear still looked worried. With his mouth tight, he took his boxers and his jeans into the bathroom and shut the door.

"Stella, Stella." Hank chuckled. "You should have seen your face when I opened the door. If only I'd had my camera ready."

She picked up a bed pillow and bonked him over the head with it. "You don't have to gloat."

"Why would you rob me of my fun?" he asked, wrestling the weapon out of her hands.

When the bathroom door opened, Bear came out dressed from the waist down. "Actually, Hank, we didn't tell you because we just don't like you all that much."

Hank threw the pillow at Bear. "Put on a shirt. Let's all go out for breakfast."

"I'll just be one minute," Stella said, ducking into the bathroom to finally dry her hair.

* * *

BEAR TOOK HER SPOT on the edge of the bed and began pulling on his socks. When Stella closed the bathroom door, he cleared his throat. "Look… I…" Unfortunately, he hadn't prepared the speech yet. And there was so much riding on it. "Uh, I know I'm not much of a catch. And maybe we caught you off guard. But this is not just a fling. I hope your parents aren't too pissed."

Hank made an irritated noise. "I love you, man. But you're kind of an idiot."

"I know," Bear said quickly.

"*No*, you fucking *don't* know. First of all, I know you'd never treat Stella like just a cheap fling. You guys have been friends forever. You don't have to explain that shit to me, okay? And anybody with eyes can see you two have been circling each other for years. But that's not *even* the dumbest thing you said. My mom, for the record, would lie down in the road for you. And not just because you've been my fucking hero for the last fifteen months. Are you listening to me?"

"Yeah." Bear was listening. It's just that the back of his throat had begun to burn, and he was having trouble looking Hank in the eye.

"My parents have always thought the world of you. And not because of all the shit that went down at your house. It's because you're such a rock. I guess my mom never said those things to your face. But she loves you to death, man. She always has. This will make that more convenient for her, okay?"

Now Bear was finding it really hard to swallow. "That's..." He cleared his throat again. "Nice to hear, man. Your mom has always been good to me."

Hank put a hand on his shoulder. "Not nearly as good as you've been to me. I don't think I would have made it through the last year and a half without you. Felt like the whole world forgot about me. But not you, man. You kept showing up. So I kept getting out of bed in the morning and putting a brave face on it. Because I knew I was going to hear your tires in my driveway eventually, and you'd knock on the door and hold me accountable. That's all that kept me going for a while, until I got over the hump. Maybe I should have said this before, okay? But I notice that shit. Thank you."

"It's nothing," Bear choked out.

"It's a whole lot more than nothing. And that's why my parents aren't going to lose any sleep over the fact that you're in flux with your life, the same way that Stella and I are. Because if you put even half as much effort into taking care of Stella the way you took care of me, that's better than anyone else could ever do. I always had a hunch you two would end up together. That's why I asked you to look after her when I left for Utah. I didn't want to see her end up with some loser."

Of all the things Hank had said this morning, none of them shocked him quite as much as that. It was a long minute until Bear could find his voice. "I..." He tried once more to clear his throat. "I plan to take very good care of Stella. If she lets me. She's even tougher than you."

Hank snorted, and then socked him in the hip. "Good luck with that, actually."

"Right?"

The bathroom door opened, and Stella marched out. She flashed Bear the first shy smile he'd ever seen on her face. "Okay, boys. Your moment is over. Let's eat breakfast. Because you know there won't be anything edible on that airplane."

"I call shotgun on the way to the airport," Hank said, opening the room door.

"Not fair!" Stella argued. "The vehicle isn't visible!"

"I saw it out the window when I was talking to your lunkhead boyfriend," Hank said.

"Liar!" Stella smacked him in the back of the head.

Bear's heart was too full to jump into the fray. He could only hold the door open for his two favorite people in the world. And then follow them out into the bright morning.

Epilogue

Two Years Later

WHEN THEIR CAR REACHED the gravel portion of her brother's mountain road, Bear removed his hand from Stella's knee, and she missed the warm weight of it. But since the man needed two hands to steer up the curing road, she had to settle for the rough sound of his voice as he sang along with Phish on the car stereo.

The surface beneath them was rutted, which made the car bounce. The motion did nothing for Stella's queasy stomach, unfortunately. For more than a week, she'd tried to fight off a lingering bug. It might have been a good idea to stay home again today. But Stella was tired of feeling tired, so she'd insisted that everything was fine. And anyway, they'd driven all the way here.

Her brother's house swung into view, and Bear parked beside her parents' car. Inside, mayhem awaited. Today was Hank's birthday, and Hank and Callie had invited everyone they knew for barbecue and cake.

Stella had been looking forward to this gathering. If only she weren't so tired.

"Are you sure you're up for this?" Bear asked, his hand returning to her knee. "You still look a little pale, buddy." There was a flicker of worry in his eye, which Stella did not like. So even though she felt pretty crappy, she gave him a big smile.

"I'll be fine," she said, unclipping her seatbelt and swiveling to grab the gift she'd stashed on the backseat. "And we drove all the way down."

She stepped out of the car, hoping she'd made the right decision. After all, she didn't want to give her three-month-old nephew a virus. But she was probably over it by now, and only feeling a little groggy from a lack of caffeine.

Yesterday was the first day this week that she hadn't thrown up. The only blessing was having no commitments right now. The competition season had just ended — she'd placed second in the world for women's freeriding — and classes didn't begin again for another six weeks or so.

These days, Bear and Stella shared an apartment in Burlington, about ninety minutes away. Living together was important since their wintertime schedules were so haywire they might never see each other if they lived apart. During the summer and fall, they both took courses at the University of Vermont. But during the winter months, their separate activities took them to disparate corners of the snowboarding world. Stella did freeriding competitions, and Bear worked on back country film shoots.

It was hectic, but life was good. Stella needed only a couple more credits before she'd graduate. And the winter travel was fun. Both of them were just coming off the busy season. It's no wonder that Stella had succumbed to a bug.

Hand in hand, they climbed the front porch together, and the cool March air steadied her. "Are you ready?" she asked Bear, squeezing his fingers. "Crying babies? Family members asking why we haven't driven down for dinner in a month?"

Bear bent his head, tucking a kiss behind Stella's ear. "Bring it," he said. And when Bear met her eyes, she found a reassuring wave of affection there. When the love of her life looked at her that way, Stella felt herself capable of anything.

The door was yanked open by Callie's friend Willow, who had her toddler son on her hip. "Hi!" she said, smiling up at them. "Welcome to chaos. But there's both coffee and beer."

"Hey!" Stella said, kissing her on the cheek. "I didn't know you were in town."

"We surprised Callie, because it's been too long since we've seen each other."

"*Cookie,*" her young son interrupted.

"You had a cookie," Willow argued, closing the door after Bear ducked in.

"Cookie," he said again, his fat little hand pressed against her shoulder for emphasis.

Stella kicked off her shoes and did not allow her gaze to linger on his chubby toddler fingers. These last few months, since Hank and Callie had their own little baby, Stella had sometimes found herself pitching between exhilaration and despair. Her newborn nephew was so cute. She didn't sit around and mope, exactly. But she would turn thirty soon. And it was hard not to wonder how her life would be different if it hadn't been for her childhood cancer.

Chin up, and all that. She let Bear lead her by the hand into Hank's swank dining area, where the table was piled with appetizers and drinks.

"Stella!" her mother cried. "Sweetheart, you haven't been returning my calls." Mrs. Lazarus crushed her against her cashmere-covered shoulder.

"Sorry, Mom," Stella said, her words muffled by the soft fabric. "I've been really tired this week. And I knew I'd see you today."

With a frown, her mother put a hand on Stella's forehead. "You look a little peaked."

"It's nothing. A little bug, and I'm over it."

That was the wrong thing to say. Her mother took a step back and looked Stella up and down, worry settling over her features. "Did you see a doctor?"

"No! Do you see one every time you sneeze?" Stella needed to change the subject, and fast. Ever since her childhood health scare, her mom became frightened whenever Stella had a fever. "Where's the birthday boy, anyway?"

"Stirring the chili," Callie answered, trotting up to give Stella a squeeze.

"Where's the baby?" Stella asked next. Because that's what you were supposed to say.

"Napping. Give him an hour, though, and he'll be all yours."

Hank called her name from the kitchen, where he was cooking and chatting with Willow's husband, Dane. "Coffee or beer for you two?" Hank asked.

"Coffee for me," Stella said, though she was not sure her gut would tolerate it. "I'd better nibble on something," she told Callie. "My stomach is a little unhappy with me this week."

"That worries me," her mother said, having snuck up on her somehow.

Stella sighed. "Nausea isn't a symptom of cancer, Mom." There was a little silence when Stella said this, but she didn't believe in beating around the bush. Her mom had been psycho about her health for twenty years now. As a teenager, she'd learned never to complain about how she felt, because it always brought on an inquisition and a trip to a doctor's office.

Pain. In. The. Ass.

She made a beeline for the crackers on Hank's dining table. In truth, Stella was rarely ill. It had been years since she'd thrown up for any reason other than a hangover. Come to think of it, the bug that she'd suffered this week had felt a lot like a hangover. She was tired and craving carbs. "Hank! Why didn't you tell me you'd made gougeres?" She loved them — a little puff of pastry with cheese in the middle. They were a near-perfect food. She popped one into her mouth, and it was still warm.

Hank rolled his wheelchair around the counter, a mug of coffee for her in his hand. "Because I knew you'd spot them. And then demolish them. I made sure everyone else got some before you showed."

"I'm not *so* bad," Stella argued, downing another one. She took a gulp of coffee, too, and then another. It should have been life-affirming, the way coffee was supposed to be. But when the acid hit her stomach, Stella felt another wave of queasiness overtake her. "Crap," she whispered.

"Are you okay?" Callie asked quietly. After two years as part of the family, Callie already understood that Stella's mother was prone to worrying about her.

"I'm fine," she said in a low voice. "I just feel really off this week. But I'm sure it's nothing." Sadly, she abandoned the mug on the kitchen counter. "Hey, I brought a gift. But it's for Little Hank, not big Hank." She held up the gift bag she'd brought in. "He's too young for it, but I couldn't resist."

Callie peered into the bag, pushing the tissue paper aside. "Is that a fire truck? He's going to *love* it!"

Bear came up behind Stella, placing a warm hand on her back. "Every boy needs a fire truck," he said. "It's supposed to make noise. But I took the batteries out and put them in the bottom of the bag, so you can decide whether it makes noise or not."

Callie grinned at Bear. "Damn, you're good. When you guys have kids, I'm going to hang out at your house and take notes."

Stella forced a smile on her face. Bear's palm pressed just a little more snugly against her back. She'd never gotten around to having *that* chat with Callie. It wasn't her favorite topic. And after Callie had gotten pregnant, the whole subject became even more awkward.

"Who wants chili?" Hank asked, heading for the kitchen again. "I chopped red onions for you, Stell. And there's avocado and cheese for toppings, too."

"Great," Stella said, even as her stomach turned over. She grabbed another little cheese puff and ate it quickly. Maybe she could help herself to a tiny portion of chili without any raw onions on top.

Ugh. Just the idea of raw onions made Stella feel nauseous. Suddenly, there was too much saliva in her mouth. "Excuse me a second," she said quickly. She hurried from the room, hoping nobody would think it odd. Sprinting through Hank and Callie's bedroom and into the master bathroom.

She made it just in time.

WHEN STELLA OPENED the bathroom door a few minutes later, after brushing her teeth with her finger and a pinch of Hank's toothpaste, she found Callie standing right outside, her arms crossed. "Seriously, are you okay?"

No. "Yeah. It's just…" Her argument lost steam as Callie raised an eyebrow. The woman was a doctor for God's sake. It wouldn't be easy to get anything past her. "I'm sorry. I thought I was over this bug. Don't say anything to my mother."

Callie's head tilted to the side, like a curious puppy. "Stella, are you stonewalling me?"

"No? About what?"

Her sister-in-law smiled. "Could you be pregnant?"

"No," Stella said quickly. "That's not it."

"But you are acting like someone with morning sickness. Seriously. Even if you've been very careful, don't rule that out, okay? It's an easy mistake to make."

"Well..." Stella cleared her throat. "It's not an easy mistake, actually. I just assumed you guessed that because we've talked about my leukemia. I can't get pregnant."

Callie braced herself against the door jam, frowning. "Stella, when's the last time you talked to a doctor about this?"

Stella shrugged. "I was pretty young when they explained it to me the first time. But I remember that my mother got all depressed, so I never doubted it was true. One time a gynecologist suggested that I have a fertility workup. But isn't that just asking for bad news? Maybe if it seems important to Bear someday, I'll ask more questions."

"Well..." Callie looked thoughtful. "I read a lot of medical research. And the latest word on chemotherapy is that even the old-school cancer treatments weren't as devastating to fertility as they first thought."

"*Really?*" Stella hated the sound of her voice when she said it. She sounded far too interested.

"Really. And if you last spoke to a doctor when you were a child... That could have been almost twenty years ago, Stella. Both your body and the science have changed during that time. Do you get your period?"

"Once in awhile." Stella's knees felt a little wobbly all of a sudden. She parked her backside against the wheelchair-height vanity. "You're confusing me," she said.

Callie smiled. "I'm sorry. And it's not like I want to give you false hope or anything. But you should see a reproductive endocrinologist. Even if you don't ovulate, you might be able to support a donor egg and still have Bear's baby." She held up her hands in supplication. "Not that you two are necessarily talking about kids. I'm just saying that your options might not be as narrow as you think."

"That sounds... expensive."

"It can be," Callie admitted. "But after Hank and I have a second one, I might have a few extra eggs lying around that you could use."

Stella's throat became tight. "You would do that for me?" she squeaked.

"Absolutely."

Stella's mind whirled, trying to take it all in. Unfortunately, her stomach went along for the ride. She inhaled a big, queasy breath through her nose.

"Oh boy," Callie sighed. "You poor thing. Have you been feeling sick very long?"

Stella flipped on the cold water tap and took a couple of gulps from her palm before answering. "My stomach has been unstable for... God, I guess more than a week. And I'm really tired. But that's it."

"No bowel problems?"

"Nope."

"Fever?" Callie pressed.

"None."

"Are your breasts sore?"

That last question pinned Stella in place. Because they *were* sore, and Stella had wondered why. "Yeah. What causes that?"

"Well..." Callie stepped into the bathroom and opened a cabinet. After fishing around for a minute, she drew out a slender box. "Look, what if you just tried this just for fun?"

Stella eyed the box. It was a home pregnancy test. "It *couldn't* be positive."

"You're probably right," Callie said. "But if you just use this one, you're only humoring me. It isn't the same hopeful thing as going to the store a week from now, buying one, getting a negative test and then having to hide it in the garbage."

"Shit," Stella gasped, fighting off another wave of nausea. But this wave was caused by nerves. "I kind of want to maim you for even making me think this way."

Callie laughed. "I'll bet. And I am sorry for making you wonder. But there's an easy way to shut me up. You just have to pee on the stick."

"I don't think so," Stella whispered, staring at the box as if it were a venomous snake. (Which were rare in Vermont, of course.)

"It takes thirty seconds," Callie argued. "And if you humor me, I'll give you that wrap dress that you wanted to borrow for the Mud Ball. It looks better on you anyway."

Stella's heart fluttered with uncertainty. How had the day brought her here? It was just a virus, for God's sake.

"Dare you," Callie whispered.

With a groan of irritation, Stella grabbed the box and tore the end open. "Is there a trick to it?"

"Nope!" Callie said cheerfully. "Just pee on it." She snapped the door shut as she left the room.

Stella yanked the yellow plastic device out of the package and dropped her jeans. *This is nuts*, she repeated to herself while she did what was required.

"Now count to thirty," Callie said through the door after Stella flushed.

"What?" She yanked the door open. "You're standing there waiting?"

"Of course I am. One, two, three…"

After Callie had chanted up to thirty, Stella still did not look at the stick. "Can't I wear the dress either way?" she asked, holding the stick in the air where neither of them could see it.

"You can have the freaking dress," Callie said. "Look at it already. I'm dying here."

"I can't." She handed it to Callie, keeping a careful watch of her face. Stella set her own face into the best mask of indifference she could master. But it wasn't easy.

Callie took the stick, and tilted it toward the vanity lights. "Oh my God!" she yelped.

Stella felt her gut twist in a completely different direction. *"Seriously?"*

"*That* is a plus sign!" Callie held the stick where Stella could see, and they put their heads next to one another, both of them staring at the unmistakable "+" on the white test strip.

"Holy shit," Stella whispered. "Holy shit."

"Callie!" Hank's voice boomed from outside the door. And then he and his wheelchair appeared in the open doorway, baby Hank on his lap. "Look who woke up."

Callie whipped the pregnancy test behind her back, but not before Hank noticed. His eyes went wide. Then he put his free hand on his forehead. "You are fucking kidding me. Seriously? We're having another one already?" His face broke into an enormous grin. "I get to choose the name this time!"

Callie cleared her throat. "I'm sorry to tell you this, honey," she said slowly. "But you're not the father."

If Stella hadn't been so freaked out at that moment, the look on Hank's face would have really amused her.

* * *

IN THE LIVING ROOM, Bear chowed on chili with his father and Stella's dad.

"Hank makes excellent chili," Bear's father said. "It's really quite amazing." His dad always seemed a little stiff at Lazarus family gatherings. Like he couldn't quite get over the fact that he and Bear were welcome in their homes. He'd stopped giving Bear grief about his relationship with Stella. So that was an improvement.

The chili *was* good, too, and so was the beer he washed it down with. But Stella had disappeared into Hank and Callie's room half an hour ago, and he wondered if she was feeling okay.

"How was your business trip?" Mr. Lazarus asked, snapping Bear snap out of his reverie.

"Cold," he answered with a chuckle. "I swear I couldn't feel my toes for two days after we wrapped up the shoot at Sunday River. But the footage looked good, and the client was happy."

"You still getting work from OverSight?"

"I am. They keep me on the payroll, and I shoot about ten days a year for them. It's a pretty good gig. But this shoot was for a little snowboard company called Genesis."

Mr. Lazarus clapped him on the back. "Good deal, kid. Sounds like fun."

"It is. And now I get to edit, which I enjoy." He'd discovered that he was good at it too. The editing internship he'd done during the fall semester had really improved his game. Every film he made was better than the last.

And the jobs kept coming in, allowing him to pay the full rent on their place in Burlington without tapping the nest egg he'd secured when his Utah condo had finally sold. A decade in the snowboarding racket meant that he knew hundreds of well-connected people. Calling them up to ask for business got easier every time he did it.

Nobody would mistake him for a movie mogul anytime soon. But Bear had found his footing, and it felt great.

Where was Stella? Though she'd kill him for saying so, she hadn't looked well all week. He was worried about her, but he hadn't made a big deal about it, because Stella wouldn't like that. He excused himself from the conversation, put his bowl in the dishwasher, and went in search of his girlfriend. She wasn't on the deck, where he looked first, so he wandered into Hank's bedroom, where he could hear both Hank and Callie's voices coming from the master bath — an odd place for everyone to gather.

As he approached, he heard Stella say, "Well, we weren't home together many weekends last winter. But that only meant that when our weekends overlapped, we went at it like rabbits. I'll have to look at my calendar."

Whoa. Even if that was all true, it wasn't the kind of thing Stella would discuss with her brother and sister-in-law. With his face heating, Bear stepped forward in time to see Hank cover his ears and belt out the first line of Jingle Bells.

Entering the bathroom, Bear gave Hank's elbow a slap. "What are you all doing in here?" he asked, searching their faces.

Callie looked up at him, her face suddenly registering discomfort. Oddly enough, Stella also donned a freaked-out expression. Even Hank dropped his hands — and his song — then stared up at him as if he'd entered the Twilight Zone.

"What's the deal?" Bear asked into the silence.

Only the baby spoke up, letting out a hungry wail.

"Right," Hank said, turning the wheels of his chair. "Let's get you that bottle."

"And I was just…" Callie trailed off, then hurried out after Hank.

Alone with Stella in the bathroom, he noticed her face was flushed, which actually seemed like a good thing since she'd looked so pale all week. Still, he wondered why. "Buddy? What's going on?"

Stella actually began to laugh. "God, I don't know how to tell you."

"Tell me what?"

"Um," she said. Then she chuffed out another laugh. "It seems like..." She picked up a strangely shaped yellow plastic stick from the counter top, and Bear's heart actually stopped. "I could be pregnant. Maybe."

"What?" he gasped.

Her eyes lifted to his. "I'm so sorry. Because it's the kind of thing you're supposed to plan. I've fucked that up pretty well. I thought I couldn't, but now it seems like maybe I can, and so I really should have been more..."

He didn't let her finish the sentence. Instead, he grabbed her in his arms and pressed a kiss of epic proportions right on her mouth.

Stella gave a surprised little whimper, but Bear didn't want to stop kissing her. Maybe it made him a caveman, but the idea he'd planted a child inside Stella really lit him up. He already had the best girl in the world, and more than he deserved. But if it was really true that they could have children?

He hadn't known it was possible to receive everything you wanted, and then get even more.

When he finally broke their kiss, he leaned back, breathing hard. Stella looked a little dazed. "I love you, lady. If we're having a baby, that's awesome. If we're not, that's all right, too. We'll sort it out. Okay?"

"Okay." She leaned into his chest. "Bear?"

"Yeah?"

"We suck at planning our lives."

He chuckled into her hair. "But we are good at *many* other things." He gave her ass a pinch. "And we are never boring."

Stella hugged him even more tightly. "Those are good points."

"Can we get married on Monday?"

She pulled her head back to look up at him, and the startled look on her face was priceless. "*This* Monday? Like… forty-eight hours from now?"

Bear smoothed the hair back from her face. "If we get married before a doctor tells us which way this is going to go, then it won't be just about the baby. Because I want to be with you no matter what."

As he watched her face, Stella's eyes filled. "Wow."

"You didn't answer the question, buddy."

She planted her face in his shirt again. "Yes." The word came out muffled.

"We can wait if you want to," he hedged. "If you want the big white dress and the party."

Stella looked up at him again. "No way. I like your plan. We are never boring."

Bear grinned down at his fiancée. "Your mom is going to kill me, isn't she? She likes to adhere to tradition. I'm robbing her of the right to pick out flower arrangements, or some shit."

"She'll get over it," Stella said. "Who's going to tell her? Me, or you?"

"This is a job for rock, paper, scissors," Bear said.

Stella burst out laughing, and then Bear kissed her, and Stella kissed him back. It took a while until they were ready to emerge and spread the good news.

Thank You

Thanks for reading *Shooting For the Stars (Gravity #3.)*
We hope you enjoyed it!
Reviews help other readers find books. I appreciate all reviews, whether positive or negative.

Would you like to read more of *Gravity?* You can see details of all the current and future books and sign up for my new release e-mail list at **www.sarinabowen.com/gravity.**

Also in the Gravity series:

Falling From the Sky
Coming In From the Cold

Also by Sarina Bowen:

The Year We Fell Down
The Year We Hid Away
Blonde Date
The Understatement of the Year
The Shameless Hour

COMING IN FROM THE COLD

Gravity #1

By Sarina Bowen

He can't have her. And he can't tell anyone why.

Ski racer Dane "Danger" Hollister lives for the moment. On borrowed time due to a hereditary secret, flying down a forty degree pitch with two boards strapped to his feet is the least of his fears. His family curse will eventually cost him everything: his spot on the US Alpine team, his endorsements, and the ability to soar downhill.

Reluctant country girl Willow Reade would never have met Dane if it weren't for her own rough luck. A few bad choices — and giving away her heart too easily — have her stuck in the Vermont boonies, and then stuck in a snowbank, too.

When both their vehicles spin off a snowy road, Dane and Willow are trapped together at nightfall. As snow thickens on Dane's windshield, their mutual attraction spirals into what should have been a one night tryst. Yet neither can guess how their spontaneous passion will uncork Dane's ugly secret and Willow's tentative peace with her own choices. Only mutual trust and bravery can end the pain and give Willow and Dane a hard-won shot at happiness.